FERNI

"And see you not that bonny road
  That winds about the fernie brae?
  That is the road to fair Elfland
  Where you and I this night maun gae.

"But Thomas, ye maun hold your tongue,
  Whatever ye may hear or see,
  For gin a word you should chance to speak
  You will ne'er win back to your ain countrie."

(Old Scottish Ballad: *Thomas the Rhymer*)

Fernie Brae

A SCOTTISH CHILDHOOD

by

J. F. HENDRY

POLYGON BOOKS

First published in Great Britain in 1947
by William McLellan & Co. Ltd., Glasgow.

Reissued in 1987 by Polygon Books,
48 Pleasance, Edinburgh, EH8 9TJ.

ISBN 0 948275 13 8

The publisher acknowledges subsidy from the
Scottish Arts Council towards the
publication of this volume.

Typeset by E.U.S.P.B.,
48 Pleasance, Edinburgh EH8 9TJ.

Printed by Bell and Bain Ltd., Glasgow.

FOR MAMIE

ONE

I

High Cartcraigs, built in 1789 as a school for the children of planters and known therefore as "The Black Boys' School", stood out of the neighbouring village of Shaws, on an eminence going by the name of "The Green Knowe". As the River Cart ran near, it was given the name of High Cartcraigs by the villagers, before being left to its lonely resources.

The French Revolution came and went. In the long field opposite, the local guard drilled to resist the Napoleonic invasion and set their bonfires. No invasion came.

The village prospered, mainly from customs-dues and the traffic of carriages and coaches entering Glasgow from the South. "The Rocket" held its trials, and a railway was built through the meadows which had hitherto been only a gigantic yellow mirror for the sun. As the Scots, in the gathering wheels of industry, lost historical vision and perspective, High Cartcraigs lay at last in a backwater, between tram lines and a railway bridge, above the old tollhouse known as "The Wee Roon Toll".

It was silent now, though once it had been full of life. On the other side of the street, like merry bells, there still came the sound of "The Smiddy". Uphill lay the Green Knowe where generations of courting couples had strolled. On the ground floor lay the school proper, and on the first and second floors the dwelling of the dominie. In the mornings the classrooms were filled with children's voices singing or at prayers, or else chanting lessons. During the interval they danced about the garden, climbing the apple trees and the rowans, and in the evenings, when they had all gone to bed, there could be heard the voice of the dominie himself, as he read aloud the Scriptures.

The district, authority has it, is famous all over the world as the haunt of "The Queer Folk". It is mentioned in Burns and in Kipling;

doubtless occurs in Scott, and, according to the Parish of Eastwood, is known even to lonely Boer farmers on the veldt, and to pedlars in the markets of India, anywhere, in fact, where the queer folk have set foot.

It is Covenanting country. That is not uncommon. Maps of Scotland are dotted like pirate flags with the crossed swords indicating battlefields, and one district in Glasgow still rejoices in the name of Battlefield. Drumclog, too, is a sound and a sentiment that still means something in Scottish ears, and the harsh Covenanting strain that severed horsemen from their saddles with a claymore was still a presence in the Shaws. Across the fields lay the "Beheading Stone". In the art galleries, crowds stood before the bloody picture of the murder of John Brown of Priesthill; and, just as David still seemed to hear in his grandfather's tones, the voices of children in the schoolroom and the dominie's theological ramblings, so he felt himself sprung from these scenes of terror and carnage.

Upstairs, he read books bound in leather, like wallets or sporrans. *The Scots Worthies*, Wilson's *Tales of the Borders*, or Rollo's *Ancient History*, impinged powerfully on his mind, like the heavy wings of some great, dark eagle in whose inscrutable eyes there lurked a drama assuaged. He was glad to run away from such pictures as these books provided. Clan battles, golden eagles and illustrations to the Last Judgement were too full of ancient sin to inspire anything but terror in the boy, and when he had read too much, he ran into the sunlight of the garden.

There he walked up the path between the flowers, chrysanthemums, the colour of burnt sugar, and tea-roses. Strange they should be called tea-roses. Some of them were white and beginning to wither. The rot was spattered on their petals like flakes of rust, or dried tea-stains.

He set down his glass jar and waited for the butterflies. There were several cabbage-whites fluttering high in the air, little dancing parachutes, at the foot of the garden where no one ever went. Once he had gone, through trees with cobweb claws, to look over the wall, against his grandfather's orders — straight into a horse's face!

He would wait for them to come up.

Now he idled about the grass, kicking the tops off dandelions.

8

Suddenly there was a spark of flame. For a moment he could not think; then, madly, he darted at it. A red admiral! A red admiral!

"Bobby! Bobby!" he shouted to his cousins in the house. Never had he seen one before. It was smaller than a white, with a web of black spots on the tip of each blood-red wing.

He careered after it, banging his net down on dandelions, cabbages, sometimes even on a clucking hen; but the red admiral rose high over the bristling, mossy wall by the blackberry bush, in a ribbon of unfurling fire, and disappeared in a dance of sparks.

Angrily he threw the net down.

"It's twopence wasted!" said Bobby. "I catch them with my hands."

"You couldn't catch a red admiral with your hands! It's too quick!" David said.

"Yes, I could!"

"Oh no, you couldn't, Bobby!"

Sandy, the smaller, a little blond with a face like the letter V, gave one of his Jack-in-the-Box giggles. He always sided with David, and that made Bobby fly into a tantrum, a veritable explosion of whimpering impotence. Coiling his lips in rage and snorting tears, he aimed a blow at Sandy.

"It's not a butterfly-net anyway! It's for catching baggie-minnows!" he screamed.

"This is a new kind," shouted David, catching his arm. "And if you touch Sandy, it'll be the last thing you'll ever do!"

Off stamped Bobby in a fury of mortification.

"He's going to cry to Bessie!" mocked Sandy merrily, a mischievous gnome.

Bessie was their foster-mother.

Together they built a tent of sacking round the rowan tree, which, though they did not know it, warded off devils from the house of turrets. That calmed David's nerves, upset by Bobby's outburst. The tent beat out the last heat of the sun and smelt of straw and earth.

Then they made a sortie to catch the butterflies snowing on the soft undulating soil among the potato blossom. When they had caught one, they returned to drink some soda from a halfpenny packet, through a tube of licorice.

"Shall we make some sugarolly water?" David asked.

9

"What's that?"

"You cut up the licorice and put it in a glass of water till it melts. It's great!"

"There's no time," said Sandy. "The sun will soon be down and the butterflies will go home."

"Home where?"

"I don't know. Sometimes they sleep on the wall alongside the blackberry bushes."

"They're moths!" exclaimed David. "I've seen them. Big tiger-moths! Ugh, they look awful!"

"What's the difference?"

"What's the difference? A moth has a thick body and small wings. It's greedy, and ugly. A butterfly's wings are wide and transparent and beautiful. It has a thin waist and furry shoulders, and only wants to enjoy itself."

Down they went again into the garden, but this time there was an interruption.

"Dauvit!" came a gruff voice. "Come oot o' the totties! You tae, Sandy!"

It was their grandfather, revered figure in hat of tweed with moustache and beard that seemed of the same material, only not woven so well, strandy and straggling, with the same tobacco strands.

"If ye want to help," he went on, "get the caterpillars oot o' the cabbages. Or dig up the wireworms!"

"What are you going to do?" said David boldly.

"Burn this rubbish."

Grandpa's grey eyes twinkled frost.

"Burn the rubbish!" they whooped. "Can we help to gather it?"

"All right! "

The old man nodded, still standing, bowed, a scarecrow in the field of destiny.

As they stood watching the flames, he patted David on the head and said: "Ye're a good lad, David."

Soon the magic of the garden mingled in the scent of the smoke from weed and bracken. In its purplish coils, so thick he could almost feel them, the dreaming boy saw ripe-red rowan berries on a branch of fern. Sparks danced at their heart like red admirals and green sap burst from the rind of burning trees like the birth of apples.

He stood with Bobby and Sandy round the fire as it mounted, but they saw nothing of his vision, except the westward sun aslant on the red and purple flames that gradually dimmed its valour. His eyes streamed smarting tears of smoke in the lazing evening. He had some of that fire and some of that sun in his jar.

Looking down, he saw the butterfly stalk up the wall of glass, clinging on hair-fine limbs, like spores of thistledown. Its green eyes, dabbled with black, stared huge as two revolving eggs; and the coiled trunk in between them seemed a fairy circus-whip, through which it sucked a nectar from the flowers.

That was part of his fire and sun, a memory of his grand-father's library near the attic where he ate "cheugh jeans" and read Tom Finch's *Monkey* or Nansen's *Farthest North*. So high and so quiet was it there that he travelled for hours in another hemisphere. The books were large and dusty, bound like ledgers and full of mysterious reckonings and figures dealing with the world of space and time, but he could not always follow the argument, sitting in the attic, near the sky, wiping dust from their bindings that somehow became the dust of stars to guide him, as the heavy tomes loomed, purposeful as the prows of ships, swinging into seas of silence and of wonder like those that once met Nansen.

Continents and years unfolded like a map below.

Somehow the garden was one of those continents. His grand-father was Nansen in the Arctic, with frozen eyes and beard, the year's hero. And he, David, was the fire and sun through the trees in that orchard, the butterfly winging towards he knew not what. Seas of silence? Chill ice-caps? He was unafraid, for Nansen had gone there before him, and now his grandfather too was there. What did it all mean?

His grandfather was smoking a clay pipe, full of thick black, and he wore mittens. His gardening was done, and he stared meditatively at the forest of potatoes and at the little orchard where the apples fell mysteriously on to the grass as if from a pendulum, marking the passage of time.

"Stick in, son," he said. "Stick in."

That meant "Work".

He turned and scraped his boots before going into the stone corridor of the house. They were caked with crumbs of earth.

David followed him in.

"What did ye do wi' the wireworms today, grandpa?" he asked.

"I hackit them wi' my spade," he said. "They're deevils. Deevils!"

"Shush, will ye," shouted his grandmother; "I cunny hear a thing oot o' this contraption!"

She was twiddling the cat's whisker on a crystal set, now and then adjusting the Ericcson headphones.

"It's a blessing to her, Teenie," said his grandfather to his mother. "She listens a' day. Ye maun thank Jock for buying it. I hae nae time for sic-like new-fangled nonsense."

They all sat down to tea.

Suddenly his grandmother slapped him across the face with a crumpet and laughed out loud.

"My, bit ye're a glaikit bairn!" she cried. "Cuddy-lugs!"

She was to him a prehistoric monster, sitting there mouthing incomprehensible language

"Here's a saxpence see. Noo awa' an' buy yersel' some cheugh-jeans!"

He went up to Gates', the sweet shop, and bought a soda-fountain, a penny "negative" and some scented cachous. Afterwards he played "Colonel Bogey" on the gramophone, while his grandfather read the Bible.

The sneck of the door lifted and his uncle walked in.

"Evenin', fauther!"

The old man looked up, but did not answer. His mother began to weep in a corner to herself. David ran out.

At the back, in the wash-house, were books in large packages, tied with string, and reaching up to the ceiling. Mr Wood had bought them at the barrows.

Exploring the garden, he found the nest still there, but deserted, on which he had once laid a stone when the eggs were in it. He was very young then, but the memory still haunted and tortured him. There were earwigs still in the washing-poles, spiders on the walls, and two ancient rusting bicycles — one of them a penny-farthing, the other a walking bicycle without pedals — still leaned against the tower, gradually falling to pieces. The sunflowers were his friends. They were hairy and strong and wore their petals like dog-collars.

He looked in at the window. His grandfather was still not speaking to his uncle. He was "grumphing". David conceived a dislike for his uncle. He lived in a modern house.

"Cartcraigs wasny good enough for him," his grandfather said.

It did not seem to matter that they were both elders in the Kirk or that his mother cried. What could have happened?

"Auld fule," he heard his grandmother say. "Him and his buiks. Ony yin wad think *Scots Worthies* was aboot decent folk. Geordie Telfer o' Trongate, who wears a lum hat wantin' a croon! Or Tinker John, who sells umbrellas and fortunes, or even Blin' Harry. But whit are they? A pack o' auld prelates! Wishart an' ithers as ill-kent. Ye're nothing but a John Grumlie. Dae ye hear?"

That was a "flytin'". It was terrible to get a flytin'.

David walked alone among the cabbages, turning over the great ears of leaves to inspect the back, and picking fuzzy caterpillars from among the straggling veins. You had to look close, for they looked a part of the hand of cabbage, green and struggling in an agony of light, like children severed from the wrist of stalk. These, too, he dropped, numb and cringing little questions, into a jar as glassy as his eyes with wonder.

When it was quite dark, his mother appeared at the back door, thirty yards off.

"Come, David!" she called, vague as a bird in the wood. "Time to go home!"

He placed the net over the jar and walked towards her, plucking the heads off flowers on the way and dropping them nonchalantly inside. Food for the butterfly in its transparent cell.

In the tram going home he knelt on the seat, looking out of the window. It wasn't sore, for his stockings were pulled over his knees. He wore his little glengarry. He should have had his rifle by his side, too — the one that fired a bullet of cork — plonk! — on a piece of string. Instead, he clutched the long cane with the net at one end, like a forlorn sceptre.

"Look!" he shouted suddenly. It sounded like "Luke". "There's a student, mother!"

He had been watching for them. It was Charities' Day, when University students all dressed up collected for the hospitals, but to David a weird day, full of irrupting red admiral magic. He looked down again at the butterfly in his jar. It lay crouched at the bottom, antennae turning this way and that, as though listening for a possible way of escape from the mirage.

Outside, Red Indians were pushing policemen off point duty. Negroes with upraised axes were chasing motor cars. Their tram was filling with strange creatures he would have liked to capture and keep in his jar. They flashed colour in all directions, like deep-sea fish he had seen once in an aquarium.

It was like Daft Friday.

He held his breath. A huge man in a blue and yellow costume shook a tin before his mother, and he dropped a penny in the slot.

At the back where the conductor usually stood was a resplendent being in blue blazer and velvet-tasselled skullcap. Irrupting magic. That was being young. These people could do as they liked, and lived a life of laughter and sun like any red admiral.

"What will you be when you grow up?" his mother whispered over his shoulder.

"A student," he breathed, "like that man over there, with the velvet tassle."

The thought was so daring he could scarcely bring himself even to think of it.

"He got that for playing football," his mother said.

Now the tram swung over the river, blue sparks shooting from the pole on the wire. This was the part of the journey he liked least, when the centre of the town was revealed, like the rotten core of an apple, as a mass of warehouses, factories, coal depots and chimneys, looking like the animals he found when he turned over a stone in his grandfather's garden.

Trams were called "caurs". There were blue cars and red cars, white cars and yellow cars and green cars, a whole hierarchy of cars in this medley of colour in the town. Red cars went to Pollok-shaws and Thornliebank, so colour was the real guide, not the direction on the roller-tape in front. People were known to each other by the car they took, and between, for example, the blue car people and the red car people, a gulf was fixed wider even than that between the muffler and the white-collar workers, for red cars went through the city, but blue cars went through the Gorbals.

He savoured the names on them. BALORNOCK. That lay out of the city to the North. It was a vast area of new factories, new tenements and soft asphalt, yet with stretches of green grass along the canal. He repeated the name to himself softly. It was forlorn and beautiful, and had grief in it, and even death. It imprisoned a day in his life when he had seen a rock-pipit there. Balornock. And they went to the deep quarry where a boy was drowned, and wondered at the fatality that lay in sheer silent water.

His head swam. He felt he was going to be sick.

When they arrived home at last, the students were gone.

"Do you remember being lost once?" his mother asked him. "In the town?"

"No."

"I went to the police station and phoned all the hospitals. When I came home you were waiting for me over there, on the stairs."

"Was I?"

"A lady had asked you where you lived, and you said: '8 Avelato Teet, Pimbim'. You couldn't say 'Laverockhall Street, Spring-burn', so you said 'Pimbim'."

In the chill lane of smoking tenements he covered the butterfly to keep it warm, but once in the small kitchen he took it out. It would be better here than in grandpa's garden, he thought.

"They live longer in houses, don't they, mother?"

"Yes," she said, taking off her hat, to light the fire.

"I can feed it on flowers and sugar and milk. It'll soon be tame and live a long time."

He took it up in his hand. The powder-grains spread on his thumb a metallic glitter, and the wings shone, glazed.

"Oh, look," he cried. "It can hardly fly! Have I hurt it?"

He stood the jar on the dresser and watched the butterfly agog on his thumb. "It's beautiful," he thought. Oh, he hoped it would live in the cold of the grimed tenements if he brought it flowers. The wind would not blow so hard. It was his youth. Every Saturday in the garden. Every butterfly he would pursue.

Gently he turned to the contortions of the anguished caterpillars. From their blunt, blind heads, and from their diffident bodies, too, would one day stream that irrupting magic. They would all be married to the sun. Carefully he placed them in the long button-drawer of the sewing-machine and stuffed its compartments with leaves of fresh green lettuce. The butterfly itself he allowed to fly about the house. It was his friend, the magic he must tame and make his own, the good and true.

Darkness fell, and he closed the drawer and sealed the jar, piercing holes in the cardboard lid to let in air.

Next morning before breakfast he opened the drawer, and at once little beads of corruption assailed his nostrils and eyes, Drawer, lettuce and caterpillars were one stench of green death. Never would they know the freedom he had meant to give them. He had made them prisoner only in order to see the actual irruption of the magic, and now the magic itself had flown away.

In the chill jar he saw the butterfly, his inspiration, lying too in death. Over its fallen brittle petal the boy wept.

II

Next day, a ghost out of the history book knocked at the door, carrying a box of rock. It had a face exactly like King James the Sixth of Scotland First of England, and sure enough it was his Aunt Bessie.

Entering, smirking, she gave him a red stalk and a white stalk, which he held up like candles till he puzzled her out. She was not Glasgow, they said. She was Edinburgh. She lived somewhere inside the Castle Rock. Some women, he noticed, had faces like scones, and tartan does not improve the complexion. He could not understand her native girn. Like his grandmother's language it was tribal and strange.

Afterwards, he was very proud to have for an aunt the only woman in Scotland to look like King James, except that she wore no ruffle and had not bothered to grow a moustache, which was pending, but now he felt so bored he made a tent below the bed, took his rifle, said he was Jack Logan and was going back to France. It was always awkward in France. There was not much room and you had to sit with your knees up to your chin. He decided to take a bit of leave, and crawled out from under the bed vallance.

She was still there. She was Sandy's mother. She stood looking at him sideways, with amusement, as if he were a stuffed teddy-bear. When she spoke, the words dribbled from her thin mouth in a meaningless sing-song. At any moment he expected her to tumble over her wilkies like a clown.

"What do you think of Jenny Campbell?" she asked, folding her hands like Alessandra in 'The Birth of Venus'. "Going to New Zealand?"

"She's daft," said his mother, succinctly.

"Her brother had a call, she shays."

Up and down went the voice in endless variations.

"Hm!" said his mother, with staring eyes, "I ken the call he had."

It was all slightly incomprehensible. It was like looking in the bird house at the zoo. He knew Jenny Campbell. She had brought him a yellow chicken once, and a boat with real cottonwood smoke coming out of the funnels. She was a Sunday-school mistress.

"Are you going to the saree tomorrow?" asked his aunt, with a simper. "She'll be there."

"Dae ye tell me that?" said his mother.

He was going. He had his ticket. It was blue, and in black capitals on it stood the inscription:

PENNY SOIREE

ST ROLLOX CHURCH

TEA   CAKES   CONCERT   ADMIT BEARER 1d.

"What's a saree? he asked.

"It's a place where everybody does as he likes," his aunt cried. "A ceilidh, only better."

For no apparent reason his mother began to recite:

> "How wad ye like tae be me?
>   Going to a penny soiree;
>   A lump of fat
>   Stuck in my hat;
>   How wad ye like tae be me?"

17

It was like all the other exciting words he saw in the town when they passed through it on Saturdays coming from Pollokshaws. There was BONANZA, where they secreted Santa Claus in a gigantic free shop full of lucky dips, and the COLOSSEUM, where people had to be urged to take something for nothing by means of huge posters, and streamers, and then, when they did so, were arrested.

These were the opposite of the Bank and the Church. His mother took him to the Bank on Saturdays and to Church on Sundays. They were next door to each other, and for a long time he thought them part of the same institution. They formed part of the same taboo. The furniture in the bank was massive — like the furniture in the church — oak and ebony. The doors, which David opened for his mother with both hands, were gigantic and swung open only very slowly. The men inside were clad in black, the lighting was subdued, and obviously operations of great significance were going on. The only difference was that no one sang out of the bank books as they did out of the hymn books, and none of the men in the bank delivered a sudden sermon from a ledger, although they looked as if they might at any moment.

On the counter stood a text: "Take Care of the Pence and the Pounds will Take Care of Themselves".

He disliked church himself. The first time he had gone, a figure had appeared in the pulpit and he had asked: "What is the man doing in the wee box, mummy?"

"Sh!" she said, and stuffed into his open mouth a cough drop, which he at once took out and found to be the shape of the moon.

The Bank was far more interesting. It was full of strange contraptions. There was a little white wheel like a mill-wheel, upon which they wiped their fingers instead of licking them, when they had to count sheets of dirty paper. He would have liked one of those. It would have saved him licking his own fingers when he had to strip the paper from treacle toffee. He watched the wheel spin round and dip into the water below. There was also a sponge sitting in a tiny basin which they used for the same purpose. It was not so good, for sometimes it gave out a horrible shrill squeak. Still, it was all part of the ceremony and rites like the altars, and organs, and choirs, and shaded lights, and thick carpets, and palatial arches, and furs, and bated breath, and self-conscious coughing. He did not like it at all.

The ticket was glossy as a negative of Tom Mix.

"Be sure and come," Jenny had said. Her hair was knotted and dry, but white too, like the cottonwool smoke.

The whole affair was full of contagious fever. Jackie Boyd was going. So were the Richardsons. Everyone took it for granted he was going too. He did not remember being asked, except by Jenny.

Darkness fell on an evening of frantic washing and donning of best clothes, and there followed the long trot along Auchentoshan Terrace in complete obscurity but for the dandelion lamp-posts, towards the gates of St Rollox Church, normally chained and padlocked like Barlinnie Prison, and thick with flakes of dust and dung. It never occurred to him that St Rollox had been a saint. Who had ever heard of St Rollox the Good? Or even St Rollox the Bad? Across the road he saw the great engine-yards of St Rollox where his grandfather had worked for half a lifetime, one of a thousand blue-clad slaves who carried the lamp of Aladdin round the monstrous locomotives, oiling the various parts. His grandfather had had rheumatism in his finger-joints. No one oiled his various parts. He was no engine, though at times he was expected to be. He wasn't even the patron saint of the railway as the dim St Rollox might be at best. He was only a man, as David doubted St Rollox had ever been.

The gates were open. The huge pseudo-medieval doors were folded back and a golden light shone forth, as if from the depths of a cave. It was like a bazaar. Sometimes they had a bazaar in church, where everyone raffled and rifled and ruffled, but the minister was not a very good Ali Baba. At the entrance, like a drinking-trough, stood a stone bowl for the "offerings". He dropped his own coin in with a loud clink, and, holding his breath, passed through. For a moment he stood as if blinded by the glare of light and the wave of sound that hit him before he could gather himself together and look round.

The pews were packed with shouting, screaming, kicking, singing, gesticulating children of every shape and colour. At each end of the various benches sat a monitor, acting as a kind of breakwater. The church was more crowded than it had ever been in its life. Of that he felt sure. Over the altar had been built a kind of stage, conveying the impression of a built-up fireplace. Ninety per cent of the howling mass of infancy went neither to church nor to Sunday-school, preferring to spend their time in stealing or breaking windows, but this was different. It was a soiree, a desecration, a demonstration they were accustomed to in the street and which they normally called "a rammy".

Suddenly he caught sight of Jenny. There was her brilliant smile, deriving from a profusion of teeth, and the dry wisps of her hair. He sat down in the tightly packed pew next to her and a bespectacled girl with eyes like a fish. She gave him a paper bag. Some of the boys had already their noses in theirs, as if it really were a nose-bag. He opened it and saw that there were cakes inside. Carefully in that barrage he counted them. There was a rock-cake, two cookies, and a doughnut with the remnant of a blob of jam still sticking in it. No snowball. No meringue.

Silently he placed it on the ledge where the Bibles usually lay. There came then a tremendous roar that made him jump.

The tea had arrived.

Above the mad clamour he could hear the kicking of seats and a dull stamping on the floor, accompanied by a monotonous chant: "WE WANT TEA! WE WANT TEA! WE WANT TEA!"

There were baskets of cups. There were jugs, pails, canisters, bowls, kettles of tea. When at last everyone seemed supplied and replenished and refurbished, the inevitable bun-fight began. Pieces of paper dipped in tea flew through the air in hard pellets. Thick as hail they fell. To escape, one had to bob down on one's seat. David was struck on the neck by a particularly unpleasant missile which flattened when it landed.

Looking round to find out who had thrown it, he saw it was hopeless to even try. Boys were standing on the seats. Others were leaning over, or bobbing and weaving in mischievous delight. The girls either imitated them or screamed.

Turning round again to his cup, he was shocked to find that someone had placed a cake in it, and stuffed it well down with paper, dragged along the floor so as to be good and dirty. He gave up.

"This is the last time you will see me!" said Jenny Campbell, above the din. He could not hear. "I'm off to New Zealand," she shouted. He could only see the bun of her hair.

Cakes followed the pellets in an endless stream. The whole church was a menagerie in which the screaming never ceased for an instant.

DAVID! WILLIE! ELSIE! ARTHUR! COME OVER HERE! LOOK! OY! HEIGH! HEY! YOOHOO! AAALLEEEC!

She gave up trying to tell him and merely smiled at him.

It seemed senseless, but it was only a soiree. It must be a part of religion, like the St Rollox Works.

Now the organist began to play, and they pelted him too, as if a Bacchic or Dionysiac frenzy, or perhaps some ancient dance of warlocks had finally thrust through the years of miracle play. Not until the choir appeared did they run out of ammunition. They were tiring in any case, and these were their friends and relatives. They were, all together, the chorus, and the tragedy was about to begin, the family tragedy.

The choir sang a few hymns, and it was the turn of the concert proper. There were conjurers and singers and highland dancers wearing breastsful of medals, funny stories and recitations by blushing boys, and finally the choir again. It was a variety show, except that there was no Punch and Judy.

"I shall not see you again after tonight," said Jenny Campbell huskily. Feeling under the seat, she produced a large box, which she handed to him. When he looked at her to thank her, her eyes were full of tears.

"I'm going to New Zealand with my brother. He is a preacher."

He did not like to say "I'm sorry", as it did not sound right, so he said "Is New Zealand very far?"

"Very far. I may never come back, David. But I shall always think about tonight."

It seemed incongruous. A penny soiree and New Zealand, where the butter came from, in the Maypole Dairy. He remembered seeing a cow from there in the window. Suddenly they all stood up and sang 'God Save the King'. Most of the children were too sleepy even to look at the orange they received at the door before being ushered out into the cold night.

He hurried again past the cemetery of St. Rollox, and past Sighthill Cemetery, the orange lying in his hand like a harvest moon, and felt the dead had risen and were hurrying after him. They couldn't have.

21

It had not been a resurrection, only a mirage. He ran faster to keep up with the Richardsons. St Rollox would be barred and shackled in dust and dung tomorrow and for ever as it had always been.

Long ago, his father had told him, there was a soldier who struck a boulder with a sword and transformed it into a warrior. There were the lines:

> Dar thighedh sluagh Tom na h'iubhraich
> Co dh'eireadh air tus ach Tomas?
> (When the Hosts of Tomnahurich come
> Who'll rise first but Thomas?)

His father said that was Thomas the Rhymer. He had been stolen away into a Far Countrie.

On he ran through the shrouds of mist and rain, back to the gaslit sunshine of the house.

"Yesh," his Aunt Bessie said, "he used to live near me. I kent him fine. He wrote the lines your mother told you:

> 'How wad ye like tae be me?
> Going to a penny soiree,
> A lump of fat
> Stuck in ma hat,
> How wad ye like tae be me?'."

Thomas, he thought, must have disappeared through falling under the seat at a soiree and never been missed when they locked up the kirk.

III

Horror-agog and frog-eyed, Mrs Greig appeared at an open door in the close, with upraised broom. David ran and ran. Out into the street, where he fell and slashed his knee on the jagged flints. His sister wept, thinking she had caused the fall; but it was Greig. The very name was the bark of the china-dog on his mother's mantelpiece, a soul-splitting crockery-cackle, a porcelain yelp — Greig! — as though the toys he played with had all come rantingly alive.

There they were, barking and shivering from the strands of her tinselled gray hair, her lidless gray eyes and protuberance of teeth: "Greig! Greig!"

At any moment she, or others as evil, might seize hold of him and pinion him with sightless glance, and he would drown, die, dissolve in the wave of terror emanating from the nothingness of the fishscale of those eyes. Always, coming downstairs after that, he stepped on pins and needles past her door and watched with awe the brass nameplate brazen on the varnished wood.

Only love overlaid these symbols of terrifying neutrality, so that he began to forget them, although, when sitting in the swing at the kitchen door, he could not enjoy the forward lurch into light for fear of the backward swing into the darkness of the corridor. They existed therefore as a background. They were the second plane to his behaviour, the undercurrent, in mortal combat with the friendly manifestations such as the aspidistra plant, which, every Sunday morning, grew a bar of chocolate wrapped in silver paper. Its leaves curled like dark green plumage out of the back of a black stucco swan. That was a mriracle if you like! So engrossed was he with the shiny crinkling paper illuminating the depressing wet plant that he left unexplored the gap between its being there and not being there. To be sure he went into the room sometimes on weekdays, but only because he was hungry for chocolate. Never for an instant did he doubt. As soon as he saw the dried tubers of the plant quite bare, he withdrew again silently, chill as the earth-mould round it.

It was probably owing to the aspidistra plant that he became aware of detail on the smallest possible scale. There were the contorted, pseudo-oriental designs on the chairs in the room. The material was green and the design in relief. He ran his fingers along the edges. In the interstices was no fur. It was horrible. Nor did the springs give. The arms, also fur covered, had a carved wooden base. They were particularly horrible.

The fireplace contained brass shovels and brushes, all highly polished. The ebony clock on the mantelpiece was equally highly polished, and had a maddening re-echoing tick, as if the makers had wanted to prove that it was going. The floor was clothed in a thick black rug of sheepskin. Thus everything within the four walls was either bald and polished wood or covered in dense hair. The only

23

available means of salvation in the whole jungle of fetish was a small organ, which, however, could in no time blow up a storm of incredible volubility, especially if you pulled out the stop marked — was it? — could it be? — BASSO VOCE. He liked pulling that. It had a smooth velvety touch and slid out, effortless as a feline claw.

At times the boy imagined that if he pedalled hard enough he would blow the whole room to fragments. Even 'Onward Christian Soldiers', however, failed to do that. All that happened was that, given particularly loud pressure, clouds of dust flew out as if it had not been an organ but a vacuum cleaner.

He was astonished. He climed down from the music-stool to peep inside behind the pedal. Yet, though he held it down, he could see nothing. It was a cave. It might easily have been a home for mice. Bobby had said that haystacks were cows' houses. He began to hoard things in it, forbidden objects, pearl buttons, toy soldiers, naked bobbins of thread made into steam road-rollers. It was a hollow mountain wherein dwelt the enemies of this existence. Sometimes he took them out and the soldiers fought in the sheepskin jungles of Brazil, the steamroller tore a path through the carpet, the pearl buttons opened up before his eyes a silver mine.

Normally, this was discouraged, and he was not supposed to go into the room at all. There were sacred occasions, however, in the evening just before a party, or on an especially cold Sunday, when the fire was lit and he was allowed to perch on a square stool with a leather top, about three inches high. A "party" was when your mother baked all afternoon, running here and there, ironing, wrestling, fighting down live dough, like a sculptor or a surgeon attending a childbirth, into the oddest shapes and consistencies. He was amazed at the transformation in the scene, and at the Sisyphean labour of his mother over tiny biscuits and slabs of shortbread which afterwards she dabbed like Auld Nick himself, with a hot fork. "If a thing's worth daein, it's worth daein weel," she said. Their shapes intrigued him. Animal biscuits bore each the outline of an animal in white icing, on a brown background. Shortbread had to be beaten all over to reveal little wrinkles and eyes, whilst cakes were fashioning themselves into birds and baskets. Yet tempers were short. Metal moulds for cakes were short. And the oven was much too small for her ambition, where David stood stirring the porridge with the spurtle.

The "party" itself was far less interesting than the tea. It consisted only in sitting around the fire playing whist, with cards advertising the C.P.R. On the backs of these were maple leaves and pine trees. On the face was a glazed real photograph of the scenic beauty to be found on the Canadian Pacific Railway. Dapper canoes throughout the pack sped over rockbound lakes, and weary travellers struggled up towering mountains. Sometimes in these scenes David sensed a brooding air of helplessness and emptiness which was distressing. Even the slopes of the Rockies repelled him, and not because of any threat of an avalanche from a crack in the card. They had merged with the shaggy empty room he lived in. He was certain that even from the train they would thrill him no more and no less than the sheepskin rug, and resolved to avoid Canada, if he could, in the future.

Easily the most mysterious person for miles was "The Gude Man". Pale, delicate, bob-haired Peggy Robertson, the girl upstairs with eyes like a mole when she had died, had, his mother explained, "gone to the Gude Man", an apparently desirable end which nevertheless cost all concerned many tears.

Her mother was much more concretely terrible than the "Gude Man", who seemed an ineffectual sort of fellow at best. She had had a portion of her cheek-bone removed — presumably for reasons of tuberculosis — though this was never mentioned — with the result that she stared though his dreams like an accusing phantom, the immense hole in the centre of her cheek tightening the single jawbone into desperate resolution. She, too, was a symbol; she was Eros oppressed, a monster with no definite features except those imposed on her by the terrible disintegration of her suffering.

The "Gude Man" seemed to be ignorant of all this. He was some-one you had to be kind to, or perhaps for, whenever you happened to remember. Sometimes David thought he was MacLacherty, who came sailing down the street every Saturday on a pony and float with a bell, selling apples or coal-briquettes in the intervals of his song:

"Aippuls, Fine Ammerrican Aippuls!" — or "Coal Brikets! Coal Brikets!" — according to whether he spun the sun or fine threads of mist and rain.

At still other times the "Gude Man" was the back-court singer, that modern troubador, 'Ye Banks and Braes', who sang the song of the same name in a tattered army greatcoat. He was old, with a drooping moustache of the Ming Dynasty, and no hope in anything except perhaps a drink. He therefore sang with considerable feeling the old lines:

> "Why do ye chant, ye little birds,
> And I sae weary, fu' o' care?"

Counterpart of the "Gude Man" was, of course, the "Bad Fire". This never meant much to David, because he could not see how a fire could be either bad or good. It was either a fire or it was not, and if it was a fire it was in a grate, and that was an end to it. So the threat "You'll go to the Bad Fire" held no terrors for him, being a piece of futile adult whimsy if they did not believe it, and superstition if they did. He had nothing but contempt for those who stood in need of a mythical fire to buttress their sagging authority. His father didn't.

He did not know his father at all at first, except as a man of mysterious movements, who occasionally appeared in the Room when he was plucking the bar of chocolate; one who had to be served with sausages and mince as soon as he came in. A man of colossal appetite, with bulldog face, he ate in short rushing bites. His bushy eyebrows, drawn down in a frown of wire, and his jaw, thrust out as if harbouring fangs, made David rather afraid. Yet there proved to be surprising things about his father that gave him confidence and made him happy to sit in a chair on the landing awaiting his arrival, watching the lamplighter clatter up the stairs with his ladder and torch, which he placed, plump, on the gas-lamp to puff it — splutter — into an incandescent hiss of brightness.

One of these things was that his father rarely if ever struck him. His mother was not so sure in her behaviour. She was capable of anything when she shouted and shook her fist at him, as on the day when he had been playing football, in spite of her admonition: "Don't kick your toes away again!"

Normally he played just the same, standing after the game at the corner of the street to let the wind blow the sweat off his face, and wiping his boots with a piece of paper. Once, however, he had forgotten to wipe off the mud, and like a fox she snapped: "Wait till you father comes home! He'll give it to you! Just wait!"

"Can I have a piece on jam?" he asked.

"No, you can't. I've had enough o' this. I'm fair sick o't," she girned. "It wad gar ye greet."

And that he knew was serious. His mother never used the phrase "sick o't" except with particular venom and emphasis that carried conviction. He slunk about the kitchen now with perturbed but fascinated glance, watching her black smoothed hair, like an Eskimo's, her sharp face, like a bird's when she turned in wonder and held her head on one side, screwing up her eyes in unspoken benevolent inquiry. Now there was no wonder visible, only, it seemed to him, boundless savagery. He began to sob, wandering round the house disconsolate and condemned, feeling his inner guilt and thinking of the coming thrashing — the unrestricted, unpredictable effects of it on all the love around him.

At nights he prayed to the Gude Man: "Make me a good boy, for I am a bad boy." His mother told him to do that. Perhaps it was really the Gude Man's fault that he was bad, but his was to be the punishment.

He heard his father's knock. "Rat-tat-a-tat!" and the quick decided downtread of his boots in the lobby. The stocky figure with the dome-like head appeared and his father threw a cap on the bed in the wall, took off his jacket, revealing arms and bunched muscles like an elm-bole, bare to the rolled sleeves, opened up his waistcoat and glanced round merrily.

"Weel, whit's new?" he asked as he sluiced the water over his head and neck at the sink, arms bent like a surgeon preparing for an operation.

"David's been a bad boy today. You'll hae to gie him a beating," said his mother, equally active and laying knives and forks for the meal, hastily, almost timidly.

He stood white-faced, waiting.

"No," his father panted, between gulps of air and great gasps as he rinsed eyes and neck with the towel, face red now as if he was throttling himself in that circular movement of rubbing. "He's a good lad you know; if you say he's bad . . . there must be some mistake."

"There's no mistake," said his mother, looking at him with needle-eyes as she poured the tea and lifted the kettle from the hob.

27

"He's been the deevil. I mean it. I'm fair sick o't. Ye'll take him into the room!"

David held his breath. This was a threat. No one was taken into the Room except for a deliberate thrashing.

"No, no, there must be some mistake," expostulated his father. "We'll talk it over. He's a good lad really, you know," until David could scarcely credit his ears. Surely his father must be either a fool, or — very, very wise? He began to walk around with his shoulders squarer now, feeling perhaps his father was right and he really was a good lad, and even if he wasn't he mustn't let his father down since he seemed convinced of it. Who knows what might happen if he found out his mistake? It might kill him. He might kill David.

His mother said he was "spoiled". He thought of a yellow cabbage leaf in the dustbin. That was "spoiled". His mother spoiled him. She picked his ears with hairpins until his father told her to take off her shoes and go in her stocking-feet. She combed his hair with a short bone-comb that was double-edged, and she cut his nails to the quick. She was to him the ogre out of Jack-the-Giant-Killer, who walked on stilts across the stage and laughed right into their box.

Everything settled again into place, the clear fire in the grate, the shining knobs of the oven handles, the hissing gas-mantle, the fender where he sat and read Sexton Blake and Dixon Hawke, hoping his father didn't see, because he said it was nonsense, although it belonged to this world of mysterious light and shade, of half-forces only dimly understood, of the balance and eternal war between "good" and "evil", "love" and "fear", his father's hands, his mother's kisses, both their voices; and the china dogs that never barked but looked as if they might; the horror of the dark; the rusting engine in the Low Park that cut your knee and hands if you slipped — between, in fact, the things that you knew and which knew you, and the things you could never know, the things that were rigid with mechanical, rebellious hate.

In the warm kitchen his confidence returned since his mother seemed to have forgotten the apparent ferocity of a moment ago.

"Can I have the tissue-paper from the bread, mother?" he asked.

Still resentful, she thrust it towards him and he pinned it by two pins to the table legs at the end of the little wooden table. This was another piece of friendly magic. The tissue-paper round the bread was brown and transparent and crinkling. If you pinned it up to the end of the table and put a candle behind it, you had a cinema. You could show the shadowy silhouettes of "scraps" and figures cut from papers.

Once right in the middle of the theatre his grandfather appeared. He could tell by the apparition of the long phenomenal knees. To his delight, his grandfather sat down between the table and the bed and was the whole audience! His head was the Gods; his knees were the Grand Circle, and his feet the Stalls.

The gods laughed when the marionettes moved in all their stilted gravity. Their actions did not matter. They could not do any harm. Set in the proper frame of the proscenium, they were insulated in space.

Their performance consisted chiefly in fighting and kissing. The figures bent over and embraced or jostled and pushed each other down. There was not much more they could do. The stage was rather small, and their reflexes therefore limited. Yet what they lacked in spontaneity and action they made up in character and exotic interest. There were coloured scraps borrowed from his sister, of Japanese ladies in nightgowns, combs and fans, winking penny-in-the-slot eyes, and pirates with their heads in turbans and a mouthful of fish-knives. There was a pale newsprint Charlie Chaplin, whose face was composed of spots, and a tomboy Pearl White in breeches. The trouble with the latter was that if you licked her too hard, you saw instead of Pearl, the printer's ink on the loss of the *Titanic*, which to David was as large and tragic as a broken mousetrap.

Between the acts there were no divisions, as there was nowhere to go had there been an interval. The cardboard theatre, which had formerly housed a gigantic pair of shoes, was not made to run to a curtain, did not perhaps believe in too great a severance from the auditorium. It was all a pleasant muddle really, rather than a play, and it ended abruptly whenever dinner was ready. The characters could all be scrapped at once. Often they would be cremated. There would be plenty more tomorrow.

His grandfather said it was a fine show, and he should know. David looked up his steep sides, amazed to find an adult so receptive.

"Are ye comin' out to the Shaws on Saturday again?" his grandfather asked.

"Oh yes; we always come out on Saturdays."

"Ye'll hae tae bring the theatre wi' ye!" the old man said, patting him on the head.

"He'll come," said his mother, "if he's no' on the training-ship by then."

He knew the dread word. It was what his father said when he took him into the room. He knew where the training-ship was. It was at Helensburgh. It was full of boys who had no fathers or mothers, or were too wild, and it was covered with black-and-white squares like Nelson's *Victory*. His father knew the captain.

"He doesn't want to go to the training-ship. He told me," his father said.

The prospect was terrifying.

Dissatisfied with the figures as they were now, because they would not stand up to their fate, David licked them and stuck them on the back of the screen until their faces and forms shone through like shades from beyond, dim ghosts struggling into life. To make the image clearer, he would bring the candle closer until, catching the paper-screen, it wrapped the whole faint theatre and marionettes of paper in a tongue of consuming flame, and David leapt back terrified, and his mother screamed.

The training-ship! Would it be the training-ship?

The china-dog barked.

Yes! Yes!

IV

When, after much daring, David discovered that he did not live in a palace-yard but in a small kitchen, which did not contain a theatre, a tent, an aeroplane and a racing car, but a table, a bed, a sewing-machine and a round-backed wooden chair, the realisation was something of a blow, and he tottered out to play in the streets.

The girls let him play with them at "hooses". That was keeping house, but it was not much more fun than really being in the house. Boys played "bools", with steelies, glessies, plunkers and jorries.

They played "rubbish" and "tig" and "conkers". "Tig" was It. "Conkers" were chestnuts. "Rubbish" was anything in your pocket, hairpins or halfpennies or buttons, thrown against the wall. If you were nearest, you threw up the rubbish in the air and if you caught it when it fell, you could stick to it. They had "peeries" they flogged, and coloured metal singing-tops if they were rich. They played "moshie", a queer game of marbles involving three holes in the ground, spaced out evenly. Into each of them the marble had to be rolled, the opponent's being, if possible, knocked away in the process. When one boy was going up to the top hole for the third time, this was called going up for "snooks", and ended the game. David never found out what "snooks" were, but they seemed definitely worth going up for.

The girls were nicer at first. They had dolls, and you were a big doll, and they played "peever", or "baw-beds", which the English call "hopscotch", imagining the Scots to be a hopping nation. They wrote on the pavements in large letters of chalk "No more playing so don't ask!". They played "bee-baw babbetty" and sang:

> "Bee-baw babbetty,
> Babbetty, babbetty,
> Bee-baw babbetty,
> Babbetty babbetty bowster!"

or:

> "Ring a ring o' roses,
> A cup a cup o' shell,
> The dog's awa' tae Hamilton
> To buy a new bell."

or again:

> "Is it hauf past ten
> An' is the morning dry?
> Hiv you got a haddy
> Or onything tae fry?"

They had their own songs and their own rhymes. When they chose someone in "tig" to be "het", they all stood against the wall and were counted:

> "1, 2,   Buckle my shoe.
> 3, 4,   Shut the door.
> 5, 6,   Pick up sticks.
> 7, 8,   Lay them straight.
> 9,10,   A big, fat hen."

and the famous:

> "Ickerty-pickerty
> Pies a-lickerty
> Pumpaleerie-jig."

These were magical incantations, recited with pride and fervour by the umpires, like Druids chanting a spell. Some were just nonsense-rhymes:

> "Dan, Dan, the funny wee man,
> Washed his face in the frying-pan,
> Combed his hair with the leg of the chair,
> Dan, Dan, the funny wee man."

There were hundreds of them. One of the girls from upstairs, Minnie Robertson, took David to school on his first day. The first day was all right, but afterwards began the real process of education, during which the boy was stripped, ragged, scruffed, strapped, caned, booted, upended, frog-marched and generally fired and tethered into a semblance of correct deportment as conceived by the Big Five (not the Yard) and the microscopically-graded Civil Service.

Not that there was a chance of the products of this school going into a bank, even to deposit coppers from a home safe, or into the Civil Service, even as crosseyed telegraph-boys. They were much more likely to go into Millar's the grocer as roll-boys, and come out again with a leather skull-pad on their basketed heads and a floury face, like "Crab" Upcraft, or into a butcher's to work up from slitting papers to a pig's throat, cheeks becoming bloodier with insolent health and dogs running cheerfully after them, even in quite a strange town, and in "civvies".

Unattractive as were the exits, however, they came to resemble Heaven to the boys, principally for four main reasons:

32

I.   They were outside the spiked iron railings ringing in the school. These grew in that particular shape in order to tempt the boys to climb over, so as they could tear their trousers and legs. They were iron plants that lived on boys.

II.   It was a different part to play in the drama of life, a part in which one's lines were to "nip" fags, take a bird out, and free-and-easy to swear, spit, puff, gurk, and generally act the tough man without any goddamned headmaster taking up the challenge to see if you meant it.

III. It was a free country. You didn't *have* to do anything. Anyone could cheat, swindle, steal, graft, bully and blackmail his way to the top as long as he had the drop on the others and did not believe in a group.

IV.   Dammit, it meant for you you threw away your school-cap and the trousers that shaved your legs for longs and a workman's "cady" and muffler. You had silver in your pocket to jingle — till you reached home anyway — and you brought in a "wage", like a loaf.

At schule they called him many names. He was "Liar Liar Lickspit in ahint the caunlestick", ninny-numbskull, toly-bungler. He was a rabble-dazzler, a tammy-tousler, a shitty breeks, a wee shauchly shaver, a dram doddle, and a scrim-shanking rapscallion skulldugger. They wrote that in their books.

Among these kittly kilties and busby-jumpers and chittering german gomerils, he was a laggardly stockjobbing sycophant, a doddering, back-scratching, mealy-mouthed tub o' guts. That was what the English teacher said. He said an Aberdeen fishwife had shouted it in his hearing. The boys thought up the answers, but they were only a set of tatter-demalion buncombe-gestators, hindlehoggish flibbertygibbets, toddly-winking corybants, snuffshifters, privy pullulators.

Before boys were allowed to "leave" school, they had by main force to pass an examination, not an examination related to anything in the scheme of things, just "an examination". The questions were not just questions either. They were Questions. They helped to create the whole complex of Questions in the world outside. They helped to make the whole Earth unhappy if it had not a Question to solve.

33

Boys left, their heads positively buzzing with Questions. They never remembered being given any list, however modest, of Answers.

Describe the cogitations of Harold before the Battle.

Construct a sentence to illustrate the use and significance of the word "fiddlesticks".

Parse Harold in the above question.

"Do you know Wee Rosa?" the boys said. Wee Rosa who? Wee Rosa Hooses.

That was what the boys said, and why in this cast-foundry, "education" to them meant less than half a toffee-ball.

The first thing to learn was The Bell.

When The Bell started ringing it was a warning that in five minutes you would be late and marked absent and need a line from your parents on why you did not come. This taught you obedience. It meant that in after-life, every time you heard a Bell, you would start running, whether it was a fire bell, a hand bell, a door bell, a telephone bell, a church bell, or, in the Alps, a cow bell. Primeval things, such as washing, having breakfast, or even putting on one's clothes, had to be dropped as soon as The Bell rang. This was the main reason why so many otherwise decent, well-behaved boys arrived at school snot-rotters, eating pieces, extracting soap from their dingy ears, or even tucking their shirts down the front of their trousers.

He always had to run to school. He was always running, at the beck-and-call of Mr Bumbletory, Francis Ponce, Jack Botabol, and old Joshua Midriff.

He rarely had time to dream or seek release from that iron obedience. He must "get on", they said, though they never told him where to go.

Yet it was in Petershill that he first learned to look at the city round him, and from Petershill that he began to explore the wastes of streets, stretching for miles away into the distance.

His own street, Laverockhall Street, he discovered, lying between Springburn and Provanmill, formed part of a pastel-desert in which blocks of tenements rose like the standing-stones of some primitive megalithic civilisation. Burns mentions the laverock often, but no laverock had been heard there for generations. Before the invasion of this stone cataract, the birds had retreated as once they withdrew from the ice. Few of the kirtled shawlies among the inhabitants even knew what a laverock was.

Towards the north spread Paddy's Park, a high waste of soil many acres in extent, on which few blades of grass ever grew. It was pitted with trenches dug by children, which invariably filled with rainwater and rarely drained. To the south there sprawled the Caledonian Railway Locomotive Works, known locally as "The Cally", with girders in place of poplars, and vast arenas of oil-drums. This, too, pinned down in idleness hundreds of ravaged acres.

Asphalt on the streets and pavements expanded like rubber into blobs of tar for boys to play with during the long afternoons when hooters and sirens were silent.

On the western side, Sighthill Cemetery hemmed in the living as well as the dead; whilst far to the east, the furnaces and chimneys of the famous Cowlairs Locomotive Works completed the design of a jagged human pen. Engines from there went to India, China and South America. The majority of the men who built them did not even go down town. Their tendency towards escape was termed "romance" and had to be built into their craft, or dissolved in tears and blows on a Saturday night at the Kelpie Inn.

It was a compact piece of territory, all the more so since every trace of spontaneous nature, including flower-pots on window-sills, had been blacked-out by smoke or erased by the knives and bibles of inhibited industry. Flowers in these former fields meant only arum-lillies under bridal-veils of glass in the cemetery. To the boy, therefore, something symbolic clung to the figure of the stonemason at the corner, who broke up all forms of the stone that was paralysing and throttling the life of the city, and shaped it into Celtic crosses. He should, David felt, have been turned loose on these terrible streets and on these walls, chalked with scorpion-like inscriptions. He might have made of them something more than condemned cells.

Masses of men in blue dungarees, shambling daily out of the "Cally", blackened mess-tins in oily hands, darkened the streets with sullen purpose. Masses, shambling without direction, like cattle moving along a country lane, bestirred themselves in his dreams and tried to break free of the iron monster they served.

35

Only the wonderful Clydesdales, with cornflowers in their manes and tails docked, trampled urbanely about their patient business. Their shoes, rising to a rhythmic crescendo as they tackled the innumerable hills at a brave trot, provided a background of music to the discordant sounds of the city. They had manes like lions. They dominated in their very nobility those warrens of cobbles and those hills of rain; and in the summer, as if the winter of work had not been enough, they carried the children from neighbouring Sunday-schools into the country on an annual trip. Benches were placed back to back on the carts. The carts themselves were painted resplendently in red or blue or green, and the horses, apparelled as no circus-horse had ever been, wore great towering bridles hung with arches of flowers and bells, on a shining harness of leather and brass fit for palfreys, and their ears and manes were decked with blossom. These festivals had a pagan origin like much in the city, but to children and horses both they were unforgettable and, though stigmatized by chimneys and the belching fires of Cowlairs as a dream, were more significant by far than the meaningless plodding existence led every day by horses and men alike.

His grandfather had worked in the "Cally" until, amid fumes and clanging fires, consumption had painted his cheek like a clown's, and his hair shone like snow. The place now meant to the boy a concrete hell that beat through his heart like a dynamo. Even if he had to run away, he felt, he must not let himself be engulfed in this morass of mad injustice. He had been on one of the trips when a child, and never forgot it. Carters and their horses were knights without armour, wandering among canyons of furnaces and yards where thistles grew, towards their final encounter with the caged engines of disaster.

Laverockhall Street, however, was wiser than some of the other streets. The buildings in it were of red sandstone. That was warmer than the crumbling yellow stone, like caried teeth, of poorer Bedlay Street, which after four o'clock in the day became a veritable Bedlam of ragged, running urchins, intent on any and every form of reckless mischief.

Though he, too, had to run, and had not time to dream, it was in Petershill that he learned to look at the horses and the men, and unconsciously to listen to the fury and the meaning of their labour.

Through the long, frozen windows and the tall forests of railings, he gazed at them in his dreams, hearing the sound of hooves coming up the long white ribbon of cart-track from Garngad. "Glasgow," he said.

Glasgow or Glesca or Glesga or Glasga or Glasgie go the iron hooves on the cobbles coming out of St Rollox, for the horses in the streets outnumber the Lord Provost and are louder than the riveters of the Empire. The bird that never flew and the fish that never swam, the tree that never grew and the bell that never rang are all buried in this city of whistles and sirens once called "Glaschu".

If it were one of its own ships, he felt, or even only a stowaway, it might go somewhere, instead of pulling the imperial cart up Buchanan Street. As it was, the rains fell through the square, aslant like Zulu spears, and Queen Victoria sat in her shroud, an old shawlie in a drunken Band of Hope. The bailiffs had moved in. The carts were carrying off her furniture in crates. Her hens were locked in wooden cages. The corridors of her home were lanes in a vast goods station. The cock crew. Her palace was a pumpkin. She was old. So Glasgow or Glesca or Glesga or Glasga or Glasgie went the iron hooves of doom in her rooms, for carters in bell-bottom trousers outbid bailies in brass, and spit on their hands as the rain spits in the Clyde.

TWO

I

At Simpson's, just before the Low Park, where a charging bull had put its foot through McAra's barrow, they sold sugarolly straps like Miss Miller's tawse. It was a sweet idea. Tawse you could eat! He remembered the legendary strap Miss Miller had, boiled and sprinkled with pepper, they said, every night. He did not believe that, though Miss Miller herself, with her silvery hair, her flowery complexion, baked face and billowy skirt, was definitely like a little edible figure, the verimost sweetiewife. She was like the cousin of old Millar in the dairy, that lactial Clemenceau.

Since the affair of his Aunt Bessie, David was always seeing relationships in faces where in fact no relationships existed. Sometimes at home in the evenings they played a game of cards called "Happy Families", and the faces in that horrified him. There was Master Potts, the painter's son, and a horrible spectre, Miss Potts. There was Mr Bunn the baker, and the frightful Miss Bunn. Miss Miller, he thought, had probably looked like Miss Bunn when she was young, her hair all done up in a prim pagoda. Most frightening of all were the chimney-sweep and the butcher with his cleaver. They were linked in David's mind with the pictures of the prisoners in the Bastille which he had seen in a copy of *A Tale of Two Cities*, filthy, hungry spectres with rolling eyes, devils which were to him more real than the ineffectual oddities represented by the others. It was not pleasant to think that in the time of Dickens, when children like himself were being ordered to sweep chimneys, their terrified portraits were liable to be put on a card for the parlour amusement of those whose chimneys they kept clean, and who represented "good taste".

The cards had been badly produced, with the result that the lips were shapeless and slobbering, as if the people concerned must be constantly wiping off blood. They were the ones who, late at night at the corner of the street, called after him: "Pussyfoot, Pussyfoot!" Mr Grant was one. He said that too.

With his penny on Saturdays he bought a sheet of dabetties. He liked the name "dabetties", and rolled it on his tongue as he did the transfers themselves before sticking them on the back of his hand to glare at him, green and blue and yellow and red, in the garish colours of nightmare. They had odd faces too, but friendly ones. When you moved your skin they did funny dances.

There were other words he had once thought "funny", like "dabetties", in that improbable world where to be funny was not to be amusing but to be strange or even beautiful. There was, for example, "glabber". That was a noise made by striking mud with the flat of a spade, or with one's hand. It was the mud itself, the original perhaps of which the Scots "glaur" was only the contraction. He had never heard it used except by other children.

Always there was a world struggling to break through, a world on the verge of the freedom it had once known, a world struggling to be born, of speech and action, of forgotten sights and sounds, the world of horses and the carters, of the Cally workers when the siren blew, of Master Potts and the Happy Families, and the filthy spectres and Miss Miller, and his father, and grandfather, and his grandmother's language, and McLacherty, and 'Ye Banks and Braes', and all his children friends. Especially in words and action did he feel that imprisoned world, against which were set the school and Midriff and Ponce and Botabol, policemen and magistrates and draughtsmen who designed better engines than houses.

There was "fankles". His kite's tail was often "fankled". It was wound in such tightness of confusion that it was almost impossible to unravel and perhaps a knife would have to be used. That was "fankled". A lot of things in the world were "fankled". It was better not to think about it, his father told him.

"Let me tell you a baur," he said. That it was. A baur, a story worth telling, sometimes amusing, always vital, and with point, true with a poetic truth.

There was Cording. He was "fankled" too. He lived at the top of the street and was top of the class, a bright boy with curling blond hair, who always sniffed and looked incredibly woebegone. His innocent eyes were inwardly puckered as though he could not bring himself to believe that the world was actually as it appeared.

"Ingins" had no such qualms. A small, wizened creature with a face like a crab-apple and a mouth as firm as a trapdoor, he made his world as he wanted it. David fought a battle with him one day after school.

"You? I could beat you with one hand tied behind my back," he said.

"Aw right," said Ingins, in his precocious bass, "I'll fight ye at four!"

The dread challenge was out. There was no shirking. A pack of screaming boys propelled him out of the stone building and down the steps into the stone quadrangle shouting: "A fight! A fight!" He was scarcely aware of what was happening. It was out of his hands entirely. It was not his fight anymore. It was a "school" fight.

He shaped up. Ingins danced before him like a firefly and suddenly smote him on the nose. It had always been his weak spot. Now it began to bleed. At once a horde of boys parted them. "Ye're beat!" they shouted at him. "Na, ye're beat!" The first to draw blood, it seemed, won. He hadn't started. It was his own private fight, didn't they know? He was amazed.

Afterwards, Ingins was much nicer, and saw him home.

"Oh my! Will ye see to that boy?" his mother shouted, putting down the teapot when he arrived, nose bleeding still. "Oh my! What I've to stand! Take him into the room I tell ye. He's been like that the haill day!"

"Whit's up wi' ye wumman?" asked his father, glancing ferociously. "I work the whole damned day and hauf the nicht and this is whit I get when I come hame! Gimme some peace! Haud yer tongue!"

"Now!"

His mother glared at his father, and David could see from the angle at which she held her head in admonition, and from her eyes, staring in wild concern, that for some hidden reason it was all she could do to restrain her tears. She looked as though at any moment she might fly into fragments like the world. "Don't address me like that in front o' the weans. I'll not stand it!"

40

Precision in speech was characteristic of her anger. David's bowels melted into water. He wanted to cry and hug her, let his father thrash him, anything to release his mother from that awful strain of temper and pathos. His father, however, only glanced up once, but penetratingly, eloquently, interrupting his eating and sucking of gravy, to say: "Hiv some eighteenpence. Is the war gettin' intae ye?"

The ugly tone, and the slang, eighteenpence for sense, cut her like a whip. Her head sank as she turned aside in a paroxysm of sobbing, and a finger and thumb stabbed her eyes to stay the flow of tears and weakness.

"It's aye ma faut," she sobbed. "When you shoot oot yer neck of course it's different. Ye gave poor wee Meg a squint wi' yer roaring last week though!" this in an accusing crescendo.

These changes of front bewildered the child. He tried to follow, to see some sequence in the behaviour, to gain some insight into the causes — but they eluded him, as did the friendly and the enemy mysteries. It seemed as though his mother was now the china dog; as though everyone, even his father, lived on the verge of an inhuman madness, exuded from the whole incalculable world of iron, glass and crockery.

"Naebody tae think o' the puir wee lambs but me," she muttered, with contorted face, and led him off to bed. What had happened? Outside he heard the moaning whistle of the long and crawling trains.

"If I don't dae a'thing mysel', it's no' din at a'."

Their mother loved both children and husband with more intensity, perhaps, than any of them suspected. Busy all day as she was, her heart was wrung with anguish for them. She was a proud woman. Her father, a man of education and real calibre, was not one who had learned how to count and how to spell merely in order to make more money; money he abhorred; but a Scotsman of the old school, loving education for its own sake, for the deepening knowledge and consciousness of reality it brought, and for the philosophy it gave him, wrung from religion.

She had seen him walk daily into work, seven miles, and seven miles back at night, for earnings that were meagre. She had noted his spartan habits and his generosity to others in need, with its small, if existent, reward. Whilst idolising him for that, and because he was capable of real and lasting affection, she had resented the fact that often his children had had to suffer as well as he himself, because of that very uprightness, in a world that had no room for a scholar and a gentleman. His son, for example, had had a good education, although he had not gone to a university but into a bank. She had married, and been twitted by her sisters for marrying "below her station", the man being only an "engineer" and coming from a line of "engineers", who were the opposite of scholars. Sometimes she thought it was true. Sometimes she thought she had missed the finer things in life by marrying as she had, that she had been forced to miss them because her father had not had the foresight or the financial ability to make possible a good match.

Yet she loved her husband, and still loved him. There was something impressive and appealing at the same time about his finely-chiselled lips and jaw, something direct, that would not be put off with evasion and pretence any more than her father could be put off by these, although he lacked perhaps her father's sensitiveness and culture, being more interested in engines and mechanical contrivances of every sort. It had impressed her when he disappeared for two years after overhearing her sister call him a good-for-nothing, and returned with nearly three hundred pounds in the bank. Not that money interested her, but one had to be careful, and she was so afraid now that the same would happen in her own family, money would go to those in need, to his parents, for example, and they themselves might be in want. That she could not stand. Love and pride forbade it. Not selfish pride, not pride of race, but the pride of her blood, individual self-denying pride typical of her stock.

When David was in bed she returned to the kitchen in silence. After the implied rebuke she was smarting and contemptuous. At moments like this she felt she could leave him without the slightest remorse.

On the grate she noticed some sparks of soot, and that gave her the opportunity for a fresh outburst.

"There'll be a blaw doon here the nicht!" she said snappishly, looking up the chimney and pulling the vent to and fro as she did so. "It's a good job we're leaving. The chimney would have tae be swept."

That, too, she hated. All the dirt of it.

"Mair expense."

Her whole surroundings, in fact, were loathsome to her, the room and kitchen in the noisy tenement; the gossiping, occasionally drunken neighbours; the dirt; the work and worry. . . .

She had to rise at six with her husband, because she did not like him to make his breakfast alone, being afraid that he would skimp himself and go out into the cold with nothing on his stomach. While he lit the fire she would fry some ham and eggs in the little yolk-encrusted pan and "mask" the tea. They never had much time for conversation in these early hours, when the light, like consciousness first breaking on the world, filtered slowly through the little panes above the sink.

There was never much time for conversation even in the evenings.

"Funny thing happened the nicht," her husband remarked. She waited intently, ready to pounce. "A went to see that shop I've my eye on. Ye remember I telt ye I mentioned it tae Alec."

Alec was his employer, a man who owned several machine-shops. She nodded impatiently, listening and watching his features.

"Well, he'll no' sell noo."

So that was it.

"Hm. T-t-t." She nodded her head backwards and forwards several times as if whilst expecting something of the kind, she could still scarcely credit it.

"He promised it tae you for £250 didn't he?"

"Aye. There's something funny aboot it. It's a nice shop. A good cycle and sidecar trade could have been built up in it, and maybe a garage one day; and there's plenty o' space."

Now she walked about, poking the fire, turning down the gas, laying back the bedcover, all, in her agitation, little meaningless gestures.

"You're aye the mug!" she flashed out at last, though as yet she did not understand anything except that he had missed an opportunity.

It was all part of his stupid goodwill, she felt. He would never get on. "The deil provides for his ain!"

There was her ancestor, who had been imprisoned as a Covenanter after signing the Solemn League and Covenant in

43

blood in Greyfriars Churchyard. That was a pride of shame he had turned into victory. In the dungeon of Crookston Castle he had made a model in wood of his prison which was now in the possession of the laird. She, too, made a model of her prison. Thoughts like these were so much air to her husband. He in his mind was comfortably off working twelve, sometimes fourteen hours a day for six pounds a week, not seeing his children at all from Friday morning at six till Sunday morning. Nor was that all. Out of his small wage a pound went to his parents living at the coast, and though they needed it, his own father being an invalid, they were not as grateful as they might be, or even as thrifty. Her children and her family were the sufferers. He might at least think of his children!

"The man must have been tipped off by Alec!" he said suddenly, and the effect was like a rocket.

"T-t-t." she was looking up now, eyes staring, as she said herself of others, out of her head "like pot feet", her hair thrown back in part challenge, part ecstasy.

"I tell ye. I tell ye," she muttered in a contralto crescendo, though what she told him was not clear. "He's no' slow, is the Big Yin. He's no' slow. That's aye the wey o't. You're aye Johnnie A'thing!"

Little meaningless phrases accompanying meaningless gestures such as putting the boots on the "spars" of the table and tucking in the tongues, snapping down the lid of the tea-caddy, wiping a piece of dust from below the threepenny bank, gestures devoid of any purpose save the expression of her excitement and indignation.

"You're too saft, that's what's the matter wi' ye! Too saft!" she hissed, and again tut-tutted, her pale face and raven hair weaving a witch of her anger.

He knew what was coming and unloosed his collar, throwing it with the bow-tie atop the coal-bunker, habits and undress she hated. The whole house oppressed him now. He felt there was no room. He was being choked. His mouth set grimly. The coal-bunker behind, serving as a dresser, stuck out in the middle of the kitchen. The folding-bed was let down like a medieval bridge; the table was larger with the wings up, and the sink shut off the window.

There was hardly room to swing a cat in. And now his wife was nagging because he would not break with his boss, or because he wouldn't demean himself by asking for higher wages.

"I really don't know how I stand it! I really don't!" she wept, eyes like slits and her face twisted into the grimaces of a clown with tears and grief in place of greasepaint.

"Some day I'll just give wey a' thegither; I know I will!"

"Listen, Teenie!" He leapt up angrily now. "You're too damned weel aff, and that's a fact. One o' they nichts I'll come hame drunk! — I'm no' Tom Foy!"

It was the direst threat possible to utter, but who Tom Foy was no one knew. He was a mythical figure, a fool, as Johnnie A'thing was a helpless creature at the service of others.

"Speak like that tae Alec, no tae me," she whimpered, and still he failed to see her real desire and need, as indeed did she. Comfort to her meant little. Love meant everything.

"I'll dae that when it's time," he said, his face a mass of thunder. "No' afore. I ken I'm makin' him a fortune. £100 a week an' mair clear profit. I know he could never dae it himsel', the big midden. Whit does he know about machinery? I ken he's cheated me oot o' startin' up for myself, gie'n the man a backhander and tell't him I'm no' tae hiv the place. I ken he's a' you say he is, and that he needs me, but Teenie, we need him noo tae!"

It was a last appeal and she spurned it.

"I don't dae it for him! It's for the sake of the faimily and the auld man. I love them. I'm like one o' the brithers, Teenie, and the auld man's like a faither tae me. Alec's in charge noo, the only blacksheep among the lot, but I canna leave the noo, jist because o' that, no' as long as the auld man's still alive!"

There were six brothers in the Falmouth family and Macrae had almost grown up with them. Mrs Falmouth had first taught him to save money in a bank.

"Dae ye think the auld man disnae ken his son is stealing the business aff him?"

"The Big Yin's gettin' the benefit though. Allow him!" said Mrs Macrae bitterly.

Alec Falmouth, her husband's immediate boss, was The Big One

45

to all and sundry, often indeed Big Mick, meaning he had a high conceit of himself.

"Mother!" David called from the room. "Mother!" terror flooding him like a sea there in the moonlit dark of the room and the jungle of green doom.

"Shut yer gub!" shouted his father, roused by frustration. "I'll gi'e ye a skelpit leatherin'!"

His wife seemed to crumple.

"Sh! The neeburs!" she hissed, but it was too late.

"Damn the neeburs!" he shouted again.

Meg, blonde and scared mite, looked up blinking in the gaslight through her sleep, from the bed in the wall, and began to cry almost before she was awake.

"Lie doon!" he bellowed at her, now thoroughly roused. Normally this terrified his wife into silence and a beggar's humility, but tonight, because of the child, she became suddenly passionate.

"Don't you raise your voice tae her. I forbid it. Don't address my children like that!"

"*Your* children?"

Macrae laughed with unaccustomed bitterness. He was rarely bitter, and when he was, it was painful to see how it hurt him, when you loved him, and with what dignity he bore it.

"Go to sleep," he thundered again, though less loudly.

In a blind access of rage she slapped him across the face with the back of her hand, forgetting her heavy signet-ring, which left a weal on the skin.

He paled, staring at her for a moment. It looked as though he might strike her down with one of those ham-like fists, in a boxer's swing, and stretch her senseless; or as if she might snatch up a poker. Anything.

Instead, he quickly seized cap and jacket and stormed out, slamming the door behind him.

Again David shouted. "Mother!"

What was happening? He glimpsed the shadow of assassins in the corner, lurking strangulation; the walls, precipitous cliffs, made him giddy as he lay looking up at them. China-dogs and brass fire-set and black sheepskin rug all went dancing through their misery, evilly pitching and tossing inside his mind.

46

From the ebony eagle clock the hour was beaten out flat, eleven times.

"Mother!" he cried again, to save her — but she did not hear.

Her head was bowed as the sobs shook her.

II

The day's ritual began. In the morning the children had to be roused, David and Meg, David for school, Meg to crawl around on errands of mischief, opening the drawers of the sewing-machine, tearing in two David's collection of cigarette cards, whimpering, wetting.

She washed up. There was the scrubbing of pans, with nothing to relieve the prospect from the one window but wickedly spiked iron-railings below in the yard, caked with rust, smoke-blackened; and beyond, the rusting iron "Billy" on the mud-flat they were pleased to call the Low Park. When she looked from the window on to this back-court, paved with tar and gravel-studded, hearing children shout "Throw me down a piece on jam! Throw me down a drink! Throw me down my barrow!" she was always afraid of seeing someone impaled on the railings. There were five such "courts", all separated one from the other into little caged kingdoms by these spear-like stanchions, over which boys swarmed and which they tugged and kicked and pulled until they were wide enough to slip through. Once a boy in the next close had missed his footing as he was climbing and the rusted spearpoint, caked with soot, had sharply entered his groin. Fearful.

Nevertheless she washed and watched. At the head of the court they shared with twelve other families in the tenement stood a low brick washhouse with an iron boiler and two primitive tubs. There wives raced every day in brown shawls and fought like sparrows as to whose washday it was.

"You washed last Friday!" Mrs Robertson was screaming, pulling at her board.

"It was Thursday! It's ma turn noo!" retorted Mrs Boyd, a small woman whose red hair gathered in a bun, pale, freckled face and thin wormy lips impressed one with their wasting bitterness.

She never liked scenes. Rather than squabble meaninglessly out there, arousing hates and gossips capable of destroying her home, she would withdraw into her kitchen to wash as many clothes as possible in the sink, until her quick, unquestioning hands were split and cracked with hacks from long immersion in water, and the gathering forks between her eyes fought against the dim light. The wet clothes would hang to dry on the pulley as she opened the window to let the steam out of the narrow kitchen that was their living quarters. The white things could be done afterwards at night, in the washhouse, when nobody was likely to interfere.

On the wall hung a picture, "The Marriage of Cana", which she disliked intensely. It was a reproduction of an engraving containing a crowd of people in togas.

"Were you married at Cana?" David asked, seeing her look at it.

"No," she said. "That's in the Bible. Christ turned water into wine there."

"Are you glad Dad and I came to live with you?" he asked again.

"Of course," she said.

He was halfway through his porridge before he asked again: "Cana is in Heaven, isn't it?"

"No," she replied. "Why?"

"It's full of pillars and people undressed and music."

"There's *no* marriage in Heaven," she answered gravely. "Neither marriage nor giving in marriage."

Did that mean his father and mother would not know each other there? Or if they did, that they would not care for each other? It was all very strange.

"Oh we'll all know each other and be together again," his mother stammered impatiently when he kept on, "but there's *no* marriage in Heaven!"

He was surprised at the vehemence of her.

Once David was packed off, the dusting began of the room where the best furniture was kept in almost holy adoration. It never occurred to Mrs Macrae that the injunction "Worship no graven image" might apply as well to furniture as to statues, or that there was an affinity between the taboos and totems of Indians and the frantic collection by Europeans of objects they neither used nor intended to

48

use, because they were too valuable or lent a sense of glory to their owners through the mere fact of possession. Nor did she realise that in both social systems, the ancient and the modern, the result was identical, deification of an object, and consequent slavery of the spirit, ultimately in the most complete and terrifying sense.

Never in her wildest dreams did she imagine that her son was obscurely terrified of just these things, nor would she have understood if she had. No one went there except for a formal reception or a formal thrashing. Dusting the organ, she remembered with fervour how David had once thrust out his lower lip and wept when she played "Jesus Loves Me". Sentiment, she thought, had mysteriously touched him, but it was the lugubrious dark-green of the room, underlined by the heavy venetian blinds, the aspidistra and surrounding darkness which cramped, sickened and made the child afraid, much as the railings, the gossip and the quarrels did her.

After supper of an evening, when she really wanted nothing more than to sit down, or at least have the long-delayed conversation with Macrae, the loving small-talk and the retailed gossip, she had to wait till he read his paper by the fire, or did his calculations and plans, illegible scribblings covering pages, up and down and sideways, without rhyme or apparent reason.

She despised him for their untidiness, while she hated him for not seeing how much she wanted to talk to him. She never had time for a paper. If he was in a good humour, which to do him justice was very often, she could perhaps take the nails out of his trousers and sew on buttons, or prevail on him to change his suit so she could wash it or have the shining patches of oil taken out.

It was up to him to speak now, she wouldn't, she decided.

The children knew there had been a quarrel. It had engulfed them willy-nilly, interrupting their sleep, making David doze at school till the teacher threw the chalk at him and asked if he delivered milk in the mornings or why was he so tired?

The outer world burgled him at school. Gone were the days when he could let his imagination run riot in hundred part stories which he told to his friends grouped round the chimney on the roof of the washhouse in their back-court. To reach the class before the Bell stopped, he had to run across the street and up a narrow, crazy lane, uneven and full of puddles, between the backs of washhouses the walls of which he had learned to "dreep". This had become a race twice a day against his own doom.

School itself was the greatest shock to pristine wholeness. This was being "educated", learning you were a hopeless fumbling fool at sewing patterns of strips and scraps of coloured paper, that you would never be anything else; that the scissors and glue and weaving and intricacy of thought and shape and loopholes in design were all forever beyond you, so no use trying. Confidence and wholeness were in the myths around you, in the family, even in the "Gude Man", myths not in the sense of untruths but in the sense of space, the standing back of all these things that there might be room to breathe, a wider environment necessary if life were to expand like a flower and not simply be crushed at the outset.

Now at school he had suddenly learned that he must not dream or feel or imagine anything, but think, fit into shape, make coloured patterns and cardboard models from rigid enervating lines. sometimes there were ridiculous coloured beads to be strung along a thread. These forms of eyestrain always took place when the rain made everything dark outside, falling in a fine ceaseless sheet against the window-panes, and the naked gas mantles hissed through the tired classroom. On all these dreary days he would be kept behind, and the teacher would bicker at him, as though the only thing worth doing in the world was fashioning strips of coloured paper into a pattern.

Yet there were many things he liked. Today, for example, the essay Miss Miller gave them, the little, thin-lipped, marble-eyed woman in blue overalls who presented him every Friday with a penny for what he had written. Then there were the stories of Danish mythology, of Sigurd and Thor in Valhalla. He would have liked more of these. They came at half-past three, and the whole shaggy class sat silent and intent for half and hour. Gaels all of them, they had never heard of their own giant Cuchulain who waited down the river, and no one ever told them of Tir nan Og, the Land of the Young.

Occasionally, too, there was question time, for fifteen minutes, before four o'clock, when picked pupils competed against each other in asking and answering questions. David often won by asking questions culled from the columns of the *Children's Newspaper*. Then he would wander home pleased, forgetting the awful mistake he had made in saying that soldiers won medals for killing Germans.

Today on the way home, however, he dawdled, balancing matters up, the quarrel and the scraps and the essay. So young, he still saw no interval between things. Old train journeys to Fairlie were swallowed in tunnels of memory, and he saw only the winking Xmas tree Aunt Nan had stood in a bare, dark room, exciting and crackling as tangible stars, swimming in the smoke of his imagination. That was a symbol of sheer pungent beauty he could never forget. Why the quarrel, though?

On he walked, past Sneddon's hardware shop, smelling of varnish, brown paper and Mr Sneddon's moustache. Over there was Millar's dairy, where Millar himself lived in a large can, wearing a face of sour milk dried in scones and singing "Soor dook! Soor dook!".

At the corner stood the grocer, a huge fat man, exactly the shape of one of his outsize sacks of flour which he shovelled into a poke. He was wearing a white apron, had a bald head, side hair, and drooping whiskers, like white meal.

David was afraid to go into his shop, even for animal biscuits. If he did, Storey was sure to say, with a walrus grin, from the depths of his tun-like stomach: "Coo's lick!"

That, he learned, meant his, David's, hair. Black and watered, it curled in a tangled knot on the point of his forehead and could not be shed, giving him the appearance of a plump, if junior, Mephistopheles.

The more concrete the contours of the city, the more disturbing they always were. The scented imagery of the Fairlie Xmas tree became hard tinsel at the window of an orphanage on top of a hill in Glasgow. Twice a year his mother made him gather all his broken toys together, with others she said he didn't want, and they went in a tram to the orphanage. "Always remember the poor little girls and boys," she said to him, although they were by no means rich themselves. She need not have repeated it so often. He knew everything she would say. He knew what she would say today — about dinner. He knew what it was for dinner.

Home now, down the lane, past the blackened ash-bins with their spluttering tongues of burnt paper like torn-out roots, he idled, unwilling and afraid to have his food. The "sausages", links they called them, would be cold, he knew, and floating in little bergs, narrow floes of grease. He would choke over them, almost vomit, as his stomach turned.

"What are you looking at?" his mother would yell. "Eat it! It's good food and you should thank the Lord for giving your father strength to earn it."

That was true. He had no idea what was wrong, and accepted the suggestion that he himself was. But his stomach would not hold it, he knew. He daren't be sick, and ye he daren't refuse. What could he do with the links? Put them in his pocket probably, as he had done before, to throw them down the lavatory later, where they looked at home anyway.

He pushed open the door and went in. His mother was kneeling on the floor with pail and cloth, washing the linoleum.

"Your dinner will be cold, but you'll eat it!" she remarked, pushing with her head towards the table. There it was at the end. He had to stand now, while she slopped around his feet great blobs of water, up and down, as he stared at the grease. Cold fog drifted through the open window and he could smell the steam from the waxcloth. Only a miracle, he felt, could save them all from the coming explosion.

"Eat it!" She thrust her head up from between his legs, glaring at him so closely that he could see the prongs in her forehead.

"I can't! I'll be sick!" he whimpered. "I'm not hungry!"

Then, thinking better of it, as he saw the table laden with potato-scones, treacle scones, muffins, tarts, pancakes, crumpets and morning rolls: "I'm only hungry for the cheesecake!"

"The cheesecake is for your father. Take a soda-scone!"

They were the only ones he disliked, soda-scones, like Mr Millar who lived in a can.

"Was it dry when you came in?"

"Aye."

He picked up a potato-scone. It was useless to argue.

They picked him last at football seven-a-sides, with a look of indifference or even disgust on their faces, during their "slave market" selection of players. Even Johnnie Robertson, of the otter eyes and deer-like movements, who could punch you round the back and had a great respect for David's father because he had once been an amateur boxer, would only tolerate him, and sometimes left him out of cricket matches altogether. Then he would field desperately, at long-stop, hoping to attract attention by catching out a crack bat and be acclaimed by both sides.

"We're flittin' tonight," said his mother, panting with her efforts at swabbing the floor. So that was it! He was struck dumb. It meant a new environment altogether, but he was too miserable to think of that. He would lose his friends, the lamplighter who came sweating upstairs with his ladder and a blue smock and funny peaked cap, like a porter's, to give him a "shine" in the face with his lantern before climbing up to lay it on top of the close lamp so that "pouf" the dark stairs leapt into spluttering brightness. He was "Leerie-Leerie Light the Lamp".

He would lose Charlie Paterson, a tall boy in a short black jersey and shorter trousers, who had unquenchable curls, ate "saps" and lived in an attic in curious intimacy with trains, which chugged on the mat and whistled along the line outside across the street. He would lose Jackie Boyd, with the red hair and freckles, whose face was like a "ginger-nut". Above all, he would lose the little niche five feet high up on the corner of their block of tenements, facing the sun, where the boys placed their penny negatives to develop into the sunburnt faces of film stars.

"Oh, leave it if ye cunny eat it!" said his mother with a girn. "We have to be ready at eight. The van's comin'. An' the kitchen's like a dog's breakfast!"

"Can I go out and play now?" he asked. His last play, when all the streets fell silent as condemned cells.

"Awa' ye go! Safe win' tae yer sail!" she said, and that was gracious consent.

Out he ran, over the sobbing wooden doorstep and down the pipe-clayed stairs of red. Santa Claus came flying with his reindeer to the sound of the sewing-machine overhead, on his way to Iceland. He was William Farnum "Smashing Barriers", Eddie Polo leaping cataracts, Tom Mix galloping over the Low Park slapping his own haunches till he fell on broken bottle-glass that poisoned the torn palm of his hand to purple gravelled skin.

He wept, wending his way home holding up his hand like a rabbit, in the company of two sympathetic maidens.

"Oh my, I'll skivver the liver oot o' ye!" said his mother. "Day and daily I tell ye no' tae run across the street, day and daily!"

"Nip it, nip it!" his father said, and bandaged up his hand. "He'll have to bathe this in Condy's Fluid."

He wept again, but afterwards he was a hero. Remembering he would have to leave all this behind, he went to the lavatory to think about it, resolved to take a last look round before going, so that he might carry as much with him as possible.

The lavatory was dark. So was the corridor. He hated the corridor. It was all draped with his father's coats, like so many ghosts. He hated swinging back into it on the swing. Yet what he hated more even than swinging back into the darkness or cutting thin strips of coloured paper, or eating cold sausage, was being washed in the sink in front of the window in the evenings when the curtains were drawn back for all to see and the yellow gaslight blared, revealing him to all his companions in a cold shower, as they stood watching him one storey up, laughing at him, shouting up at his nakedness: "Ho-ho, wee Mac! Look at wee Mac!"

That was the rack and that was tragedy in almost a dissolution of personality. It was seven times worse then being in the stocks of horse-whipped through the town, yet his mother seemed entirely ignorant of it all — was she made of china? — and went on rubbing and scrubbing, even to waving down at them, inflicting on him far more than the tortures of the stinging soap that blinded his eyes with foam and tears.

"Scuddy!" she said, slapping him. "You're scuddy!" Then he felt like:

> "Wee Willie Winkie, running through the toun,
> Upstairs and downstairs in his nightgoun!"

But there was no escape.

He went to bed, dreaming through the concretisation of shadows, of the Low Park over which they had played out their curious, grim wars; of the Wandered Building, a lone tenement standing on the other side of the park, like one of the American flat-iron buildings

54

built by engineers, not architects. These were all grim stages and grim monsters, that thrust up through the green grass of his dreams like pitiless barbed-wire battlefields. He would have no truck with them. Even if his father were an engineer and his great-grandfather had built the Forth Bridge and another cut the First Trans-Scotland Canal, he would have no truck with them.

He called out many times to his parents in the kitchen: "Goodnight!" to see what they would say. There was never an answer, though there might be a shout: "Go to sleep!". And he drifted uneasily into a land where the "Shows" came with their lights and music and games and caravans and lulled his fancy till his mind, almost broken up, like a dissecting-map by the hammer, through any quarrel, was like a pool into which a stone had been thrown. The ripples widened, exploding fantastically into ever-expanding circles, seeking perhaps their own cause, only to launch themselves against some unyielding shore, as waves or dreams or reflections, like those in the green and red bottles in the chemist's windows, where, they said, babies swam before they were born.

III

It was not that he had been unhappy in Laverockhall Street. There was the constant serenity of Saturday morning to buoy him up, when the flint streets filled with the cries of flower and fruit vendors; of giants in leather jerkins carrying coal on backs of black-dust; or of carters with vegetables, and mysterious old women who deposited miraculous baskets on the door step, full of china and pots and vases. They were called "bowel-wives". "Bowl-ladies", said his mother. They might have come from Spain or Africa, so ageless and so gipsy, so knowledge-laden and so redolent of energy were they. Sometimes his mother took a jug from them, and somehow a jacket of his father's would be missing next time he looked for it, since these incalculable Furies dealt in old clothes, like moths.

While his mother was washing up floor and sink, polishing taps to bright gold and battling against voluminous dust, he would be sent out then into the warm sunshine to the Co-op, against which his father harboured some inscrutable animosity, to buy a sixpennyworth of "snowballs". These were small cakes, with macaroon on the top and jam inside, which were indescribably sweet when hard. Eating them was like biting icing. Remembering, too, was biting icing, sweet and sometimes agonising, as the sugar sought out a hidden nerve.

And there were the Saturday afternoons when he still went to Pollokshaws with his mother, in trams full of the odour of chrysanthemums.

"One day we'll live there," she said. It was the opposite of all Springburn stood for. It was old Scotland, a garden of gold bees and breasts of fruit, bright as a patch of sun in the drab life of these streets, and inspiration.

On the wall there hung a little picture in an ancient Celtic frame of a man wearing a Tam O'Shanter, sitting on top of a hill. Beside him lay a collie dog, and underneath was a poem he had written. The chorus was:

> "Eirich agus Tiuginn O,
> Eirich agus Tiuginn O,
> Eirich agus Tiuginn O,
> Soraidh slan le Fhionnairaidh!"

That was one of his ancestors. Now they had all to go. He knew now why the old man looked so sorry as he gazed at Fiunary.

He was sitting on a fernie brae like the Green Knowe.

His games, too, had been inspired by the solitude of his own imagination. Besides the theatre and the rudimentary cinema, the tents below the bed and the wars in the park, there were the weekly magazines he read increasingly, the *Union Jack* or the *Gem*. Sitting by the oven-door of the grate, so thrilled was he reading these that he would not have been surprised, turning over one of the pages, to find it suddenly soaked in blood. That was what his father called them — "Bloods". Dixon Hawkes or Sexton Blakes he threw angrily on the fire, but he would buy for David himself *Comic Cuts* or *Boys' Cinema*.

He had few toys, therefore, to take away, apart from some soldiers with wooden legs, more often than not headless as well, so that he felt it was unjust if not indeed slightly ludicrous to expect them to fight well, or even to submit to conscription. He did not want a Meccano set like Jackie Boyd next door. Unlike his father, he had no aptitude for such intricate, concrete mysteries. Their skeletal construction seemed to him the bones of nightmare. What he desired was the flesh and blood of dream.

It was the same with games outside. Always he fought to preserve something of his own world. He had sat for hours on the roof of one of the washhouses, by the broken smoking chimney, grotesque as a boar's head, telling stories of fictitious heroes to his comrades, to Willie Hodgins, to George Milne, to Alec Patterson. If they showed any signs of impatience, he would lard it with more excitement. If they made to move away and "dreep" the wall — which was hanging by the fingers full length and then dropping — he would call after them: "It's a hundred-part story! You can come back tomorrow."

He liked Hodgins. He was a small boy with a pale but plump face and serious brown eyes, exactly 364 days younger, so that for one day every year they were the same age.

The art of story-telling he had learned from Mr Johnson who lived up the next close, and filled the night with the hideous laughter of his Indian war cries and tales of Blackfeet and Sioux.

"Sou-ix," he would say in two syllables, "Sou-ix," gnashing his jaws and licking his lips till David could *see* the Indian in his face, conjuring up in the lanes of shadow black and blanketed assassins.

He was leaving Petershill and wee Ingins, "Onions", with the crab-apple face; the toffee-balls made by Tammy Anderson, a man in a cap and huge waistcoat surmounted by a watch and a chain of gold or toffee. Tammy always coughed sharply. He had a very red face and a black moustache. His eyes were brown as two of his own toffee-balls and as pointed.

"Cheugh-jeans," said his father. And there was Bill, who had fallen through a plateglass window from a dyke, and had his leg encased in plaster of Paris, the street hero.

"How would you like *your* leg in sticking plaster and stucco?" they shouted at him.

He was leaving them all, Bill and George and Alec, the red close and the smell of pipe-clay and the iron banisters, leaving the swarming street cries of a community where he had begun to feel at home, to go and love on Balgray Hill.

The air was better on Balgray Hill, his father said. For some reason, the people on Balgray Hill thought themselves better than other people. For one thing, they lived in houses that were larger and had gardens. They were "semi-detached", and they were near Springburn Park. It was almost like their own park, they were so near.

They could go every evening, instead of every weekend like other people. They "commanded" a view of the city, as if it appeared only when they wanted to look. The wind was keener.

They lived in another world, his father said.

When they finally left Laverockhall Street it was certainly the beginning of the end of the world he had known. He was sitting in the back of a delivery van with knives and bolts and screwdrivers jangling in his ears and over his head, lying on his back, unable to sit upright, with the light coming in through chinks. The van was a clanging mass of metal travelling with the speed of light. He could think of nothing but the people and the places he was leaving forever, and how long was forever?

As soon as he stepped out of the van he felt friendlier to his sister. In the past he had ill-treated his sister.

"Beat it!" he had said. "You can't play with us. You're not a boy. Boys don't play with girls. Go on, beat it!" And he kicked his toes away at football, his mother said. When he stood at the corner of the street to let the wind blow the sweat away before he went upstairs, his sister put out her tongue and shouted: "I'm going to tell! I'm going to tell!" His sister was a "clipe".

Here she was his only link with anything. He took her hand and together they went into the little garden and sat among the gooseberry bushes. It was nicer than Laverockhall in a way. There was a lovely new private washhouse for his mother, his father said; green dreams in the grass, and from the garden next to them they could hear the cooing of doves.

It was summer, and they ate one or two hairy gooseberries, like strange and minute crustacea. If they peered through the bushes they could see a big house, from which came the sound of piano-playing. They were very high up. David felt very elated. It was like Alec Patterson's, high and empty and somehow mournful in the waning light, as they looked down upon the plains of the city where the tall

58

chimneys stood like trampled wasted grain and the whistling was the whistling not of birds, but of trains that slowly crawled along like black slugs.

They sat blinking in the light. Suddenly, they heard a voice: "Would you like to see Ian's pigeons?"

Looking over, they saw a girl's face peering at them through the bushes behind the white-cemented washhouse. She was like a cannibal, unkempt, teeth large and protruding, and eyes bright with glee as she stared at them, relishing the liberty or the new sensation they brought.

"My name's Jessie," she announced, and as she stepped out, they saw she was short and plump, with yellow skin like an old woman. She wore a tattered gym costume.

Behind her appeared her brother.

"This is Ian," she slavered.

"They're ma pigeons," said the scarecrow behind her, edging forward.

His nose was running. He wiped it frequently with the sleeve of his jacket. The seven-league boots he wore pinned him to the ground, which perhaps explained the mud on them. His blue and white striped tie was hanging out of his waistcoat and his collar was open at the neck. Watching the small, shrunken face, coppery as a pear, and the hair curled under the skull-cap on the back of his head, David conceived an intense dislike. It was as if he were looking at a rabbit.

However, they obviously expected him to be friends. He was made to feel he and his sister were adopted, so together they stumped through the mud of the back garden, up four wooden steps, to find themselves in a maze of boards and planks and hen-coops and dovecots and toolsheds, with tumbledown whanging fences leading to a wheezy gate which in its turn gave on to a disused quarry.

All over the back of the quarry were similar ramshackle constructions, a nightmare of fictitious and largely fortuitous privacy, where families scrabbled not for gold or oil, but for a stake in stony soil, like soldiers under a barrage with entrenching tools.

For the moment David was too occupied to notice that they had merely exchanged the barren Low Park for a disused quarry as a playground.

59

He tried to tell Ian some stories, but found his tales engulfed in the feathers and down and eggs and shit that seemed to be the sole components of this new world.

During the long summer they played from early morning till late at night, and the sun did not go down till midnight. It was the Land of the Midnight Sun. They went up to Springburn Park and fished for baggies with a butterfly-net. They picknicked on lemonade and biscuits and hunted frogs among the yellow jungles of broom beneath the bamboo flagpole. High above the smoking city, like a pyre or an ancient sacrifice, higher than the highest chimneys and masts of the fiery forest, they swayed in the wind on the "swings".

They wandered through tall palaces of glass in the Botanic Garden with jam jars, canes, and flushed faces, alone with the aristocratic tropical plants of Africa; staring into fountains rusting with goldfish, walking along duckboards like gangways, sitting under sweating palms, wondering at the change in the climate, and coming out of a dream and walking down wide avenues of trees and cushion-flowers in an almost empty wonderland larger than Pollokshaws, yet full of the same sweet geography.

He went on these excursions with his sister and the Seymour clan — of whom there were five. On other days he played on the lot with Adam Hamilton, a boy with porcelain features and a light blue jersey, who always seemed on the verge of tears. He had a brother called "Hammy" whose head swung like a pendulum in a tick, or tilted backwards like a globe, and whose eyes squinted though he always grinned. "Hammy" was popular because he was supposed to have a wild temper, but Adam whimpered too much about the "hammering" he would give you to mean it really.

David read the papers to find out about Music in the Parks. There was a small column about it. He never "read" the papers. He did know what they were about. He wasn't old enough to read them; but he read the column about Music in the Parks.

It said:

GLASGOW GREEN:	Scottish S.C.W.S. Band.
KELVINGROVE PARK:	Besses o' the Barn Band.
QUEEN'S PARK:	Round the Clock Concert Party

| ALEXANDRA PARK: | Scottish Light Orchestra. |
| SPRINGBURN PARK: | Band of H.M. Scots Guards. |

In Springburn Park they played under a bandstand like a Chinese pagoda. Along the road, however, lay school, waiting to put a stop to all this nonsense. It consisted of two stone buildings and a ramshackle structure of red corrugated iron nicknamed by the boys "The Tin Building", which was really called the Higher Grade Department, exactly as if it housed a lot of salmon.

During the first week there he met his friends and his enemies, Chick McDougall, the chick being ironical; Galt the bully, with a mouth like a bear. He was a beefy youth. The calves of his legs terrified his schoolfellows. Not that he was very much of a bully. Scuffles with him never got beyond the stage of handing round pepper in the classroom instead of snuff, or of rolling up his handkerchief, tying it tight, cutting the end in strips, dipping it in vinegar and cracking it round your knees to make you jump. He was not as bad as some of the masters — Stalker, for instance.

The teachers, Mr Bumbletory, former laird of Burriecrassie; Francis Ponce, the science master, formerly full of indiscriminate if rambunctious female fructification, a believer, they said, in tart for tart's sake; Jack Botabol, the salmon-tanner and mind-reader in English history, bowed at the Head, old Joshua Midriff, descendant of a somewhat long line of baked-bone manufacturers, who rammed into the barbarous empire of children he had the dishonour to command, every known law, so that they might know exactly what it was they were breaking besides adult adulterers' hearts.

It was a famous school, as David found out. In its time, which was mainly before now, it had produced galaxies of panhandlers, corn-chandlers and haberdashers; a man who made a living by getting out of a straitjacket of mail for a wager; a policeman who swallowed his whistle when wetting it; three honest clerks; 76 greengrocers; 3,594 fitters; three pumpkin-purveyors; one apothecary; six heretics; one professional and highly qualified burglar; as well as 65 members of the leisurely dispossessed classes, 22 bookmakers' touts, three pimps and a beekeeper. There was really no end to what it might produce. Oh, and a plumber who became a minister to stop the evil leak.

These were but a few of the testators of ability, the inheritors of the cobbles that ran down the lane.

Once it was Cardboard and Stalker was walking up and down in front of the class. One of the boys had wet himself with excitement although it was only half-past three. Stalker had been in the war. He had a "gommy" leg. His face was long and dry and vicious, like a clean-shaven wolf's. He would eat you up. Once he beat up Donald Levens.

On top of his desk play a pile of models from last week. He picked up one. There was a breathless silence.

"I don't know what this is supposed to be," he said. "I asked for a tray. Look at the corners! Not even gummed up properly. Look at the outside! All finger marks. What the hell is this, Graham? What is it?"

He stalked up and down. He was six feet.

"Please sir, a tray," whimpered Graham, holding his stomach.

There was a muffled series of snorts from the others.

"Out to the floor, boy," roared Stalker.

At those terrible words, the chaps looked at each other fearfully. A few wriggled uncomfortably in their chairs as if they had had it. David sat quite motionless, holding his breath, hoping he would not be noticed before four, when it would be too late. His model was a wreck. It was to him the continuation of the torture of the coloured paper and incomprehensible design of childhood. The measurements were beyond him. He lived in another dimension, outwith measurement. Paste stuck to his fingers like fish. He could not always borrow the scissors, and anyway, he had no idea what he was supposed to be making. Sheriff was cleverer. So was Geordie Low. They did it all. He had to wait until they had finished to see what it was, and then it was usually too late to put it together rapidly himself. Out curled the strap like a snake from Stalker's hip-pocket.

"Crossed hands, Graham!" Swoo-oosh! Smack! Smack! "Back to your seat!"

Stalker smiled. It was a quarter to four.

"Here we have a beauty!" he said. "It's fit for — hm, let me see —" He held it up. Then suddenly he let it drop, raised his gommy leg and stuck his foot through it. "The wastepaper basket!" he screamed, in a horrible warcry.

"Whitna a lovely drop-kick," whispered Easton.

"Easton, the floor. And you, Macrae. It's *your* model!"

He picked up the rest of them, trays, boxes and pinholders, reading out the names of the owners like the lists of the condemned. "Murray, Gregg, Carter, Frame, McDougall, Galt!"

They all trailed out to the floor, crowding to the rear so that his arm would be tired when their turn came. For ten minutes, only the sound of the strap like a steady waterfall could be heard in the tired classroom, and the weeping of a few boys not terrified into silence. Stalker knew it was close to four. He meant to have them all strapped by then. It was a game he played, cat and mouse.

When the gong sounded for the Relief of Mafeking, Stalker picked up his things and left, and the boys stampeded over desks, kicking models, throwing maps, yelling and fighting in the unutterable glee of tension released.

David ran home along Edgefauld road and along the back into the kitchen. Jenny McArthur was in. She was consumptive and had large teeth. Everyone treated her with peculiar indulgence because she was going to die soon and they were not. But she did not die. She, too, went to New Zealand.

"Is ma tea ready, mother?"

"There it is, see, at the end of the table."

He still ate standing up at the end of the table.

"Can I have a penny?"

"Whit for?"

"The Wellfield."

He was quick. He wanted to be off. Jenny McArthur was looking at him with amusement, like his Aunt Bessie.

"I haven't a penny in my purse."

"A halfpenny, then. A halfpenny and a jam jar'll do."

"There's one in the scullery. — Don't scliff!"

The scullery had a bunker. On the top was the bread-bin. Jars were stacked there, jam still clinging to their washed sides like little pimples.

Outside he met Fagan trotting to the same destination. They arrived together at four-twenty. Inside the hall was a seething mass of boys, whistling, shouting, jostling, chewing, spitting, and fighting, and running up and down the narrow corridors like thunder in the clouds.

"I'll gie you a hammering!"

"Whit, you?"

"Aye, me."

"Where's Mac?"

They sat back, drenched in catcalls, sneers, and the winged threats of snakes and eagles.

It was best before it began, because then the hall you knew was fully of happy anticipation, and nothing could really go wrong.

No programmes were announced for matinees.

As soon as the lights were lowered a loud cheer went up, almost entinguishing the gas–jets, and they descended into a miraculous dakrness. They saw Buck Jones stopping a runaway stagecoach, but at the most exciting moment of the chase the lights went on again and they gazed at each other like strangers, stupid in that sobriety. Shouts arose, like the shouts of awakened sleepers.

"Hoy, hoy! Lights! Whit's the big idea?"

The manager strode on to the stage wearing a bowtie and the face of a snarling lynx. His bedraggled hair, but for its dryness, might have been a wig.

"Silence!" he bawled, "or I'll clear the hall and give you all your money back! *And* your ruddy jam jars!"

That was an old threat of his. It stilled them at once.

"Is Willie Macfarlane here? His mother wants him at the door."

"Macfarlane! Come on, Macfarlane!" they shouted. *"Buzz off!"*

A small figure, bowed with grief, huddled out.

"He's tae mind the wean!" a voice cried out.

There were a few laughs at the sally, and then there spread again before their hungry eyes the panorama of a dream as they rode through sun-drenched reels.

When they came out it was dark and raining. Drugged with wonder, they stood for a moment, but could think of nothing else to do. There were no "Shows". They had no money for a Tizer, and they did not know there was such a thing as a public library, so they launched out into the rain and the shock was just like being in the Baths. Round the back and up over the trenches and uneven ground to Hill Street they ran, all the way home, bracing themselves against the drenching and the chill in their shoulders and knees.

The lot was their usual playground, though not at night. It stood between the wings of tenements, where they chalked up wickets on one gable end. Sometimes they had to run if a slop came, and then it was easy to get through the bent paling into Hughes's close. They were safe there, Hughes said, because the slop couldn't get through the paling and he didn't dare come in the close. It was their close — Hughes's close — very pink and very private. You could only get in if you were with Willie.

If you had 2d, Mrs Denham was next door who made tablet. It was like a speak-easy. You only had to knock and ask. She hadn't a shop and you just had to know.

"Here's a googly!" shouted Hughes. He had long lanky legs and a very thin nose. He walked with a bounce, his legs were so long. He could swallow anything, like an ostrich, and his hair stood up on end like an ostrich's when he was annoyed.

He had buck teeth too, which snarled when he smiled. He was a fast bowler, but Adam Hamilton clouted it.

"Run! Catch it; oh, catch it! Oh, butterfingers!"

Bunny Fergus ran for it, his podgy little legs knocking against each other at the knees in their eagerness as he ran. He was shortsighted and fat. His peering through his glasses gave him a constant frightened look which his bulk should have dispelled. He pelted on, knees wavering ever more wildly until he stumbled and fell, hands outstretched in an attitude of payer — to receive the manna of the ball.

It dropped past him like an egg.

"Yah, butterfingers!" shouted Hughes, his hair like a cockatoo's. "Yah!"

Hoohoohoo, tittered Fagan behind his hands, the cunning eyes full of glee.

Bunny blushed.

It was Saturday afternoon. Somehow the atmosphere was totally different from that of Laverockhall Street. There was no flood of grimy men pouring out of the Cally or St Rollox, no hurrying of dense

65

crowds on pavements and trams away from the stillness of the cemetery. It was the highest point in the city. The flood lapped around the base.

Leisure was reflected in three large pools left by the rain.

The people around were accountants or plumbers, and therefore had leisure on Saturdays for the dogs, or Rangers, or Johnny Fisher's rabbits, playing in the small square of green before their house.

On days like these David usually went to the pictures. They had 2d. seats in the gallery, and they threw paper wrappings of their caramels at the girls. If they giggled and looked around, they loved you. If they didn't, you cared as much as Hoot Gibson.

"Catch!" shouted Hughes again, and he looked up out of the window of his daydream to see a ball, directly overhead, shooting down on him like a gray star.

Instead of waiting, he dived up to meet it and his knuckles struck against the rim.

"Yah!" screamed Hughes again, in his anger, running up to David and shoving him out of the way, so that he fell, and cuffing and swearing.

"Butterfingers!" he shouted, making a menacing gesture with the back of his hand.

David and Adam left the game. Hughes was much bigger than either. His ears stuck out on either side of his head like enormous wings. They dandered tearfully up to the porch to wait for his father.

"Big swine," said Adam. "Damned bully."

He couldn't understand why Hughes had done it.

The figure of his father came hurrying up the hill. Now, he thought, justice will be done, one way or the other. Ian Seymour's father had cuffed Willie Hemphill once in sight of the whole street for hitting Ian, and they were the same size. That was not right, but it was possible to talk to a fellow.

"Whit are ye cryin' aboot?"

"I'm not. Willie Hughes hit me."

"He did? Listen here."

He looked up. His father seized him by the nape of the neck.

"If ye don't go back now and give as good as ye got, so help me I'll gi'e ye a slugging."

66

"But . . ."

"Nae arguments."

He went. On the vacant lot, Hughes and Fagan and the others were still playing cricket. He gathered a clod — a dirty, big clod, they said, with worms hanging out of it — and leapt on Hughes's back, rubbing the clod over his face. It was the only way to get near him, he was so tall. Half-blinded and furious, Hughes lashed out with hands and feet, but David and Adam were gone by then, to the orchard up the street, which often served as a sanctuary.

It was full of apple trees and pear trees, and surrounded by a high wall. Entry lay through a small wooden door, like a trapdoor, set in a large gateway. Up to the castle led a winding path. Though all overgrown with weeds and only partly inhabited, it had great prestige in the neighbourhood and was still referred to as The Castle. The Russells lived in it. Charles Russell was a slightly pompous boy — not quite a prig, but not far off — who went to the High School.

"What'll we dae noo?" asked Adam, as David was admiring this totally new country.

"Take the milk up and get some apples."

Milk cans, with long shoulder handles, stood at the gate. Boys sometimes carried them up to the door. It was a good excuse for being inside.

They stuffed into their pockets a few wizened and shrunken pieces of fruit — the white hair on which imparted a sweetness, they thought — picked up the battered milk cans, and walked up to the house in trepidation. There was said to be a large dog in front of it.

Mrs Russell was in a laundry where one of the towers had been. Charles was playing with his sister on the lawn. That was sissy. He looked suspiciously at them as they dodged under the trees.

"Oh, thank you, boys," sang out Mrs Russell. "Give them an apple and some pears, Charles."

"I've a good mind to set the dog on you," whispered Charles as he did so.

David was furious, and disgusted. The castle was yet another of his ruined illusions. For two pins he would have knocked Charles through one of the windows.

"The castle," he said. "I've built better out of blocks."

Out of the other gate they went over to Springburn Park. When it rained the frogs came out of the gorse under the flagstaff. There was always wind, and the waves in the pond lapped merrily over rudimentary piers.

Glasgow's parks were studded with yachting ponds, but they were not, properly speaking, children's yachting ponds at all. The City Fathers, always in over-evidence, had here thoughtfully provided boathouses for large and costly models, to enable other fathers to dominate their sons even at play, with an ample supply of keepers in uniform to dampen down the ardour of children who might imagine the park was wholly theirs. The Art Galleries boasted one Rembrandt and the largest collection of model ships in the country, but here again it was less a question of Clyde tradition and love of adventure than an indication of the juvenile mentality of so many male Glaswegians, who in any case were unable to distinguish an early Rembrandt from an early George Stephenson.

It was heartbreaking for a boy to place a proud schooner in the water and watch it turn turtle on its first voyage. That did not happen ever with the yellow and black models marked "Clyde Built" which you could buy in the Arcade for one-and-six. David had one of these. On its bows, stamped in tin from a machine on Gourock Pier, was the gleaming name *Elk*. He liked the *Elk* best when it was dripping with water after a race across the sea. He bet it was one of the fastest for its size in the whole of Springburn. Once he sailed it over with a frog tied on as captain, lashed to the tiller in case of a storm. Captain Frog arrived unhurt.

Today they had only a glass jam jar. They played for a while on the swings near the bandstand, but dusk was falling and it grew chilly. The pond, too, was stormy, and they dragged for a bit with their improvised nets — a cane and an old rag — without catching much. You could see, if you looked closely, thousands of baggies, little dark forms swarming under the surface in minute shoals. Adam caught one with the palm of his hand while David looked along the path toward the duck-pond. That was where she and Miss Cott walked on a Sunday, their coats and ribbons and haughty demeanour all part of the flying park, with a law against trespass that was even in the Lord's Prayer. Trespass to him meant only Mary then. That must be why she and Sally went to Sunday school before coming out on their flirtatious walk. It did not seem right.

It was cold when they returned, between the long beds of eternal flowers, red and yellow and blue, and they were tired and footsore. They had hunted frogs, fished for baggies, looked for birds' nests over the railings among the rhododendrons in spite of the keeper's whistles, and even looked for girls. They had trailed bubbles again through the tropic seas of the winter gardens and studied intently the stuffed fauna in the little museum. Fauna was a large bird like a penguin.

The nicest thing you could see in the evening was the red railing surrounding the park, before you went down the quarry and home for a fish tea.

IV

"O-o-o-u-u-u. O-o-u-u. O-u, o-u, Ou, ou, ou. Le Coup.
E-e-e-u-u-u. E-e-u-u. E-u, e-u, Eu, eu, eu, il a eu."

It was like listening to a gramophone record.

Beau Tibbs, the French master, was six feet tall, with a long protruding nose like an anteater, delicate in his movements and simuously furious when aroused. He wore a high stiff collar and a tie, the knot of which was bunched like a fist. All day he walked around holding up his book like a prayerbook and uttering strange sounds, like groans.

They learned to recite with mechanical regularity, not know a word of the sense, one or two pieces of verse:

> "Enfin nous te tenons petit petit oiseau
> Enfin nous te tenons et nous te garderons."

The boys said:

> "Ongfang nootitinong pitee pitee wazo
> ongfang nootitinong ay nooti garderong."

"Now you, Macrae."

Through the long summer afternoon they drawled. Even afterwards, there was no relief, for two periods of English followed, with

Paddy Marshall. He wore an equally stiff collar, but turned out, as if it were a dicky, with a bow-tie or an artist's tie pinned on. This was the proper aesthetic touch required of an English scholar. When he was angry, which to do him justice was quite often, his face went purple and swelled up out of his collar like a frog's.

"Here are the exam results," he said. "McDougall 54. Not bad, McDougall, not bad at all."

McDougall was just backward enough to confirm Paddy in his idea of himself as a *teacher*. He didn't know just the very things that Paddy did, so they complemented each other. McDougall smiled his shy, wry smile, happy, not that he had done so well, that did not matter in the slightest, but that he had succeeded in pleasing Marshall and escaped the lash of his tongue, and even "the tongs".

"Low, 61. What's the matter with you, Low? You can do better than that. You're lazy, that's the whole trouble, bone lazy. You've thrown marks away right and left."

Paddy bit his lips and showed great yellow fangs, lowering his bald head in anger. Low sat blinking; for a year he had been one of the brightest boys in the school, but of late never seemed to do anything right. He had to deliver milk in the mornings before coming to school, and could not concentrate afterwards, but the masters did not know that.

"Macrae?" Marshall stared at David, livid.

"So you've never read a dry book?"

"Nossir."

"The question was 'What is a dry book?' 'Describe some dry books you have read.' Macrae, who only gets 64 by the way, says 'I have never read a dry book', and draws a bloody line! What do you mean by it, boy? What do you mean by this impertinence?"

"I don't know, sir."

"Answer! You don't mean to say you like Scott?"

"Oh, yessir!" That class tittered.

"Well, what about Thackeray? Wouldn't you say he was rather dry?"

"Oh nossir, not Thackeray, sir."

"You're a liar. And so is your 'essay'. You'll stay in after school. Lord? Very good, Lord. Lord has 67, the highest mark in the class. *Vanity Fair* is rather dry, isn't it, Lord?"

"I thought so, sir."

"Quite so, quite so."

It was all a question of confirming people in their prejudices and characteristics.

"Poor old Mac!" they said. "Never read a dry book. Do you read the Bible every night, Mac?"

"What if I do? There are good bits in it."

"Haha, hear what he says? Dirty dog. He's a sly dog in'y? You're a sly dog, Mac!"

"Should I bark?"

"Yeah, bark, Mac! Mac's going to bark!"

They went from one classroom to another, for each lesson. Science was the worst.

"What's the boiling point of water Macrae?"

"The point at which water boils, sir!"

"Oh, is it?" smiled vicious Russell.

"What is heavier? A pound of lead or a pound of feathers?"

"Please sir a pound of lead!"

"You nitwit! You numbskull! You're up the spout!"

"I'd rather be hit on the head by a pound of feathers, sir!"

And the birth of kings in history was set out in a series of goalposts.

⌐⊥⊤⌐ Why?

The whole tin building smelled of ink and rubber and rulers. Often they met Joshua the Head. He cut the end of his strap into thin strips and steeped them in vinegar to make them bite. He was always besting new leather, and had found a whopper he kept like a pistol in his hip-pocket. As he walked across the playground in his striped trousers and tails, his hands tucked under his coat, he looked always as if he were going to a wedding. He wore eye-glasses and his hair was cropped close like a German's. His eyes were bright with merriment or sadism.

"Boys," he said, "when you are asked in after life which school you attended, I want you to say with pride, 'St Albert's."

He was liable to break into this peroration in the mornings after prayers, in rooms where he had no business to be, and, of course, at prize-givings; so often, in fact, that he almost seemed to be doing it for his own benefit, as a morale-restorer.

71

"There's Joshua," said Sheriff, and picked up snow in his cupped hands. "Let him have it."

He threw the snowball and aimed better than he knew. It hit the Head on the back of the neck. He had six of the best.

All the staff firmly believed in the virtues of the strap, all except Higgins, perhaps, although Higgins, the maths master, could use it when he liked. Higgie had a sense of humour. Somewhere he could see that David and maths did not go well together, and although the thought confounded and appalled him, so that his mouth repeatedly fell open with astonishment, he was still kindly, even when he shouted, and did not insist too much on the impossible.

He stared, eyes wide open like a child's: "I can't understand how a boy like you, who can do so well in French, has to fail in mathematics! It just doesn't make sense!"

That was exactly what David thought of mathematics, though he did not like to say so.

The one class in which they all felt free was Maggie Scott's. Every Wednesday after "the baths" she let them do what she called a "Five-Minute Essay" on any subject they cared to write about. David wrote on a film he had seen: Ibañez "The Enemies of Women".

She had a long nose and walked with long strides in a tweed skirt and Fair Isle jumper. She was a "sport", they all said, but she did not like his essay.

"Where did you get all this stuff?" she asked. "Is it really what you think?Because, if it is, I'm going to give you the strap."

"Yes," said David, "it is."

"Come out to the floor."

That was what you did with Maggie. You had to be fair. She gave him two.

"It's not fair!" they shouted. "It's a free period!"

"All right, we'll have a vote," she said, "and if you think I was wrong you can strap me."

The show of hands showed she was wrong. They picked "Stork" Hughes to strap her because he was the biggest, and he hit her hard. She winced.

"You wait, Hughes," she said. "Next time it's your turn I'll belt you as hard as I know."

They howled with delight.

In the second year, those of the pupils who "were going on" were allowed to take German and the others Latin. David was offered choice of neither.

He immediately bought Hauff's Grammar and began making obscure noises to himself in an attempt to catch up with the others. Dass houz, dee frow, der man, were easy enough, but he said der nabe instead of der Knabe, and decided he had better not go on, except when they did prep in Muriel's German class and he had a chance to listen to the reading of Storm's *Immensee*. He murmured to himself over and over again his introduction to the language: "An einem Spätherbstnachmittage ging ein alter, wohlgekleideter Mann langsam die Strasse hinab. . . ." It was commonplace enough, but for a long time he remained caught in the web of glittering words and sentiment thrown around him by this opaque language.

It was the story of a love-affair, and held him possibly because one of his own was just beginning, and it seemed a curious prophecy or anticipation of his own experience.

Mary lived at the end of their row of houses. She was to him the personification of the perfection he had begun to seek. Once his mother had given a party at Christmas and she came unexpectedly along the corridor at the back, which was piled high with snow. She wore a white dress shot with blue, and it sparkled with flame enveloped in ice against the glittering darkness. It was a picture he would never forget. He remembered his shyness as he opened the door, in case she should see the love in his face.

Adam Hamilton went to sleep on the couch in the room. They handed round little sweets with messages written on them.

You are sweet. I would like to kiss you. When can I see you again? None of those he received were any good for passing on to Mary. He had only messages like: *A stitch in time saves nine,* or *Tell me the old old story,* or even *Keep a civil tongue in your head.*

It was like being given the wrong instrument if you were a musician, or a code you did not know, if you were a wireless telegraphist.

He watched her coming up the road from the front room window for so long that his mother wondered what he was doing, and called him away. He was full of vague longing that began to plague his dreams. He watched her, too, as she walked along the road to and from school, sometimes with Johnny Fisher, who was in a different class. He was jealous of Fisher, for he was very handsome, with an air of easy assurance. He was going to be an accountant. Evidence of such familiarity with figures was breathtaking. He fully expected Mary and Fisher to get married almost any day.

They were fifteen.

His whole story, he felt, was in the book by Theodor Storm, the obscurantist German of which he could not dissolve quickly enough to allow him to follow the plot. It seemed that the hero, Reinhardt, was an old man, and that he had been in love in his youth. What had happened? Why had he not married the girl?

It was not only that there had been another fellow, like Fisher. This Reinhardt had gone away, and seen much; he was a kind of tragic figure, a romantic hero almost, and the tragedy was that he had grown away from the girl he loved. There could be no other explanation.

"Meine Mutter hat's gewollt" was the title of the chapter. "My mother wanted me to marry the other man" was the explanation in the tale, but it was not the true one. The girl perhaps had not loved Reinhardt at the time, or had not known she loved him, but Reinhardt had grown away from her, attracted by the allure of a world he did not know, believing himself born to grapple with some problem involving humanity, and forgetting his deepest desire.

Mary left school and went to work with a firm in the town, returning by tram in the evening. David could see the drama unfolding before his eyes. He wanted to leave school to be with her, and yet he felt he must go on. He took to going down at 5 p.m. to buy a paper, so as to meet her coming up the hill.

They were mostly all leaving school, but David wasn't, though his father wanted him to come into the shop. He had a talk with him about it.

"You're growing up," he said. "One of these days you'll meet a nice young girl and you'll want to marry her. You've nothing to offer her. Have you thought of that?"

Had he thought of it, when the question was beginning to fill his mind? He resented the knowledgeable way in which adults talked, and the way in which his life was being mapped out for him beforehand. He could not bring himself to mention Mary, knowing only too well the consternation it would have caused, especially in his mother.

"Yes," he said.

"I need help onywey. Your great-grandfather was an engineer, ye know, and a good one. He cut canals, built bridges and lighthouses, like the Stevensons. In my way, I'm an engineer, though tractors and engines are my line. I could have gone further if I'd had had the time and the education, but I've learned the value of practical work. Do you feel like it?"

"Not yet," he said. "Could I study for one more year and then tell you?"

His father was surprised. He was not accustomed to being crossed. He was a man of action, an engineer.

To David he was the symbol of the wrecking, crippling process which was destroying, not liberating, his country.

"All right," he said, after a while, "I'll give you a year. But you'll have to make up your mind. Think about what I've said."

If he went to work he could pay for evenings out with Mary, and even after a while offer to support her. The thought was terrifying in its attractiveness. What was the price of this love of his? Slavery. Corroboration of his father's errors in helping to build the mechanical cackle called civilisation.

He thought about it, even in school.

He was thinking of it when he saw Howden, a crosseyed ragged urchin, cunning as a weasel, come up the street, dressed in the resplendent garb of a telegraph-boy.

"Hello," said Howden. "Hoo d'yi like ma claes?"

"Hello," said David, coolly. "It's a marvellous uniform. Does it mean you've left school for good?"

"You bet," said Howden. "I'm leavin' the morn. Gee, I'm gled. Where iyi gon? Iyi gon a message?"

"Yes," said David.

A message in Scotland is passive and intransitive. It is gone.

"Haud on a meenit and I'll show you something," said Howden, disappearing. At the end of five minutes he was back in his ordinary clothes.

"The erse is oot ma troosers," he said, "bit it disny maitter."

"You mustn't play with boys like Howden," his mother said.

Why not? His eyes were bright with mischief like a magpie's. It did not matter in the least to David that he was as filthy as human ingenuity could make him. His feet were bare, his knees black, his trousers holed, his jersey in tatters, and his eyes, alternately horror-struck and filled with animal gloating, squinted through his hair.

"Iyi comin'?" he asked.

David followed him down the hill to a grocer's shop. Stalking in like an Indian, Howden said: "Kin I hiv some o' thae pickles at the back?"

Fetching a small ladder, the grocer climbed up. As soon as he did so, Howden whipped a handful of biscuits into his pocket.

Astounded, David could not utter a word.

"This kind?" asked the unsuspecting grocer.

"Naw, that other kind," said Howden, pointing to a bottle at least three feet along.

The grocer climbed down and moved along, during which time Howden stuffed more biscuits, chocolate ones this time, up his jersey.

"Is this whit ye're wantin'?" asked the grocer.

"Is there ony ingin in them?" asked Howden.

The grocer looked closely at the bottle.

"No," he said, "there's nane!"

"They're no' the right kind then," said Howden. "My mother likes ingin."

"Whit wey?" asked the grocer. "Did she ask for ingin?"

"Oh, aye," said Howden. "She says Napoleon aye ate ingins."

In a sudden rage, the grocer climbed down.

"Ye bluidy wee deevil," he shouted; "ye've stolen ma biscuits!"

"Me?" said Howden, the picture of injured innocence. "Me? I never did! Did I pinch ony biscuits?" he asked David.

"How do I know?"

"Ye did; I saw you," said the grocer.

Howden flew into a fierce temper.

"Whitna lie!" he screamed. "Catch me snaffling biscuits. I widny eat them. It's the last time I'm comin' intae this shope," he went on, holding up his hands. "Come on, search me! Search me if ye're so sure!"

"Gae tae hell oot o' here," shouted the grocer. "Wait till I come roon' this coonter! Ye impident deevil!"

They ran outside, feet covered in sawdust, but once out: "Hiv a biscuit," said Howden; "they're good yins. I bet ye never saw me!"

"No thanks," said David.

"Whit wey? Jeez you're daft, they're the dodds," he said, wiping his nose convulsively on the sleeve of his jersey.

"Iyi wantin' some chocolates? I'll get ye some!"

"No thanks," said David; "don't bother."

"Are ye feart?"

"No."

"Watch me."

He was worse than "Ingins".

What appalled David was less the deed than the swift ruthlessness, the resolution and decision it revealed, which he had been unable to read in Howden's face.

They went into R. S. McColl's together.

"Hoo much are thur sweeties up there?" asked Howden again.

"Where? There?" asked the girl, trying hard to help, and twisting her head round.

For no apparent reason he remembered a rhyme in *The Rainbow*:

> "What are little girls made of?
>   Sugar and spice and all that's nice,
>   That's what little girls are made of."

"Naw thur," said Howden.

As she reached, David, hypnotised, saw the hand of Howden snake over a heap of chocolate cracknels.

"How many do you want?" she asked.

"I don't want nane," said the incorruptible; "I want to know how much they ur."

"Sixpence a quarter," replied the young lady, nettled.

"Too dear," said Howden, and stalked out.

David was again amazed at the transformation. In school, Howden had been invariably either asleep or in a furious temper. His abnormal good humour was a revelation. Howden had solved his problem in a radical way. He was "seeing life". In time he would settle down, with luck, to the steady career of a respectable burglar, unless any victim was unwary enough to rouse that homicidal temper of his. David felt sure that, as an old Albert boy, he would never rest content to plod through life as a pilfering postman.

"Where iyi gon noo? Iyi comin' tae the Tally's for pea-brae?"

"No, I've got to go and see Summers. So long."

Bernard Summers was his best friend. His hair was blond and curled over one eye. His eyes were blue and he had a long Roman nose. He spoke with an English accent. He was best at drawing in the whole school, and they both saved stamps. He lived on Orange Terrace.

The light was beginning to fade, and he could see in the sky the cloudy wisps of white and purplish smoke that spelt drops of gathering rain. The Summers' house was one of a group of three semi-detached dwellings of which there were four rows, clinging to the side of the hill that straggled down to the locomotive works. As he walked up the flight of stone stairs, washed and combed with fantastic curlecues of chalk, and knocked at the wooden varnished door, brass-plated like a coffin, he felt both astonished and vexed. Summers had sworn to be there. This was no way to treat a friend after he had walked all the way down from Balgray Hill and put off seeing Al Jolson.

Disconsolately he knocked again. No reply. He remembered: "'Is anyone there?' said the traveller, knocking on the moonlit door."

He hung about the close-mouth, watching the dripping ghosts of clothes strung on the palings and railings and ropes and crumbling dykes, or staring gloomily at the hordes of purple and bright-blue men streaming uphill from the maze of steam and hooters and pistons that was St Rollox.

He remembered one night on that moor when he had won a coconut at a shy in the Shows. Gypsies, his mother called them, or "tinkers". Sometimes she called him a tinker. It was not a pleasant word. It was like being a terrier and wild and doing things you shouldn't, or being an incorrigible wanderer.

78

At last he saw Bernard coming up the street with his mother. They were very jolly.

"What a pity," she said. "David has been here all the time, Bernard. Come in. Come in." When they went in, Bernard showed him some drawings of a man called Ally Sloper, which, privately, David thought very silly, though he assumed he must laugh politely.

"My father did these."

"Did he? He must have been very clever."

"Oh, he was. He was killed in the war, you know. This is Ally Sloper's Cavalry. He was in it."

"We're going away soon, you know, David," his mother said.

Shocked, David went pale.

"Far?" he managed to say. "Are you leaving the neighbourhood?"

"Yes," said his friend, "we are going to Stockton-on-Tees."

Equally well might he have said Wurtemberg or Ortisei.

"Look," David said, "I've brought my autograph book along. Will you draw something in it for me?"

"Certainly," said Bernard, in his queer English way. With a ruler, which David considered brilliant, he proceeded to draw a toy soldier.

"You can have this stamp-album," David said, "I don't want it anyway. It's an old one. Have you one of these?"

He showed Bernard a triangular African, with a snake.

"Mar-vellous," said Summers ingenuously, touched by the beauty and frankness of that smile.

"Keep it," said David simply.

"For me?"

"Yes. And here are some transparent hinges."

"Tomorrow is my last day at school," he said.

"Albert won't be the same place without you," David said.

Summers was supposed to be rather effeminate, but they were like David and Jonathan. The only love he admitted was for Summers.

In the morning as he went into school he saw Galt and Prigg standing looking down the gravelled hill past the church. They were watching a young girl. It was Ian Seymour's cousin.

"Could she take it?" Galt said.

79

"Could she!" agreed Prigg with a grin on his pimpled face like a scar. "Look at these hips."

He was a tall boy, almost six feet, and his pale face bore the embarrassed expression of a camel, perhaps because of the short trousers he was forced to wear.

He moved loftily among the other boys — like a giraffe, not looking down.

"Take what?" asked Summers, coming up.

They laughed.

"Take what he says," sniggered Galt.

"You don't mean to say you don't even know how you were born?" asked Prigg with a sneer.

"He's a baby," Galt said. "He'll shave in about ten years. Do you know the difference between a man and a woman?"

"Have you ever watched dogs?" asked Prigg.

Summers slowly blushed.

"Git," Prigg said viciously. "This is a man's conversation. Some paps!" he said.

McDougall, Galt, Hughes, all the precocious, tall, tough ones, gathered admiringly round Prigg, the fount of wisdom.

Bernard turned away and began to kick a tennis ball.

"Did you hear, David?" he asked. "What do you think?"

"About what?" asked David, miserably.

"Is it true? About men and women. Sleeping together and all that?"

"What they say isn't true," said David.

What had it to do with them? He could not really understand Summers' embarrassment. He did not really know if it were true. He hadn't thought about it. He supposed something like that went on, but he thought more at the moment of Summers.

"Forget them," he said. "They're a lot of rogues."

Prigg was shouting now.

"It's the bluidy miners," he said. "They should get a bluidy good thrashing."

His father was a policeman.

"There'll be a bluidy riot tonight," he said.

"Whit's up?" asked McDougall.

"The bastards are on strike."

80

Workers in revolt were strange. He did not associate them with his grandfather or with the thousands in St Rollox. They were like men at the dogs, or drunk at the foot of the hill, full of strange power, determination and tension. You could not argue with them and it was wrong of them to starve their children.

"What has it to do with us?" asked David. Prigg looked at him.

"If there's nae coal in the school cellar, ye'll bloody soon know what it's aboot."

David walked away.

At four o'clock they all ran down the hill to see what was going on. There were students driving trams in blazers and women in shawls shouting "Blacklegs". People lay on the tramlines and had to be forced to rise. A procession passed with red banners. The police tried to break it up.

"The mounties!" came a cry, as the horses bore down on the crowd. There was a scuffle and David saw a man fall through the window of the Balgray Arms. His leg smashed the glass. He was drunk, but unhurt. It was a wooden leg. Others were not so lucky, and there were many bleeding heads.

He was furious. He did not belong to the dice-capped, mounted and blue-clad, besotted, jigot-faced cavlary who rode down with criminal indiscrimination a crowd of workers complaining in the street. He did not belong to the yellow belly cop-touts, or the gay young students who were making General Strike Day into a carnival like their Charities Day. To him it was no prank, or jape, or chance to dress up and break the law and still be a hero. He saw the masks of violence hidden behind even Hallowe'en. He did not belong. He hated students and police alike.

Every year they went to Fairlie for their holidays and met their Uncle David from Belfast.

Uncle David always believed in a good time when he came, he said. He always stood ice-cream all round, the expensive kind, in glasses, not just sliders, and putting for all on the golf course, and he always went for a row.

This time he went fishing as well and took David with him — nobody else — because he was his namesake.

"Where'll we get the boat?" he asked, and his moustache wagged, muffling his voice. "Fraser's?"

Fraser was a real sailor. His chest grew out of his jersey like the roots of a tree in the ground, and he was burly as a bottle. His boats were well tarred, but before he let you have one he always looked up at the sky and his eyes fused.

"No," said David, "Knox White's!"

Together they ground down the sucked beach, crushing shells and crinkling shingle, striding the hungry tongues of red-reefed sandstone. Knox White was the only other boatman in the village and his boats were a by-word. So was he. He wore a Tam O'Shanter, even in bed, had a beard like a goat and face all mottled like a sea-urchin. He rarely changed his clothes, and rarely washed. His boats were never repaired. Half of them had stove-in bottoms. He was mean, too. Even the tins he handed out for bailing were given grudgingly, yet everybody liked him, for he was a landmark. He gave the village character and made it feel superior.

His jetty lay just beyond the yacht-builders', a huge barn of corrugated iron like a granary, where the long, black trunks, shining with rain and fungus, were trimmed and shaved into knife-edge racing craft white as swans.

Knox did not speak, but nodded the nod of an old gray crow, and hobble-de-hoyed down his crazy landing-stage.

"You kin have this 'un!" he shouted, and cast off a small-boat.

"Goin' far out?"

"No," said Uncle David. "We'll fish a bit in the bay. Have you tackle and bait? A line will do."

"Mhmh," gruted the old man, meaning yes, and fetched the weighted line, bait and two tins.

"For bailin'," he said. "You'll be needin' them," and stood still till they were well out in the bay.

At first they did not go far, for Grandma in Fairlie was watching from her window, and she did not like them to go out far. She was a bad sailor, she said, and even made David sail his schooner on the green at the back with a piece of string in case he was drowned.

They paddled about a bit, and cast the line far out plump into the water a lot, so as to please her make her think they only meant to bring back fish for tea. Then they drifted below the pier where the stakes were black and encrusted with limpets, and Uncle David caught three mackerel. Right out of the sea's maw, out of shell-stump teeth and an acid salt-bite!

"Grandma will be pleased," he said. "We can do what we like now, eh? It's mackerel weather all right. Look at the clouds! A mackerel sky! We could catch them all day, but we have enough for tonight. See over there," he went on. "That's the Big Cumbrae! D'ye think it's far?"

"No, it's quite close," said David.

"Could we be over there and back, d'ye think, by teatime, and Grandma would never know?"

"Yes," said David. "I'll take an oar."

Even if they were late, they could always give her the fish.

David pulled and pulled and the water slapped away from the bows at a smacking pace, but the boat kept spinning round in the wrong direction.

"That's because I'm rowing harder than you," said Uncle David. "Put your back into it. Take that jacket off, and that cap!"

When he had done so, David pulled harder than ever, and the bow did not spin quite so much. He saw his uncle rest oftener on his oar, as if he were tired.

Still the water swirled and smacked away from the blade at a merry pace, and every now and then he turned to see if the Big Cumbrae were any nearer, but, although it was plainer, it looked as far away as ever, for the distance was plainer too.

Once he caught a crab, Uncle David said, though David saw none in the water, and fell full length back in the boat with a creaking of timber.

"T-t-t-t-t!" went Uncle David. "What if this was a race? Oxford and Cambridge? Eh? You'd have lost the race by one mistake. They'd tip you in the river! *Dip* the oar in the water, just below the surface, not too deep or you'll never get it up. At an angle! And turn the blade whenever it comes out, at the finish of the stroke."

He said so much David couldn't follow it all, especially as he was trying to think what Grandma would say if she saw him now, halfway across to Millport in a Knox White boat! It made him shiver. She'd have half screamed that tomahawk face off. And yet he couldn't help feeling superior to anyone who ever talked about the Boat Race now he'd such a coach.

"Feather it!" said Uncle David.

The Cumbrae they did not reach for half-an-hour.

"What about climbing that hill?" asked his uncle. "We can get some heather to take back to Grandma along with the mackerel."

When he looked at the hill again he saw it was a cliff.

"Can ye do it?" he asked.

"I think so."

"Come on!"

The sky was mackerel coloured, with flaky clouds. It took them twenty minutes to reach the crest of the hill, and David was puffed. He could not even gather any heather.

Uncle David was tramping all over the moorland, into holes and burns that soaked his feet, and even though he was supposed to be Grandma's favourite son, David wondered what she'd say if she saw him.

He liked being there. It was so high you could see the Cloch Light and Largs across the bay, and a liner booming up the Firth for a pilot. It was like the roof of the world, and as if the heather extended right up into the clouds. If you kept on walking you came at last into the Plains of Heaven.

"Is this enough?" asked Uncle David, his little cheeks blown like a bulldog's.

"Let's wait a bit longer!"

"Remember the tea," his uncle said. "Grandma has to fry the mackerel, and I'm hungry. It's a long way back."

He knew that. He was beginning to be a little afraid. He didn't know why, maybe because he didn't want the good time to end so quickly, and he knew it would.

If he had known what was coming, he would have waited for Fraser's motor-boat to come and rescue him, then Grandma would have been glad to see him all right.

"Come on!" said his uncle. "Race you down."

He had been a harrier.

"The tide is with us this time," his uncle said as they pushed out.

84

"When we came over at first we had to cross at an angle and row against the current part of the way."

They had to be careful now and not drift too far, he said. You could stop drifting just by putting an oar into the water. When they were only halfway, however, the old tub sprang a leak and then he began to shout.

"Quick! Stop rowing and bail! Bail like Old Nick!"

The wind sprang up and carried away breath and voices.

It blew the boat off its course and Uncle David had to row till the veins stood out on his head like knots and crosses.

Tin after tin of water David threw out, splash into the sea, and either the oar or the spray flung it in again, or it seeped through the floorboards lurching in drunken riot.

"Stuff your jacket in the hole!" shouted Uncle David again. He was breathing regularly now, like a pair of wheezing bellows.

"There isn't any hole," said David. "It's the floorbeams. They leak like old boots!"

One of them began to float as he spoke.

He was really scared now. They had no rockets and there were no coastguards or anything. He could not swim more than a length at the baths. He hoped Uncle David might take him on his back, but that generous figure had shrunk to less than human proportions with exertion.

The whole of the bottom was covered now and his uncle was trying to row and bail at the same time.

"Sit at the stern!" he ordered, and stood up in the boat. It wobbled.

"Never stand in a boat, even a paddle-steamer," his grandmother said. "It's dangerous."

She knew everything.

Edging along the side, he sat at the bottom. His uncle followed.

"To keep half the keel out of the water," he said. "We're still a long way off."

His hair was blown and curly, like bubbly fankled seaweed.

"How fast is it rising?"

"I don't know," said David. "I haven't a stopwatch."

"It's a stopcock you want, not a stopwatch," his uncle said.

Soon there were four inches, then five.

"We'll start to sink when there are about six," his uncle said. "Jump for my neck then."

It crept up to five and a half, five and threequarters. It was at six!

Then David saved their lives by catching sight over his uncle's shoulder of a motor-boat heading straight for them.

"A motor-boat!" he screamed.

"Don't dance," his uncle said, "or we'll go down."

He lifted the mackerel and they both stood in the stern so the boat was almost perpendicular.

The other approached and David caught sight of the bottle-shape of Fraser.

"Third sinkin' this month, sir," Fraser said when he was alongside.

"What'll Grandma say when she finds out?" David asked through chittering teeth.

"We still have the mackerel, haven't we? We can say we only did it to get her a tasty tea. She only worries in a storm. There's no storm now; can't be with a sky like that." And he slapped the fish in David's face.

The house was right on the shore, up limestone steps all dotted with pebbles, chuckies and shells, like currants and icing in a gray dumpling. David pulled the bell.

"A present for your Grandma," his uncle said, wiping his walrus moustache when she opened the door, because she liked it.

"I've been watching!" she snapped. "Through the glasses! A fine cairry-on!"

Sure enough, the binoculars lay on the hall table.

"What's this?" she said, unwrapping the paper. As soon as she saw the fish she ran screaming down the path to the breakwater and threw them far over, farther than he could have done, her face all blue with anger and fright, and one eye staring.

"Mackerel! Mackerel!" she shrieked. "An' the spots on their backs! They turn into maggots! Swarming maggots! Ugh!"

She twisted her face into one spot and let her scrawny hands dangle in the hair like a dead bird's claws.

David saw the sky suddenly darken with gulls in a gathering shriek and swoop that made him shiver. A maggot swarm! It was a mackerel sky all right! They fell like bullets on their prey. He was afraid to look on the fish.

THREE

I

In the kitchen where his mother kept her special dishes there was a lead-rimmed cabinet. It was in its way a work of art. The sliding glass doors, of which there were three, bore on their surface elaborate designs inlaid in semi-precious stones. There were three shelves, and underneath, nine drawers, with a protruding ledge on which he had sat at times, though it was narrow and his mother discouraged the habit. Here she kept all her precious cups and saucers, with coats-of-arms from all over the country, and occasionally from other countries. Edinburgh, Ayr, Largs, Braemar, Goslar in Germany, figured among her treasures, but David was always fascinated in particular by the arms of Helensburgh, depicting a man clad in skins and bearing a huge club. Dimly he associated this figure with the seaweed on the shore at Helensburgh, and with Charlie Friel, who had once looked pretty much the same, except for the club, but its significance occasionally disturbed him. Was it an antique, or a portent?

He liked to sit and read over the mottoes when he had time. There was *dum spiro spero*. That was rather good. And the proud *nemo me impune lacessit*. He was proud of being able to read most of the Latin.

In one of the small cups — mostly the size of demi-tasses — lay a threepenny bank. It held twelve pieces, and when it was full the lid sprang open and a small fortune was at your disposal. This gave rise to a very unfortunate incident.

As he and his father were walking home one evening from the garage, which was in Sanny's Piggery, they found his mother in tears and terror. She had discovered the top of the bedroom window down. Someone had been in the house during their absence. His father set to work methodically to find out if there was anything missing. Opening the door of the cabinet, he found that the threepenny bank was gone.

"It's been a kid," he said, "after the bank."

"Oh, my oh," said his mother, "I'm tellin' ye."

Uncle Norman was standing behind her in contemptuous neutrality, working his jaws.

"The question is how did he know it was there? Had you anybody in here?" his father asked.

He hated his father just then. Why did he have to be so clever? How did he know these things?

"No," he said.

"David wouldna do a thing like that," his mother said. "I'm surprised at you. And when could he do it onyway?"

"He must have had somebody in," maintained his father, coughing through his nose in the way he did, which might have been because of asthma, "but when? Try and think!"

The situation was desperate. He did not want to give anything away. He knew how jealous of the house his mother was. The penalty for having it overrun with tramps when she was out, he shuddered to contemplate.

"Come on, when?" said his father. "I'm damned if I'm going to have Teenie frichtit in this wey!"

When he was angry his father always talked in Scots. It sounded so much more abominable, like swearing in German.

"Maybe on Saturday," he said timidly.

"What happened on Saturday?"

"Well," he said, terrified, "I had some of the boys up in the attic in the forenoon. We ate a plate of ice-cream, then we had boxing."

"Boxing?" — "Yes." "With my horsehair gloves?" — "Yes."

He thought his father would be very angry, but he wasn't. He was quite pleased.

"That's when he must have seen it," he said. "Who had you in?"

"Alfie Fagin, Adam Hamilton and Malcolm Hemphill."

"Hemphill, that wicked wee deevil! There ye are, ye see."

"Oh, my oh," said his mother, leaning over so as to miss nothing, but not not understanding it all, looking to her husband's face to read his mood, in perturbation. "I'm fair flabbergastit! It's an ill-win'..."

That was what he hated. Couldn't his father see that? Couldn't he read her face? What right had he not to reassure her immediately?

88

"I'm sorry," he said. "I didn't know."

"I'll away to the polis," said his father, putting on his jacket. "Don't worry. It wisna your fault, David. Had ye a good scrap? That's the main thing!"

"Oh my, oh my oh," said his mother. "Nae sooner dae I turn my back! I tell ye!"

He awaited the inevitable storm.

"I feel as sick as a dog," she said.

The police interrogation was a thrill. They had found the little bank outside, in the street, empty as a nest. He wondered whether, against his father's will, they would arrest him. In the small house the uniforms looked absurd and somehow obscene. Were they human, or did they pretend to be. Why did people become, not inhuman, but unhuman because of the limited ridiculous activity in what they called their "job"? They took themselves too seriously. They forgot that others in other "jobs" also took themselves seriously, which meant elevating the Position of Responsibility into a Thing *per se*, in which humanity, and other people, might count for very little. They were cursed by the superstition of abstraction which makes a Government sacrifice a people in the name of the "nation".

Fortunately, it seemed that in the absence of proof they could do nothing even with Malcolm. David both could and did. He remembered his mother's face as they had come in that evening. He remembered his father saying "I'll no' hiv Teenie frichtit this wey!". The idea that a malicious Hemphill could terrify his mother in that casual, bold way made him furious. Meeting him going a message, he took a vow in the street where the Seymours could hear that he would punch Malcolm's nose — hard — every time he met him, and thereupon proceeded to do so.

He himself, he felt, might well have been blamed for the theft, had he not been unjustly accused two Sundays before. His father had placed twelve pennies one on top of the other on the ledge of the cabinet. They fell off, scattering in all directions, under the table, below the bed, down wedges and cracks in the floor, and finally out through the door.

"Pick them up, David," said his father.

He was unable to find a single one.

"They've all gone," he said. It was a mystery.

"Don't be a stumer," said his father. "There must be one or two lying aboot where ye can see them."

"No, there aren't," he replied, crawling about on hands and knees, poking his head under the bed-vallance. He could not see there, so he crawled into the light, where seeing was easier.

His father lost his temper.

"Dae ye take me fur an eediot?" he shouted, jerking him to his feet. "Gimme the money!"

"I haven't any money!" he said, appalled, not understanding.

"I'll gi'e ye a last chance and then ye're comin' up to the attic, wi *me!*"

"I can't help it," he said, the water running down his legs. "I haven't any money."

His voice sounded very far away.

"Come on, you're fur it! Big as ye are!"

Upstairs, he was slapped and punched around like a drunken man. He could not see where the blows came from, and dared not look. His father had always been a good man. He did not keep a strap hanging up by the fire like so many other parents. He was enlightened, but now he seemed to have lost all sense of justice in the face of overwhelming if circumstantial evidence.

"Confess!" his father shouted. "Tell me what you did wi' the money and it's finished. Come on! Spit it oot!"

More blows. There were so many now he didn't care.

"I didn't touch a penny," he said, weeping. "You can go on as long as you like, but I didn't touch a penny."

It was the change in his father that appalled him, not the blows themselves. There was always a hidden reason, he believed, for these changes. It was his own stupidity kept him from seeing them.

At length his misery touched the man. The storm subsided, and David was led downstairs feeling drenched and dazed.

"I believe he's tellin' the truth, Teenie," he heard his father say. "They're gone! Fancy! I never heard onything like it! The whole twelve!"

Not one was ever found.

His father had lost face. He knew it. His attempts to remedy

90

matters were as absurd as his accusations, and when he noticed this he covered it up by being very gruff and drawing down those brows of his.

"We'll hae the Bible reading noo," he said.

"God made a Covenant with Abraham," he went on sternly, as if not believing it himself.

There was not much to be said after that. David felt humble, like Abraham.

"So you have the word 'Brith' again. 'Brith Ish'. 'Covenant Man' in Hebrew. And God said unto Jacob, 'In thy seed shall all the nations of the earth be blest'."

That was a nice thing to say to anybody. It had started quite a bit of trouble.

"Such was the Union with Jacob. Do you see? Union of Jacob. Union Jack."

Once, he thought, his father forbade him to read the *Union Jack* because it was the name of a "blood".

"It's Gospel truth," his father said.

"Oh yes, David," put in his mother, head on one side and eyes rolling slightly. "It's B.I. truth you know."

The woman in her underlined the dreadful seriousness of purpose inherent in the race. Equally appalled and adoring had she been as a child at the thought of her father, whose affection she had craved.

"It's not scientific," replied David defiantly.

"Are you one of those Modernists?" asked his father fiercely, his brows sewn together with thick black cotton. "There's an article you should read this week in the *Banner of Israel*!"

"No, no," he had to say. "I know nothing about them. To me they are as mistaken as the others."

"Mistaken! I'll show you who's mistaken!"

Outside, people fought to get on. In this house you had to fight to stand where you were. He picked up the *National Message* in a white passion.

On the cover the world sat between the flags of the U.K. and the U.S.A. while a scroll underneath said *Ephraim, Manasseh*, and *In Thy Seed*.

There were so many trumpets and pyramids and pillars and

battleships and rising suns that it resembled rather an illustration of the Battle of Omdurman than a religious tract. Signed Paul Klee, it might have sold for 200 guineas.

"The ideology," David said, "is 1878. It's jazz and religious Kipling."

"What's the matter with Kipling? *The Light That Failed* is a great book."

"So is *No And Where To Say It*," David said.

That was the name of a prize his father had been given for regular attendance at a Victorian Sunday school.

The veins on his father's temples were standing out. He took up the paper with obvious difficulty. "'Some Symbols of Identity between Britain and Israel', by the Rev. Pascoe Goard," he read.

"Is that a name," said David, "or a title? It sounds like a kind of Rabbi, or a Ben."

Such literature poured from his father's cornucopian pocket. There was, in addition to the *Banner of Israel* and the *National Message*, implying, of course, no Semitic ancestry in either case, a galaxy of pamphlets, all seeking to prove that Britain and America "represented" the Lost Ten Tribes of Israel.

You could prove it easily between reading *The Mirror of Life* with Tancy Lee in tights on the cover, and the *Sunday Companion*, with a picture of the Queen Mother looking down the muzzle of a naval gun. For Brit-Ish meant Covenant-Man, or even "Covenanter". That was only the first step in what was really more fascinating than word-making and word-taking, acrostics, or any parlour game so far invented.

There were countless variations of the one infallible proof. The Keltic tombs in the Crimea, the Scotii-Scythians, the Cymry-Cumbrae-Cambrian-Cimmerian-Sumerians; the Rivers Don in Russia, England and Scotland, named after the Tribe of Dan, with all their ramifications, Daniester, Danieper, Danube, Drava, Drina, Douro. There were the original megalithic civilisations of England, Scotland and Ireland and Egypt; the similarities of syntax between Celtic and Hebrew, the relation of Druid to Tibetan philosophy, or vice-versa, and of Gaelic to Hindu — Sgeind, Ind, Indus in Gaelic meaning "swiftly flowing". There was the mysterious Basque

"Euskara" meaning "Basque", the "B" being aspirated so that it was really "Eusk", the same word as in the Esk River.

It was a fact that the Celts had travelled across Europe from the cradle of civilisation in Asia Minor, leaving everywhere imperishable traces, even among the Mongols (a Celtic word) and the Georgians. There were even those who identified the Slav word "Nemets" (meaning German, or foreign) with the Gaelic "Naomades", indicating links with Noah and the Nomads.

"I suppose you know the Stone of Destiny is Jacob's Pillow?" said his father.

"And his coat of many colours was tartan?" said his mother. "What else could it be?"

"I always thought it was a patchwork quilt," muttered David, "like the one on the bed."

"Now wouldn't he look silly going around in a quilt?" his father witheringly said, and, quick to follow up his advantage: "Ye have only to turn to the Bible, Genesis 12, verse 2," he said: "'I will make of Thee a nation and a Company of Nations and I will bless Thee and make Thy Name Great.' What does that mean? Tell me that? If the Bible is true it means this nation. No other nation is called Great, except 'Great Britain'."

That was taking things very literally, he thought. To him it was a strange grotesque morality-play in which his grandfather was Abraham, his father Isaac, and he himself expected to act the part of Joseph.

"And the vines shall blossom and hang over the wall," his father said.

"Does that mean anything? The vines are in the four corners of the Earth, 'and the branches run over the wall'."

It was a nice picture, but David was thinking of the blackcurrant bushes at the foot of the garden.

The lesson was ended. Although his mother liked old Scottish psalm tunes, they did not sing hymns on Sunday evenings like the Seymours next door.

II

"You can believe what you like," said Easton, staring straight ahead, to Jowett, "but I believe in evolution, like Hardie."

Hardie was the history master.

"Your soul will roast in hell-fire," said Jowett, with indifference. He wore glasses. They had thick lenses. His nose was thick too. So were his lips. When he smiled, he bared his teeth in a cold sneer. Something potentially vicious in him made David shrink. Jowett was "saved".

For a long time he could not think what that meant. It was so final. Jowett's parents, he decided, had made some private arrangement with solicitors by means of which Jowett need not work so hard or play so hard as other boys, or even make the effort towards elementary kindliness in human relations required of others. He was "Saved". He went on living in this parody of a world merely as an act of grace on the part of the Ego of Master William Jowett.

"You will all roast in hell-fire," he said, smiling like a fish in a bowl.

"There is no Hell," said Easton scornfully, still not looking at Jowett.

"Oh yes there is," said David quickly; "what about Whitehall?"

Whitehall was the name of their school.

They laughed.

Once they had had to draw two circles and write underneath: "Graphical Illustration of Spiritual and Temporal Power". That was the height of silliness.

It worried him, because he did not trust the pronouncements of Hardie, the history master. There was something slightly smug and wrapped-up about Hardie. His opinions were too glib and two a penny to be taken off the premises. You felt, when he talked to you of evolution and Genesis, playing billiards all the time in his pocket, that he was not so much concerned with your education as he was with his own nimbleness in scoring off people who were probably dead and who didn't matter anyway. He was a Rationalist. Not that evolution itself worried the boy. It was absurd if it meant a monkey for an uncle, while if the relationship were much more distant, it lost much of its urgency as an issue. It was a word to describe the process and not the purpose of Creation.

"Will you come along to the Bible Class tonight?" asked Jowett.

"Yes," said David.

"There's a lecture against evolution," said Jowett, "illustrated by lantern-slides."

"Will you come?" he asked Easton.

"OK," said Easton, "if Mac comes."

"There's the bell," shouted Sheriff, "run!" But as soon as he began to run the books fell out of his strap all over the muddy road and he was late.

They had to wait in the school hall to be seen by Baby King, the maths master, a man who combined a furious temper with a complexion like a cherub and an expression of the most satanic pride and malevolence.

"Why are you late?" he barked at David.

Surprised at the absurd squeak in the man's voice, David stared at the spots on his bow-tie.

"Why are you late?"

"I had to come from the end of the Parade," he stammered.

"Which end?"

"The other end."

"Are you trying to be funny?"

He began to sweat, in a nightmare of injustice.

"Take a hundred lines!" cried Baby King.

The masters at the new school were as mixed as they had been at St Albert's. There was "Charity", or "Stinks", who whined through his nose when talking and wore a hat turned up at both ends which Easton at once dubbed "The Show Boat". Then there was the maths teacher, who wore outstanding ears like those of an orang-outang, a forked sarcastic tongue, sinositis, and such an air of worldly content that David lost all interest in mathematics whatsoever. As the class was now approaching the calculus, this was a serious matter, and he never recovered. Always he was afraid of the lash of that tongue and the malice in those little eyes. It was:

"Macrae, can't you see the board?" because he was peering, and:

"Yes sir, but I can't see what's on it!" Or:

"Macrae has been playing with the rope all afternoon. Why do you come to this class, Macrae?"

"Because the Education Authority lays it down that mathematics is a subject for study, sir."

Often they were asked to buy a new copybook for the class. These cost 3d. As David had no interest now in the man or his subject, he failed to see why he should buy one, and steadily refused to do so all through term, borrowing pages or odd scraps of paper from the others, who were fast coming to regard him as a "clown". It was:

"Macrae, you will buy a jotter for the next class."

"Yessir" or,

"Macrae; why have you no jotter?"

"No money, sir."

"Haven't your parents any money?"

"No sir."

"You boys will not lend Macrae any pages in future. Understand?"

"Yessir, yessir, nossir!"

It was:

"Macrae, what are you writing on now?"

"A brown paper-bag, sir."

"Where on earth did you get that?"

"I brought my lunch in it, sir" or "I found it, sir, down the back of the pipes, sir."

He began to write on the backs of desks in ink, and was given up as hopeless; yet not insolence, but nervousness had inspired the entire episode, plus knowledge of and dislike of the maths master himself.

At the first exam he received 5% for maths and 10% for general neatness. That made a total of 15%. In other subjects he did better. English, for example, had begun to be English, instead of the mere naming of parts of speech, and a beginning was made with poetry, though *Lycidas* sounded strangely excruciating between the lips of Mr Walsh, who tore at the lines:

> "Yet once more, O ye laurels, and once more
> Ye myrtles brown, with ivy never sere. . . ."

as though they were so many bones.

Yet "English" was less remote than the history class of Mr Vey who, in a mincing tone, would talk for hours about the Ostrogoths and Visigoths as if they were so many ladies in the chorus, and even made jokes about them. This was to hide his own pronunciation. "Ostrogofs", he said and "Visigofs".

96

David could not help wondering what he would have done if a Visigoth had suddenly entered his classroom there and then, complete with horns and spear. Vey, in spite of his interest in prehistory, or perhaps because of it, was a pansy but he also sailed a yacht, which raised him in the estimation of a class apt to judge him solely by his profusion of silk handkerchiefs.

Nevertheless, it was a strange bias which in a wholly Celtic country had steeped these children first in Scandinavian mythology and then in an entirely irrelevant and alien "Germanic" history, dominated by the equally mythical Goths — with whom they could feel no kinship, but only hostility. There was an apparent conspiracy to separate them from their identity, and the "B.I.", as his mother called the British Israel Association, at least informed and furnished their unconscious revolt with precisely those elements it needed, heralding the downfall of "Germanism".

There, Keltic prehistory was admitted and recognised in the placenames of Europe, and the Goths relegated to the barren political barbarism from which they had never in fact finally emerged.

Thus, again there was a division between what he learned at school and his private life. More and more he distrusted the glibness of the existing order.

Throughout the fourth year David worked as hard as the others, since ambition was now beginning to enter the lives of all. They were out for the Higher Leaving Certificate, the Highers, they called it. *Altiora peto* was the motto of the school, which they translated freely as *I seek my Highers*. He liked work but not play, which was made into work.

Across from the main school buildings stood the gym. It had a queer, brown, tiled exterior, which looked both cold and treacherously slippery. Inside, they wore gymshoes and shorts, going through the series of exercises from the buck to the ropes in the greatest cold and inconvenience. Against the walls were parallel bars. Down from the roofs slid beams for vaulting, and every form of physical contortion. The mat and the rings were so many instruments of torture unnaturally evolved from the torture-mechanism of the Middle Ages, just as so many bloodsports — instead of being the spontaneous exercise the body demanded — were so many excuses

97

for the martyrdom of the spirit, like hectoring and bullying in the army in the name of discipline — which is either organic or non-existent. He loathed the trotting up and down the gym. Still more he loathed the sandalled teacher who stood in one spot jumping up and down and shouting, "Look, I'm not tired! One, two, one, two, one, two!"

Hating this, he was bound in honour to hate its external manifestations such as Rugger, in which again the scrums and tackles seemed devoid of purpose except the general one of throwing one's weight about.

"Give him the beef!" they shouted. "Give him the beef!"

Day after day he stood on the gym field with Mackay. He was idle.

"Idle! That's what you are! Bone idle!" shouted the gym master. "Come on now!" If he had had a whip, he would have cracked it across the cinder field.

"Let them chase around if they want to," said Mackay. "I'm not playing rugger anyway. I'm going to stand here against the fence and read the *School for Scandal*."

That was breaking a great taboo. Mackay was a dude. He was chi-chi. He wore light tweeds and a bow-tie. He had a very attractive manner, but he was not perfect, because he was too aesthetic. He was also practically a "cad", because he did not share in the myths the others recognised.

He organised the Dramatic Society and produced its plays. He was going to be a Dramatic Critic, he said. David liked to sit next to him in class, for he read unashamedly through *Androcles and the Lion* or *Outward Bound* no matter the subject for study, and David therefore felt it safer to concentrate on *The Ancient Mariner* or the *Scottish Ballads*, to the exclusion of all else.

The two were heartily despised for having no interest in sports. Mackay was even said to be a ladies' man. Together they borrowed books from the library in the Great Hall. One was in French. It was called *Servitude et Grandeur Militaire*, by de Vigny. The style was sonorous and dignified.

It was his father who put a stop to all this.

"You're not getting enough exercise," he said. "I've arranged for you to go and have boxing lessons from Carswell's. He's a friend of mine. He has a private gym."

In some ways that was not so bad. They had medicine-balls and punch-balls and they did Swedish drill. In other ways it was worse. They boxed for at least half-an-hour towards the end of the lesson. He hated the smell of the gloves, but at least the Ring was honest.

Once he ducked below a boy's left and hit him in the stomach.

"Good," said Carswell. "Now you must try that with my son!"

David had only been taught the straight left and ducking under a straight left. Carswell's son knew all the answers. He was a beautiful boxer. He knew what was coming and blocked David's blow easily. Then he sailed into the attack. David was driven round the ring and hit from all angles. Punches he had never heard of gave him no time to recover, and he was supposed to use only his left. Two wicked right hooks caught him on the point of the chin and he almost fell. He felt jarred and dizzy, and had barely enough presence of mind to shamble round the ring. Then he saw Carswell's son coming at him again, with a grin on his face, and found the prospect rather upsetting. His nose had begun to bleed, but no one paid any attention, as once with "Ingins", so instead of waiting, he leapt at the figure before him and threw out his right suddenly, striking the chin and knocking Carswell straight across the ring. He pounced forward, but they all became very concerned suddenly and said that would be enough for today.

"What are you goin' to do now?" his father asked him again. "When you were fourteen I asked ye that, and ye said could ye stay just a wee while longer, as a favour. Well, it's long enough I think."

"I'd like to study a bit more," David said, "and get to know things."

"Whit things? You're just wastin' your time."

"No I'm not, really I'm not."

"Well, what *are* you doing?"

"I don't know."

"I wished I saw you settled down," his father said, "like other boys. There's Fisher in an accountant's, and Willie Hughes a draughtsman. You could be a mechanic."

"I don't know what settling down is.."

"An' you don't know why you want to go on wi' this stuff either? Is it a fad?"

"I know I like books. I'd like to go on to the sixth year, then I might leave if I'm not clear about what I want to do."

"Just another year then," his father had said. "We don't want any faddists in this family!"

Now the year was up he had won two medals. It said so in the school magazine. They were not important medals, French and German and the Rosebery Burns Club. The dux of the school and the second dux and the runner-up and most of the others, prefects and captain of the school, looked on him rather pityingly as a popular wit and no more. It was not expected that he would appear anywhere on the bursary list. There would be Violet Smythe and Cameron and Kirk and a few dark horses. When the list appeared in the *Herald* one morning, however, there was a sensation. Kirk was 85th, Cameron and Smythe were nowhere. David, it seemed, was 52.

They could not understand it. Neither could he. He slunk around the school playground with his cronies, hiding from prefects and teachers alike, till the maths master saw him on the stairs.

"Macrae!" he called. "You've done well, haven't you? Congratulations!"

It was painful. It should never have happened.

"Where did you learn Spanish?" Miss Barr asked him.

"In the evenings."

It was a dirty trick, learning Spanish in the evenings. Why couldn't they leave him alone? What business was it of theirs? He had no use whatsoever for their absurd conventions and pretensions and prejudices.

"You've certainly kept up the honour of the school," she said.

That was how they put it. Having done everything possible to prevent him from learning anything, now they said he had kept up the honour of the school. He had kept up his own honour — at the cost of a lot of extra work at night — not the school's. The school could go to blazes.

Yet, if the school could go to blazes, why did he wait after four on that last day, at the foot of the stairs in the hall, listening to the marching feet that no longer came? Listening, and trying to remember the sound of the waterfall behind the stair, as boys, in countless classes, filed into school, their footsteps beating an iron music on the stone? Why did he stand and listen to that sudden silence, and softly move into the hall to gaze around at the books and up at the high glass roof over the welled stair, if not because of a sudden feeling that a part of life had ceased to move for him? He felt no different. What would he be found to have lost, apart from the quick friends who were so swiftly gone?

"David!" shouted Sheriff outside.

He left the deserted building and walked over to the corner they always stood at, outside the shed, and picked up his books.

Low was there, and Easton and Jowett as well, four lonely figures in a bewildered playground.

"Howdy! Are you going on?" he asked Low.

"Na, I'm leavin' the day," he said, shifting his feet and looking across the road, so they should not see his mortification.

"Is that why you've a hooker on?" asked Easton with a laugh.

"He's a tough man," he said to Jowett, and they both laughed unkindly, David felt, at Low's checked cap. He had never worn one before. It was the symbol of his sudden servitude.

David's face fell.

"Got a job?" he asked.

"Aye," replied Low, "Millar's."

"A rotten shop," said Easton as he walked away with Jowett. "Terrible wages." His father was a Labour man. None of that for him. In some ways he was not unlike his friend Jowett. They were both "saved" and had little use for folk beyond the pale.

It must be comforting, David thought, to be so exclusive. You could be exclusive in blood, politics or religion, all so many shawls to be wrapped round the chilled and flagellating ego.

Geordie smiled, hitched up his trousers and sniffed.

"It'll be fun," he said.

David was overcome with sadness. He liked Low. He had been very brilliant at school and in the third year was one of the hopes of his class. Now he seemed always to be tired, his life a constant fight against falling asleep and falling in people's estimation. As soon as he awoke his mouther shouted: "George! George! You've to deliver the rolls remember!"

His breakfast was cocoa and bread and dripping.

Nobody had known of the rolls at school in the old days, neither immaculate "Stinkie", the drawing master, whose pansy breath smelled, nor Felix, who told the boys so often never to be ashamed of the school, that they felt quite ashamed for the first time.

When George was really awake he was clever. In German he was one of the best, although he was a "corry-fister". Muriel, the teacher, was quite certain he would get a bursary and go to the university.

He had worked only for that. Easton, always neat in his blue suit and skullcap, as becomes the son of a respectable Co-op man, and Jowett, who walked sedately under his cap as though balancing a basket of rolls, and who would go far in insurance like his florid kirk-elder father, had made George woefully conscious of his own torn corduroys, missing handkerchief and comb. At the sight of them he would pass his hand through his hair. Only in study had he hoped to equal them.

At four he had been one of the little band who stayed behind for special instruction before the bursary exam. He left at five and then began the long swotting of isotherms; longitudes; Pitt, Peel and Gordon Pasha, date of birth, death and deed; potted biographies, geographies, and word derivations, as well as other subjects enlightening because unrelated. It was difficult to swot in their little warm kitchen beneath the naked gas-mantle, with five human beings chattering around him and him tired. He kept falling asleep in the chair at the side of the grate.

Now he had to leave because he could not afford to go on any longer.

"I'll come and see you," David said. "We can go hiking together. Let me know how you get on."

George smiled and said yes, but it was as though he knew something David didn't, and as though he did not really believe that they would continue to be friends. It was the parting of the ways.

It was strange. He wondered what his father would say now, on this day of the breaking-up of old associations.

He was not left long in doubt. Before he had a chance to explain things himself, his father came into the house. His face was white, his mouth hung open as he threw bags of sweets, comics and newspapers on the table, laid keys and heaps of small change on the mantelpiece, took off his cap and tossed it on to a hook, to hang swinging on the back of the door.

"This is a fine thing ye've din tae me!" he said.

"What?"

"In the *Herald*," his father said, dropping his jacket round a chair and sitting down. "A bursary to the Uni? A hundred quid? Was my money no' good enough for ye?"

"How did I know I would win anything?" asked David.

"Ye knew damned weel! Put it there!" said his father, rising impulsively and holding out his hand. "You're a tryer!"

This was embarrassing. His father was jumping to all kinds of conclusions, as he often did.

"You make me feel that size!" his father said, holding his hand above the floor. "Will it buy your books and pay your fees?"

"Yes."

"It's terrific, isn't it, Teenie?" he said, undoing his collar and bow-tie.

"I wanted to go on studying."

"An' I was going to make you a mechanic! I could have put you through. It's a smack in the eye to me. You're sure you didnae mean tae insult me?" he asked again.

"Don't be silly."

He was still apprehensive. Only yesterday he had read a bit of Hendrik van Loon aloud, because it struck him as funny, about a bird chipping away a piece of rock every second, taking one million years to wear away a mountain, and beginning then to take a fraction of eternity.

"Bloody rubbish!" his father had said. "I don't want to hear any more of that tripe!"

"The money might not be enough," he said, "and then I won't have to go."

"If ye need any help, jist say the word. But remember, keep shovin' yer ain barra. Helpin' other people is aw very well, but this socialist stuff is tripe. Ye hear me? Tripe!"

He thrust his face close to David's own, so he could see the brows drawn down and the jaw thrust out for all the world like a dog about to bite.

"Capitalism isn't tripe, of course," said David. "Two million out of work and living in hovels is quite normal. If it's economics to let all that labour rot, let alone humanity, all I can say is, let me out of here!"

"Ye bluidy eediot," his father said. "Is that whit I've spent my money on yer education for? I know what I'm talkin' aboot. My best pal, my best pal," he repeated, the veins standing out on his forehead in an effort to be earnest, "dipped ma pocket once when I bought yer mother a silk scarf! Naw, if ye shove somebody else's barra, dae ye know what happens tae yer ain? Eh? It slips back. Doon the hill."

"A stoot hert tae a stey brae," said his mother, sitting in patient resignation, her hands folded. He looked at her. She shook her head from side to side like a peasant woman in lament. There were tears in her eyes. She was "keening".

"I've seen the day," she said, "when ye wad hae seen that wi' yer ain een!"

He was mystified when they began to talk like that. The language he understood, but what lay behind it was incomprehensible. They seemed to be carrying on a performance which had only a partial reference to what went on in the world. They were living a past tragedy, the tragedy of a proud race that had lost its way. They were hating a cruel humanity, and scorning and fearing a future when the fight for survival might become more bitter than ever. Yet they said none of these things. They were Celts, and they acted it out in gesture and proverb.

"That's a' I hiv tae say," said his father heavily. "Hiv some common eighteenpence. Look at what yer daein' tae yer mother. I mind o' a man, I mind o' a big man, a big man . . ."

"I'm not the only one," said David, fatally interrupting the incantation of a tale.

"What do ye mean, ye swine!"

His father's temper was notoriously quick.

"I mean you."

"Oh my, oh my," said his mother again, tears standing out in her eyes like nails.

"There have been other rebels in this family," he said, in a subtle effort at compromise and flattery. "What about my great-great-grandfather?"

"That was different," his father said vehemently. "He was fighting against Romanism."

"Nonsense," said David. "He was fighting against Episcopacy as existing in the English Church, and against Feudalism. He was fighting for freedom."

"Weel, whatever it wis," said his father, "he wasnae a Communist."

"Grandpa always says Christ was a Communist," said his mother, eyes wide, as if pleading for clemency.

"Aye, an' he votes Tory."

"There was John Maclean," said David.

Silence fell. The name of John Maclean was not one to be lightly set aside. During the Great War he had died of starvation in Barlinnie Prison. He was said to have been highly regarded by Lenin. A Shaws man, he was the true Scottish revolutionary of the Muir type. His fight was the fight of the workers of the world, but no more welcomed by the English than the fight of James Connolly in Ireland. Something in his complete intractability appealed to the Scot everywhere.

"A madman," his father said. "A madman. One o' the wild men."

"Les fauves," said David.

"I've heard them a'," he said finally, dismissing everything and turning to his wife. "Are ye fur the B.I. the nicht, Teenie?"

She looked at the clock.

"I'll jist mask the tea," she said.

"Tim it oot, then," his father said. That was a joke. "Tim" was a funny word in the family. "Tim it oot or we'll be late."

They did not know it was the old word for "toom" they were using, as in John Balliol's nickname, "Toom Tabard".

His mother was treasurer. Meetings were held in the Christian Institute in Bothwell Street. To David, there was something wild about the name "Bothwell Street", but there was nothing remotely wild about the Christian Institute. Sometimes a mass meeting would be held in the Great Hall, complete with maps and dates, on the "Great Pyramid of Ghizeh and its Significance in Prophecy". The words always seemed put together with a trowel.

These lectures were conducted by an engineer called Haroldson, of whom his parents spoke in bated breath. The dates, corresponding to inches, indicated that the Great War began in 1914 — which few were likely to dispute or forget, or, even if they did, to construct a

Great Pyramid as a mnemonic — and that another war would begin in 1928 or alternatively 1936.

The sands of time, it seemed, were again running out.

In retrospect, the prophet pointed out, there had been no war against Russia (which, note, was ASSUR speltbackwards, or nearly so) in 1928, but instead a drastic fall in world commodity prices, doubtless the same thing as Soviet aggression to the affluent promoters of this new totemism.

The BIFW, with which was affiliated, as his mother used to say, the Scottish-Israel Identification Association, had been introduced to his father by a Freemason called Mr Finger. There was a photo of him at home, wearing an apron like Salome; white gloves like a conjuror, and a frockcoat. Standing before a table of trowels and maces and glasses of water, he was unquestionably the man who had just built the Pyramid.

His father and mother took it all most seriously, and indeed there was is in it much that merited serious attention.

"You are an Israelite of the Tribe of Benjamin," said his father.

"I thought I was a Scotsman!" he said.

"The Scots are all the Tribe of Benjamin!"

An old gentleman in striped trousers who constantly sucked his whiskers — adapted rather to tobacco and black-striped balls than to public speaking, insisted on giving a sermon that evening entitled *Cui Bono?* This led him into incredible predicaments of self-questioning which the small audience saw straightened out with considerable relief.

It occurred to David that he was talking to his own conscience. Congregations were really audiences, which accounted for the apathy in the kirk. They went only to be entertained to an exhibition of histrionics, or individual catharsis, much as they watched cripples dancing in the streets. When they "caught" religion, as in some of the cults, where it came to resemble a bad cold, that was bad. They ought not to be "religious". Only sinners had the right to be religious, and they were by no means sinners. The sinner, with all due respect to him, stood in the pulpit, as the murderer strode the stage, and the judge clung to the dock.

The Christian Institute was full of halls which were hired at least once a week by various sects of which there was a formidable list docketed downstairs, together with the number of the room, much as if it had all been a list of firms in some block of offices.

There were the:

Assemblies of God,
Associated Bible Students,
Anabaptists,
Bethel Hall,
Bible Students,
British Protestant League,
Canal Boatmen's Institute,
Christian Brethren,
Christian Scientists,
Church for the New Revolution,
Church of the New Jerusalem,
The Gaelic Free,
Elim Tabernacle,
Congregational,
Mains Street United Original Secession,
Railway Mission with Singer,
Reformed Presbyterian,
St Silas' English Episcopal,
Shiloh Hall,
The Church of God in Glasgow,
The Four Square Gospel,
Unitarian,

as well as the Wee Frees, the Quakers, the Parish Churches, the Methodists, and the Scottish Episcopalians, plus:

Adelphi Radiant,
Camphill Communion Healing Circle,
The Greater World,
The Rosicrucians,
The Good Shepherd,

and last but by no means least, the 'chapels' — which here meant the Roman Catholic Churches — the synagogues, and Mr Campbell, who gave trance addresses all by himself, every Friday, which seemed on the whole very sensible.

Each of these multitudinous churches vociferously complained of small audiences, and of the decline in religion in a country the size of London in population. All maintained that not only their particular religion but their sect, their parish, their district, and ultimately of course they themselves were more religious than any other, a defence and denunciation in itself most suspicious, reminding David of Howden protesting his innocence. It would indeed be curious if 'religion' should prove to be no more than a complex of unacted guilt.

They talked of everything from the expansion of life and the latest novel to the future of Europe and the coming struggle for power. Rarely if ever did they speak of the Saints. They were all wild exiles in their own perpetual conflict, as their fathers had been imperial exiles, transforming that conflict into geographical terms and building up domination abroad to cover an inner fission — more explosive than any atomic fission. They were all escapists from themselves and Scotland, though only Mr Campbell perhaps, speaking in a trance, might accidentally stumble on the fact.

They did not read St John of the Cross, nor the Bhagavadgita, nor the mystics. They had lost all knowledge of their own earliest Christian church, the Culdee Church, now extinct, and only by hearsay did they know the Druids, whom they regarded as a species of Ku Klux Klan. They did not consider spirit the greatest possible realisation of the potential in the actual, but a polite fiction. Yet they did love freedom without realising what it might involve, and they preferred the right of choice, though it led them where they were.

Easily the best of the evening was his mother at the organ, slightly flushed at times when they sang the wrong note, or the wrong version, or even the wrong hymn, but always adjusting herself rapidly to the meeting, always playing and singing well 'The Old Hundred' or 'By Cool Siloam's Shady Rill'. He loved to see her sitting there, head turned, watching the proceedings and intent on her "cue". She looked so helpless and embarrassed now and then, and it made her very attractive. It was a pity she always had to wait behind and count the money. It was a waste of her time and talent, which she regarded as sordid. He hated, too, to see her inward indignation and excitement as she marked up the various small sums, feeling as she did that the meeting was not really to be judged by the amount of alms collected.

David was most impressed by the B.I. but he could not help feeling strange when he saw, streaming out of the hall across the way, a band of equally eager, equally convinced and dogged Apostolics, who regarded others as being quite as lost as others apparently regarded them.

It was most confusing.

The Christian Institute did not, however, exhaust by any means the activity of the city. When you came out there was The Evangelists Association in the Tent Hall, Tron St., Saltmarket, with Miss Longshanks illustrating addresses with a story-graph, and the singing of West African Choirs, including at 8 a.m. a free breakfast for the Adult Poor.

That night at prayers they read together the 39th Chapter of Ezekiel. It was an appalling chapter. The fury of the prophets haunted the boy. They were filled with terror of Him. They believed in Him, and yet, in an outburst of hysterical violent oratory, they prophesied universal downfall.

It was the old Story of Father and Son. In prophesying Christ they foretold their own ruin at the hands of that omnipotent Father of theirs, who had no more to do with Jehovah than with the goats that give their children milk. Tribal conflict, he felt sure, lay at the root of it all, and if the clans had broken up, tribal spirit among the Scots existed in plenty, with all its hates and unresolved violence and inhibition. He had not been entirely wrong in developing a feeling for historical faces. These were so many unresolved lives peeping through history. Aunt Bessie was one.

It seemed that whenever the Father motif in a society weakened, terror broke loose which He had held concentrated on Himself. This was the real reason for Fear of Freedom. God was not the Father. He was the Trinity. He was all three, Father, Son and Holy Ghost, and the three phases of the human spirit on its journey. Society made Him the Father, held Him prisoner in His Fatherhood, because only thus could the very worldly fathers maintain their tyranny. It was disgusting. Scottish society had never recovered from Culloden. The defeat in battle of the Scottish fathers then had left an ugly, festering sore. The defeat of the German fathers had been worse. Neurosis had spread like a weed where there ought to have been only happiness at relief from tyranny.

The German solution had been to rivet terror of the father even more tightly on to a leader who was at once new father and scapegoat son of the Fatherland.

He heard his father and mother whispering about him as he was reading by himself, imagining doubtless that he read only the more salacious chapters of The Buik.

"When I came in the day he was on the fluir readin' it. Whit dae ye mak' o't?"

"Dae ye think he's all right?" asked his mother anxiously.

"Oh aye, but it's no' good for him, Teenie. It's no' good for him at a'!"

"Maybe we should ask him aboot it? Dae ye think he'll be a minister?"

The scholarship, of course, made no difference to David's attendance on Sunday evenings at the Institute. In time he knew the inside of the Pyramid as well as the inside of his own home. It seemed you entered high up on one face, as if the opening were a cave on a mountainside. Then you went down a long passage called the Grand Gallery. This was high and broad. At last you came to a small cavern, along which you had to crawl on hands and knees, and which was known as the Ante-Chamber to the Queen's Chamber. A similar cavern followed the Queen's Chamber, leading to the King's Chamber, inside of which you could at last stand upright.

The amazing thing about the King's Chamber was that there had never been a body there at all.

"Now," said the orator, "does that not prove that the Pyramid was built for a different purpose from the others? It is our contention that it provides an illustration in cross-section of human history, and especially the history of Israel."

You started off with the Pyramid inch. It was only slightly different from the British inch, owing possibly to what in other spheres was called the Displacement Factor. This was a very variable constant. He found himself imprisoned in an expanding cage of mathematics, as at school, only this time it was not so easy to escape, for they had been given divine sanction. God, it seemed, was a Scientist, the first step in making the Scientist God.

The main point emerging from such deliberations was that counting the number of inches from the entrance to the final narrow corridor, and allowing an inch to equal a day (Gregorian Calendar) you arrived precisely at the date, August 4th, 1914. It was from there on that you had to crawl on your hands and knees, and when at last you emerged into the Queen's Chamber the date was said to be November 11th, 1918. "Crawling", of course, meant the War Years, known to the authorities as the Years of Tribulation.

The audience, as the speaker unrolled his maps and tapes and charts, sat enthralled in apocalyptic rapture. The man was a prophet. He forecast a new era of crawling to which everyone looked forward with morose glee, to begin on May 28th, 1928. Reading between the lines, and taking it all in conjunction with the 37th Chapter of Ezekiel, one sinister purpose revealed itself behind this gallimaufry of nonsense: war with Russia.

It was now April 1928 and the prophet was a little nervous. He emphasised that no man could foretell the future — though he omitted to mention that not a few mediums on the Stock Exchange actually sold it — and only afterwards would the actual event become known. May came and went, and the sun was as lovely as ever. The waves at the coast maintained their serene regularity. Golfers went by with unhurried swing. Apocalyptic urgency was seen to have its origin in deep-seated repression amounting to a hatred of nature in the highest degree Puritan, unhealthy, and even, paradoxically, irreligious. The Crucifixion itself had been just such a hatred of nature and the whole ridiculous mathematical scheme to imprison the nature of things in a formula — including even human nature — was bound to burst as it had before in the blind fury of human resistance, called revolt of the unconscious.

"He may be all good and glorious within," said his aunt Bessie of the prophet.

"It's a pity you couldnae flipe him," said his mother.

He didn't understand that at first. It seemed that after socks were washed you turned them outside in. They were then "fliped".

III

In the winter air, pictures froze his mind into visions of loveliness that already, he could see, were passing so swiftly that they ought to be cherished far more than they were. There was the picture of Mary Watson coming up the hill, her head lowered on account of the wind that wrapped her skirt around her figure with a loving hand. For a long time he thought she lowered her head when she saw him coming, out of shyness, and forgot about the wind. He still felt strangely unhappy when he saw her talking to other boys on Saturdays. That was her free day. She seemed rather brazen, somehow shameless then, and most certainly free and mature — a woman, in society, whereas he was condemned to remain a "schoolboy". When he passed, she smiled at him sweetly, but absently, and went on with her conversation. Yet he was exactly one year older than she, and coming to "know" much more from books about the ways of thinking and feeling and living that did not make him altogether happy because they were deliberate instead of being spontaneous — as she was.

For long he stared through the window at five in the evenings to see her coming up the street. Through his sister he sent her invitations to go to concerts with her niece. He knew he was in love. When he looked closely into her face and saw she had freckles, they seemed miraculous. There were large brown checks on her coat, too, and they seemed to match the patches of sunlight on leaves against the sky, and in her eyes, where hid such heaven, he was afraid and could not bring himself to kiss her as he wished. Was it that he no longer believed in heaven?

Sometimes he saw her come home late at night with someone else, and stand at the little gate under the lamp, parting from the man with a swift kiss; or he lay awake in the attic under a heap of old rugs and blankets, wearing headphones attached to an old crystal set, and taking them off every now and then to listen for the quick step and the bang of the door that meant she was home after an evening out. If for some time he heard voices in conversation it was worse, and worse still to hear her silvery laughter, and know she had been to a Palais de Danse. One day he hoped he might marry her, and she did not even know how he felt. She could not read what was in his face because of the rather bitter mask which hid it, and there was nothing to be done but lie and listen to the Savoy Orpheans from 2LO playing 'Valencia' or 'The Waters of Minnetonka'.

He thought of asking her out himself, but something always seemed to crop up, a visit to his grandfather in the Shaws, or work at home. Now and then he managed to slip downhill to the tram-stop towards five o'clock, saying he was going to buy a paper. There he walked nervously up and down, watching every white car that came along, until he saw her, but then he strolled past the stop as though he did not see her.

Opening the paper, he walked on slowly up the hill, reading politics and expecting a war. There was a headline, 'Japan Invades Manchuria', which almost made him forget that she was coming up behind him. Closer she came, with long strides and her wide, attractive outward arm-swing.

"Hello," she remarked. "You're a stranger."

He leapt at the words like a dog at a bone. What did they mean? Their conventionality distressed him, but he strove to find what they meant to her, if anything.

Together they walked on uphill talking and laughing for a few fugitive moments, and he noticed again, with a pang, that her eyes were as blue as cornflowers in wheat. He wanted more of her, yet he hated to have to plot in order to see her. In any case, when he did see her, he did not know what to say.

"Are you busy?" he asked.

"Fairly busy," she said.

It made him angry, impulsive, impatient, in contrast with the wonderful sensation of looking at her, and of walking with her.

Soon he began to see her in the mornings too, as he rode in the tram. Climbing proudly upstairs, he would take out *Immensee* to read in German and she would sit down beside him, admiringly he hoped. He opened the book. They were together, she and *Immensee*, two of the things he loved.

"Look," he said, and began to read a passage to her.

> "Heute, nur heute
> Bin ich so schön;
> Morgen, ach morgen
> Muss alles vergehn!
> Nur diese Stunden
> Bist du noch mein;

> Sterben, ach sterben
> Soll ich allein."

"What does it mean?" she asked.

"It is a piece of poetry," he said. "Listen to this.

> Mein Mutter hat's gewollt,
> Den andern ich nehmen sollt;
> Was ich zuvor besessen,
> Mein Herz sollt es vergessen;
> Das hat es nicht gewollt.
>
> Fur all mein Stolz und Freud
> Gewonnen hab ich Leid.
>   Ach, war das nicht geschehen,
> Ach konnt ich betteln gehen
> Uber die braune Heid!"

"You mean you understand all that?" In her face there was only a puzzled look and a hidden distaste.

"Nearly all."

"What does it mean?"

"It is the story of two lovers who have to separate, because one is a student. When he returns he finds his sweetheart married. She says it was her mother's wish, but she realises she has made a mistake. This is how they separate at the end:

"Upstairs in the house he heard a door close; steps came down the staircase, and when he looked up Elizabeth was standing before him. She laid her hand on his arm, and his lips moved, but no word came.

"You won't come back," she said at last. "I know. Don't lie to me. You will never come back."

"Never," he said. Her hand dropped. She said no more. He walked to the door; there he turned again. She was standing motionless in the same spot, looking at him with dead eyes. He stepped forward and held out his arms. Then he forced himself to turn away, and went out."

"Silly," she said. David was hurt.

"What's silly? I think it's wonderful. Only he wouldn't really step forward and hold out his arms. That *is* rather silly."

"I think it's rather nice," she said, glancing out of the window, almost casually.

"One day I'll come back and find you married, I expect," he said.

"Oh no," she laughed, "not me. You'll have found some nice girl long before that I suppose."

"Never." The very idea shocked him.

"Oh yes you will!"

"It's time I left," he said, putting the book away and rising.

"Cheerio!" she smiled, and the commonplace word at once became one of the loveliest words in the language, a red gem on her lips.

Three mornings before, he had seen a reporter waiting for her at the car-stop, a man he knew who had been out with her, and *they* went upstairs together in the tram. That filled him with a cold fury and yet with fear, because she seemed so talkative and merry. Either, he thought, she was doing it to make him jealous, or she considered him very dull, since he never went anywhere. He decided to ask her now.

"Are you doing anything on Saturday?"

"All right!"

"I'll meet you at 6.30 at the car-stop!"

It was done.

Was it imagination, or did her father, an elderly man with curling white moustache, eyeglasses and grim granite exterior, *really* begin to nod to him churlishly in the street? When he passed their house, where her mother sat at the window, did she really beam at him? He hoped they would not talk. He was not ready for that yet. All he knew was that he wanted to be with her.

They went to the Regal. He bought matches and a box of chocolates for her.

"Here you are," he said ungraciously. When they sat down to watch the film he found himself sitting behind a pillar, but it did not matter.

He could follow nothing. Mindless characters talked out of turn. Beams of flickering light and shadow were to him less than his cardboard theatre compared with the girl at his elbow, and yet he hardly dared glance at her in case his expression gave him away, so he sat in the dark, feeling how wonderful it was merely to be with her. The evening was expensive. He could not afford many of them. One and six each for the seats and one shilling for the chocolates made four shillings; a small bribe really to have her in his company, but a large sum for a student.

"Enjoying it?" he asked.

"She looked at him and said "Yes" in the low voice that always stirred him, and he was overcome by panic. He imagined he saw tears in her eyes.

Could there be? Of course not. She would not waste a single thought on him. Might there be? He did not know.

Perhaps he was a brute not to take her out more often, not to take her hand and not to kiss her, but how could he, till he was sure she cared for him at all? It was brutal to kiss her if she didn't care for him. Others did, he knew that, and it was none of his affair, but he loved her too much to do so, casually, though his whole being yearned for her.

He stole a glance at her and saw she was following the film intently. David tried to do so too, so that he could talk to her about it afterwards, but the pillar blocked his vision.

He must not be too late or his mother would ask him where he had been, and then it might all come out. He did not want Mrs Watson and his mother laughing over the two of them or saying knowingly: "Yes, there's something in the wind all right!" He could not have borne that.

A comedy film came next, and he laughed uproariously, unashamedly, until he saw . . . no one else was laughing. It was her turn to look at him strangely, almost wistfully; but the moment was all too swiftly gone.

"We shall have to be going soon," he said. He had not held her hand. Not once.

Outside the neon lights glared redly through the fog. David, reckless at the thought of losing her for another week, or perhaps longer, said: "Will you have a coffee?"

It had been a very pleasant evening, but there was a gulf between them. She seemed to think that being employed in the town made her a woman of the world, and he felt the tragedy of moving away from her into the dark forest of books. They were both friendly, but shy, and they could not compose this difference.

"How is school?" she asked.

He hated her for saying that. It made him feel so young. Girls matured sooner than boys, they said, and already she used scent.

"I'm at the University now."

Couldn't she see the love in his eyes? Couldn't she see that he adored her? Couldn't she read his anguish? Then there was no use in anything. To her he was at school, and she longed for smart clothes, a car, cinemas, dances. They were still drifting apart. "Education" was a wedge being driven between them, as between him and George Low. He wanted her to understand the things he read so that they could enjoy them together, poems of Mörike and Heine and Eichendorff, but she was not interested.

The restaurant they entered became luxurious with her presence. The carpets took on an added gleam and the flowers sprang up at her approach. Out of the radio a mechanical man made love for him because he did not dare.

"Did you like the film?" asked Mary.

"I'm afraid I didn't see much of it."

"How do you like the University?"

"I like it, but I don't like moving away from my friends."

"How do you mean?" He told her about Low.

"He's a friend of mine. We were at school together. Now he works in a leather shop, making soles for shoes out of compressed paper for 15 shillings a week. It's no job for him. He was very good, but he has to take what he can get.

"It won't last long, so he says. He can make the soles now so you don't feel the nails for months, but he'll get the sack. The firm is feeling the draught."

"I don't understand. He's still a friend of yours."

"He doesn't think so."

He could say no more. He could not tell her how he had met George coming up from the library, and of the last talk they had had. George was on the dole now.

"The buroo's no' sae bad. Nuthin' tae dae bit go and sign on once a week. I've ta'en up wrestlin' noo. You should come to the classes. Last night, a fella, ye should a seen 'is muscles, caught anither man a beauty right on the chin wi' his fit!"

As he said it, George's eyes shone and his shoulders bunched.

117

There was a smirr of rain.

"I'll tell ye what," George had said in an embarrassed tone, "come hikin' wi' us some weekend."

He sniffed less.

"Last weekend we wur away for four days, sleepin' in the open, lightin' fires. We got a lift as faur as Loch Lomond. Gee we hid a lot o' fun pinchin' totties an' tumshies. On Sunday we hid tae walk twinty miles hame!"

"I'd like to come," said David. "It must keep you fit."

"Oh aye, I hid a wumman up there. One night we were sleepin' in a barn. I didnae know her. We had a bit o' a talk in the dark, ye know, then I crawled ower."

He braced himself, in a gesture of bravado.

("We're clubbin' thegither for an army tent," George said.)

A wedge had been driven between them. They were pals. They wanted to remain so, but the old friendship was split asunder like a piece of wood.

"I might go abroad this summer," said David.

"Oh?" Geordie put his head back as though politely inviting further news and his blue eyes tried to smile, but nothing came. There was only a glaze.

"I told him I was going abroad," he said, "and he thought it was swank."

"Was it?"

"What do you think?" ("It must be great there," George said: "David's no' what he used to be," he was thinking. And David was thinking "Geordie's no' what he might have been.")

"People change," she said.

"So now," he thought, "he'll live out his life in Wellfed Street, near Buggery Brae, next door to the Starvation Army." That was what they had called Wellfield Street, Balgray Hill and the Salvation Army.

She did not know what else to say. "We'd better go," he said.

As they rode home together on the tram, he tried to make her laugh by talking politics. Mary said she knew nothing about politics.

"How do you expect to get on," he said, "if you never read the papers? There's going to be a war, don't you know that?"

"I leave that to the men," she said.

"I leave that to the men," she said.

"Aren't *you* interested in going abroad, then?" he asked.

"Why should I be? I haven't a chance." She looked squarely at him and he felt a fool, felt as if she were looking through him and as if she knew very well that he watched her through the window coming up the hill and that their "meetings" had not been accidents. It was to as if she might be saying, "My only chance of anything like that is with you!"

"Well, you could now!" he said.

"How?"

"You could save up," he concluded miserably, and she turned her head and looked out of the window again.

They stood at the top of the hill, watching a flurry of lights.

He frightened her, too late he realised it, as he said in a sudden access of hate: "Are you going to go on living here?"

"Yes," she said, with mild surprise, "aren't you?"

"No," he said, looking savagely across the sea of lovely dusk and moonlight that formed the city beneath them.

"I'm going to get out of it all."

In a way it was only that he could not bear to be with her when she seemed even slightly indifferent.

"You *are* strange," she said at last, rather sadly.

"Why?"

"The way you talk about getting away."

"Do you blame me for wanting to get out of this?"

Dramatically he pointed to the factories, the smoke, and the red glare in the distance of the blast furnaces, called "Dixon's Blazes".

"It's all dead, a dead Inferno."

She shamed him. He knew she would always live there and there too would always be his place, no matter where he might go. He had a vision, absurd, perhaps, of her beauty stifling in years of smoke, and he could not bear the thought.

Now they were standing outside of her home, beneath the lamp-post where he knew she had been kissed before.

"Well," she was about to say. "goodnight," when a sound at the head of the lane made her look round. A figure at the top appeared to draw back into the shade, peered and then slowly descended the hill. Softly she laughed.

"What is it?" he asked her, watching the golden face.

"That woman thought we were going to kiss or something," she said, and looked at him.

They were standing very close, under the green lamp. He looked uphill, thinking it was a lie.

"Did she? She should have known we'd have told her first!" he said bitterly.

"You are a card!"

"What?"

"You are a cool one," she said.

Yes, he was a cool one, standing there, wishing he could take her in his arms and yet mocking himself for the thought. He was more than a cool one, he was a futile one!

He wanted to tell her so much, that it was difficult to explain. She did not always speak his language. She might not understand. But need she understand? Was that not being futile too, to 'understand'?

"Goodnight then," she said cheerfully. "You must come in next time and meet Mum and Dad!"

Shocked, he looked up at the house. The room was comfortable and inviting, with the flames of the coal fire flicking the walls and shadows gesticulating through the windows. There was nothing he would have liked better; and yet — to meet Mum and Dad! It sounded terrifying. It would mean he was practically the chosen one. He'd seen it in the case of her sister.

"Goodnight," he said to her sincerely, almost affectionately, as she ran off. He felt hopelessly in love, but how? In a different way from others? He adored her. She was the most significant thing in his life, but he was not ready to face at once that significance. He could not reconcile it with his image of the world. It would not be fair to go in there, until he could. That would take years.

There would not be a next time. He would never see her again. He would not even write. That was the kindest way. He would go, because he loved her too much to see her hurt in all this ugliness. He felt absurdly like Reinhardt and could not get her out of his mind. For him the freckles round her limpid blue eyes were made of gold dust.

Along to the front of his own house he walked in an agony of remorse. Why had he not acted? He did not know. Always he was remaining mute and motionless at the wrong moment, as if his will were paralysed, or shrinking from decision, so deep was inhibition burned into him, and hatred of his prison. He did not realise how important a part in his life his father had played, how every decision paled into insignificance beside the decision of taking matters up with his father and opposing that iron will.

He would say he had no job! He spun in the shell of his own torment. He would not have his life determined by anyone! Or was he shrinking from the rebuff he feared, a rebuff more than once received from his mother, who naturally gave his father pride of place?

At cricket, rugger, football, he had always been picked last for the same reason, that he shrank from any form of self-assertion. He had an inferiority complex. Why should a girl differ from a football captain?

Inside the house he ambled about with such an expression of unhappiness on his face that even his mother was affected by it.

"Whit's the matter wi' ye? Take yer tea."

"I don't want any tea. Nothing's the matter."

"I'll no' thole it," she said. "Look at him! If this is how he's going to behave when e comes back from the pictures on a Saturday he'll no' go at a'."

"I'm damned if he will," his father said. "I'll slaughter him!"

He did not mean that. That was stupid "British" heartiness because he did not know what was wrong. It was boring.

He remembered how she dropped her head when she saw him coming down the street. Why had he spoken as he did, or run away from her and himself, making himself a permanent exile even in his own country?

"Comfort me with apples and stay me with flagons, for I am sick of love."

Now he knew the meaning of the Song of Solomon.

"He's been to the Shows. He's been to some coconut-shy ," his mother said.

"I don't know what eating you," said his father, "but always remember this: don't get het up. A wee bit pits ye right, and a wee bit pits ye wrang."

IV

Now David had to study at home by bright gaslight, on a table covered by white waxcloth — the same chair he had once pretended was a racing car — an obscure drama of Hebbel, when there was in the little kitchen a far greater drama waged, the drama that his father wanting the light out and yet expecting results from his study, could not see, a drama of hidden guilt, a battle between "work" and "culture", and love.

"I've tae be up the morn's morn' at the back o' six," his father said. "I've tae work!"

He never knew what was meant by that masterpiece of a phrase "the back o' six", but he resented the implication that no one else besides his father worked.

"I don't work, I suppose," he replied. "This is all a lot of stuff and nonsense!"

"You said it yoursel'," his father said.

He read for a little then, his mind full of the secret drama burning his life into the white incandescence of the fragile mantle that yet gave so much light. He knew he was hopelessly in love, yet, having gone so far in developing the intellectual approach to organic love, miscalled culture, he was forced to study further, and to derive such consolation as he could from the cold classicism of Racine's *Phèdre*. Its deadness sickened him. He turned to Marshall's *Principles of Economics*. That was marvellous. It was a watertight system, but it postulated scarcity. Economics was defined as the science of the disposition of scarce means among unlimited ends. He read Henderson and Cole and Stamp and Keynes and Gregory and Beveridge, and, as the days went by, Cassel and Withers and Robbins and Jevons and Hobson and Smith. As the worldwide economic blizzard blew up outside, he read steadily through their theories of over-production and under-consumption and even sunspots, with increasing bewilderment, and would not at all have been surprised had the Great Pyramid been brought in again to explain a sudden decrease in supply, as once he had heard it used to prophesy, or defend, a fall in commodity prices.

What kind of "science" was it,. he thought, which explained the trade-cycle in terms of sunspots? What gave such scientists the right to laugh at superstition? The fact was they were all equally scared and superstitious men, with an equal interest in obscuring the truth. Their voluminous books were merely an attempt to put 1,000 pages between them and the reality that mended their taps.

It was gradually borne in on him that the immediate causes of what was now called The Crisis were the transference of financial control from the Bank of England to the Bank of France and the Federal Reserve Bank, and the consequent complete cessation of foreign lending on a pre-war scale. *The Waste Land* was an American export in more senses than one. Their financial wizards expected to hold all the gold in the world, without lending it to anyone for fear they lost it, and at the same time expected no effect either on capitalism or on international trade. It was the final proof that the whole legion of economists were "liars and lickspits".

A more fundamental cause, however, was simply that Smith's insistence on labour as the real creator of wealth had been overlooked by the subjective philosophers, until wealth had come to mean gold as it had to the Mercantilists though that was merely the mechanism to which it was tied. The growth of vast urban populations had created an enormous potential wealth which gold was quite inadequate to measure at all. He read the Report of the Gold Delegation of the Financial Committee of the League of Nations.

"Britain was built on the Bible," his father said; "God, not Gold, that is what we believe in."

It was wide open to cracks about missionaries and soldiers and capitalism, but perhaps in the final analysis it was true as most things, in that what counted was the faith of a man in himself, his motives, and in those of his country, his country being simply the way men such as he lived together. Again he came up against the sense of community he had lost on leaving school.

He remembered a text his sister had had to learn by heart when she was five. They all had a text to learn every Sunday, illustrated and in colour, and they were always happy if it were short. Hers read: *Thy faith hath made thee whole.*

Poor Meg. She could scarcely talk at all. She said: *The face has made the hole.*

He thought, too, of the ludicrous philology of the B.I. Christ was not a Jew, they said, He was an Israelite of the Tribe of Benjamin. He said so Himself. Ten Tribes had been lost, including Dan.

"Dan shall judge his people. . . . Dan shall be a serpent by the way, an adder in the path that biteth the horse's heels so that the rider shall fall backwards. . . . Dan is a lion's whelp. . . . And they called the name of the city Dan, after their father."

It was incredible how many Dans there were in Europe. Dan-mark — the boundary of Dan. And Don? And Dun? Most of them were Irish: Donaghadee, Dundalk, but also there were Dundee, Dunfermline, Dunedin, Dunoon. The sounds were the sounds of the river he rowed on: the Clyde, Caledonia, Caledon, Chalcydony — philology on holiday.

He drifted into an attitude of scepticism. Where the Gold Standard was kept, what was Vitamin B, or the Nature of Idealism, were things of which students had even less idea than he had once had of Santa Claus. Less, in fact, for they did not distil little lightnings of snow, nor did the wear a scarlet cloak. They were not sweet in the mouth, and they certainly had not been met with *in practice*, yet they thought themselves more scientific than ever, hearing them in the words of their teachers. They grew more gullible in fact as their scepticism grew. The gap, the old hole in the chimney widened, and a stream of sooty words blew down which they picked up and ate with the ashes, though they constantly crumbled and made them filthy. Perhaps if they had ever grown sceptical they would have been a lot less gullible. Perhaps the first myth was the best, the more organic, the living poetry that would have given them freedom. Only most of them had lost sight of it, and for each of them it differed.

Living, it appeared, was not enough for some of them. So terrified were they of mere lives that they invented and willy-nilly hunted down mythical enemies, heretics, scapegoats, witches, with the entire paraphernalia of paranoiac finance. That grew to be his name for the system: paranoiac finance. It was paranoiac finance that caused wars, and lay at the root of greed. To his professors, however, it was only a glib phrase and not "scientific".

As a relief, David joined the Boat Club, situated on the banks of the Clyde. He always regretted that the windings of the Kelvin made boating on it impossible, otherwise it would have been an ideal site.

As he walked through Glasgow Green to the river, the first day he caught sight of Currie.

"Hello, whit are you daein' here?" Currie asked, tall and thin, standing stiffly till David came up, as though he were on stilts.

"I'm joinin' the club."

"Gee, so am I. How do you get in?"

"Here's the door, I think."

Inside, the place was like a stables. The air was coated with dust, and in an inner room they found a student with his coat still on and his feet on the mantelpiece. David remembered the student he had seen on the tram, when he was a child, wearing a velvet-tasselled cap of an athlete. The comparison was odious.

"Can we join the Boat Club?" asked Currie.

"Set ye back ten and a tanner," was the answer. "What weight are ye?"

"Nine-ten," David said.

"A bit light. You might make bow. You?"

"Six stone," said Currie.

"Good God!"

The man leapt to his feet and walked round Currie as though he had discovered a phenomenon.

"What?" he asked. "Jeez, are *you hollow?*"

"No," said Currie; "a clear case of malnutrition when an infant."

"I don't care what it is. You're hired. You're cox in the first boat, starting right now. Get your clothes off!"

"I don't know anything about rowing," said Currie. "I came here to learn!"

"You'll learn! Here's a megaphone! Get going! We'll have to start you on a tub." He turned to David. "Bill will take you out. He's coach. Hey, Bill, freshman here."

The tub was not so bad. It was like the boats young men took their girls on when he had been on the River Laggan, but it was hard work. He sweated and pulled.

"Come on," the coach said. "You're not trying. I can see that."

Now and then there passed a skiff or shell in which there sat a crack oarsman pulling at the sculls. They went four times as fast as he did, but sometimes they overturned and had to be rescued.

The river, too winding to allow of eights, restricted their racing activities, and they had to have fours. Under the bridge the currents were swifter and below the middle span there was quite a whirlpool, which invariably cost ten minutes of invaluable time. They called it "The Tunnel".

So David came to love the river and the rain, the walk along the towpath and even the speakers on the Green on a late afternoon, when yellow lights went on shimmering in the mist like tall crocus. Along the banks as they rowed upstream there rose against the evening sky the bare branches of poplars, shaped like feathers, and the river was silent and morose, murmuring only to itself as the oars plashed. It was his bed.

Far down towards the coast they could occasionally hear the sounds he had heard from childhood, and almost heard no longer; the sirens booming mournfully in the far distance, like great birds travelling over seas and continents. He used to ask his mother what that was.

"A ship in the Clyde," she said, "going to America, or India, or China."

He watched them from Fairlie, steaming down the river, telling from the colours on their funnels the line they belonged to and so whither they were bound. There was the Anchor Line, White Star, Burns and Laird, Blue Funnel, and countless others, steaming into the distance like incarnations of destiny. One day he hoped to take one of these ships. Meanwhile the river was a good substitute.

"Where does this river run to?" a stranger had once asked a Glaswegian.

"It runs to America, ye silly bugger," was the answer. Down past the boathouse and the lights it ran, to America.

Eirich agus tiuginn o, he thought.

In the morning he awoke, stiff as an oar.

FOUR

I

Every time he climbed to the top of Gilmorehill he stepped into a dream. It was a dream in which there lay below him a wild panorama of buildings, where thousands of people still lived in the Victorian Age, out on the mudflats of civilisation, on drear islands of English industrial towns untouched by any tide. Side by side with these, the Middle Ages strangled like creepers the lives of Balkan villages, though ghosts and dwarfs were more alive and gentle there than the cold, inhuman horrors and shadows cast by twentieth-century industry and inhumanity wearing the mask of science, or the cones and triangles of factories and chimneys building a geometry of trance.

The thing was to bring abreast of each other these contemporary centuries of the mind until they too were spread out and visible as in the panorama below. It was very difficult. To those who still lived in the Victorian Age that Age was very real. To those who still hoped for the return of the good old days of golden sovereigns there was no other criterion of the normal. They felt no other history. One and all they finally swarmed like flies around any one of the gigantic buildings and institutions that still seemed to promise them some thwarted form of salvation — the Bank, the Infirmary, the Church — in them depositing their panic, their savings and their wounds.

He stared down.

By Alexandra Parade, where his father worked, stood the giant block of the Royal Infirmary, a strange Sing-Sing, redolent of skyscrapers, courtyards, small doors and endless haunting corridors; frozen with mirrors, stiff with women in white, like secret nuns, overflowing with fast cars and alarums and flowers and knives and sudden, overpowering chloroform.

Once his father had had a weight fall on his head, cutting it open, and had rushed round, clothed from head to foot in blood, to the Casualty Ward, where a small staff fought off immediate disaster amid blood and repression.

They took it for granted he had been in a riot, or perhaps a fight with the police, who were not always scrupulous in their choice of heads.

At the entrance to this factory of devotion there stood a large clock which punched you a ticket saying when you came in. He had one of these every time he went round to the bacteriologist's with a parcel of piping, to watch by the laboratory-door through a haze of aprons and flames, the slow pickling of disease. It was a mysterious process, grim with ordered purpose, unlike the jungle peering through the small windows outside.

Beds lay out in the drowned sun. Patients coughed and the sound was like paper softly blown over wide playgrounds. Out on the verandahs old men, paler than primrose, lay back into breathless white cushions.

Once a year from its towers of mercy there started out through the imprisoned city a strange white chain called the Children's Flower Procession. It had one small band, the B.B. (standing for Boys' Brigade), with pipes, flutes and drums. Long files of children in white, escorted by their parents, walked along the cavernous streets on a carnival of thankfulness, bearing collecting-boxes for the infirmary of wounds. The girls dressed like brides, the boys like pages or clansmen, marched to George's Square, where they joined May Day processions of joyful horses, red banners from the ironworks, silken Masonic emblems hung with Orders, until, in waves that scattered into a thousand rivulets by the river, there swept over Glasgow Green one giant tide of mercy and revolution and temperance and labour and love and charity and fruitfulness.

Glasgow, from the hill, was always attempting in incoherence to free its own rude pagan vitality, and anything served to rouse the currents hidden in the recesses of these canyons.

Next door to the Infirmary lay the Cathedral, where the blood was dead, the Regimental, the Highland, the Covenanting blood, draped in the grapeshot of silken colours, and the receding waves of headstones in the Yaird. Next to that again stood the silence of sealed and turbulent Barlinnie, a feudal castle of broken hopes and criminal intentions, more feudal, more criminal than the blood and neglected death lying opposite. Farther down still, the North British Goods Station, releasing fleets of drays, wove steadily through this whole incomprehensible politic a python of horses swallowing carts, and a long rope of tails, mooring to the banks of the Clyde undesirable economies of dirt and abuse, until finally the city came to resemble a ship boarded by pirates.

These were the activities going on around Whitehall School and Gilmorehill. They deafened the still tomes in the libraries. They drowned the ineffectual voices of the teachers. They made drunk with the illicit stills of romance the sober schoolboys with their books, in which the real pirates were symbols of romance. The colossal plunder of Nature in the mining of one and a half million human beings was ignored. The pirates were in command. The defeated walked the plank of poverty and death.

There lay the Tron Steeple and the Tron Gate, dating from the days when the city had gates like floodgates, and down from Barlinnie, the Gallowgate — foundation of an orgy in the "Killing Times". By Langside lay the Battlefield where Mary Queen of Scots was utterly defeated in 1580 by the followers of Knox. That to Scotland he thought was the greatest defeat ever suffered, greater than Flodden, greater than Culloden. He could see the Queen poised on a white charger, awaiting the outcome of the battle, and her dogged, glib-tongued opponents tearing down her cavalry as at Drumclog, fighting down first all the love for women in their hearts to build a grim prison of Calvinism for their country. The ruin of that image, he felt, was the ruin of the Scottish matriarchy, as Culloden was used to discredit Scottish manhood.

It was why women could not rule and why men ruled too harshly; why his mother was unhappy, her father dour, and his own father a relentless fighter. It was why his mother said to the minister: "We don't think enough of the Virgin Mary in the Kirk!" surely the most daring thing said since the time of Jenny Geddes.

It was why religion was the one vital thing left in an emasculated country, though he felt obliged to renounce it. Above all, it was his mother demanding the whole love of his father; Mary and Knox,

E

Eros and Ananke. Yet her love too could turn to violence and tyranny, from the multiple poisons of disappointment.

England, they said, was a matriarchy still. In Scotland the matriarchy was dead. Women there were good housekeepers, not good mothers. At least, he thought, they had avoided that horrible concatenation of corrupt power which produced the doggy English female, the English matriarch, supreme in the riding-breeches, tweeds, bowlers and blotches of over indulgence in physical appetite for power, with all her absurd pretensions to agility of limb and potency inexhaustible.

"At least," he said aloud, "we were spared the pervert and the lesbian for rulers when our rulers were betrayed. Power may consist in the inhibition of conscience, as conscience is nothing but the inhibition of power, but women have no conscience and therefore can have no real power."

"You're telling me," said Rollo. "They're pussy-folk. Ever notice them in the German tutorial? Men pool their sex. You know what I mean. They neutralise it, in a kind of comradeship. Women sit in isolation, like creatures of prey, doing nothing but growing their hair and painting their nails."

It was true. Only motherhood matured them, yet in spite of that they remained largely immature. Even their cosmetics and their rouge, derived from days of blood and gunpowder, were stored against the cadaverous obedience of some future love.

"I hate them," he said.

"I love them," said Rollo.

"Well, the bourgeois ones, those who have so inherited cadaverous obedience that they feel their very bones to be property brought to the marriage."

Why? How could he? Did he hate his mother? Was it hatred of his mother that made him hate Mary, and hatred of Mary that made him hate his environment? Did he hate his environment because he hated women, or vice-versa?

"You must suffer from mother-fixation," Rollo said.

"OK," he said. "I'm not an engineer, so I have a mother-fixation. There is no escaping industrial perdition is there? No escaping the conical sections of perversion!"

There lay the adult dream, where the figures were not the spontaneous emanations of his fancy, but animals, in various stages of rut and fetish. He could not stand aloof as with the cardboard-theatre. The vision was stereoscopic. The figures walked out of the screen and ran round him, claiming validity, infecting him with their own nameless excitement, demanding interest and approbation, participation in their schemes and ultimately even his servitude; after which he would cease to be of any interest.

First it had been violence in the fist-fight with Ingins.

Most, it seemed, never grew out of that stage. The strange fear of sex which had conceived these children in violence also embedded and rooted them in violence, so that they could never grow up, but lived out their lives in a wasteland, a class division, a mental age and country within the frontiers of the comic strip.

He, too, was ashamed of sex. It was sissy. Emotions were sissy. It was sissy to cry and sissy to love and sissy to have anything but hard muscles bunched for action like Buck Jones. None believed violence derived from emotion, or that emotion was the mainspring of action. Accepting action and aggression as independent phenomena they sought them everywhere — in the boxing booths to which his father took him, at the markets, and on the battlefields, where they were confirmed and canonised, and condemned.

That was still a battlefield down there. He saw the O.T.C. coming back from a route march. Miners were a finer army. Any man in the street with a cause and the average amount of courage was a finer soldier than these dolls. Theirs was a ritual mania, a khaki Hengler's, a form of ballet unrelated to any conception of war. The rifle and the bayonet, the 36 grenade, and tommy-gun, were not the important things in that secret society, but the drill, the inculcation of a correct attitude of mind they had the impudence to call character. Such leaders, he thought, over-anxious to step into the harness of type and tradition, were less the embodiment of the social virtues than the expression of the ruling social neurosis. Rulers wielded power, and power, Lord Acton said, corrupts. Already they were corrupted. They had begun to imagine corruption a prime necessity for the attainment of power. They had become a fount of disease.

Like the great bell in the tower, its clapper silenced, the University hung suspended over the city, a shell. Noticeboards in the empty rain stood like shop windows with nothing to sell. Around the quadrangles drifted black gowns and red, whispering of corporate life and social events, but ultimately the students walked apart, so many doctors intent on diagnosis of their own reasons for coming thither.

This pile was indeed visited only by doctors and engineers. It was one of the first martyrs to science. It had become a factory for industrial design, a clinic for inventive practitioners, since vivisection on the social body was to be encouraged. More rarely, it was a museum or grave for the Humanities.

From the front he looked across the drifting cloud and smoke toward Glasgow. Tenements in the foreground loomed like gigantic ships' hulls. Behind lay Townhead of the royal-blue lights and bleeding heads, light-blue suits and red ties, with the Cathedral and Barlinnie Prison, like Fort Bay. He always thought of the Bastille as a kind of impudent Barlinnie. The horse-droppings helped. Nearby stood the City Hall, amid dung and straw and houses like horse-boxes in the rain. Over them the clouds floated like wraiths.

Nothing had happened between these walls since Adam Smith.

With Stott and Currie and Rollo, he walked through the tiny doorway and joined a group of medicals.

"Nice corpse this morning?" tittered one.

"Was she a virgin?" sang Stott.

"Tee-hee-hee!" smothered Currie. "Anatomy, what crimes are committed in thy name!"

"You are discussing Glasgow and you don't know it," he said.

"Glasgow," said Currie, the wit, the Polonius. "Let Glasgow flourish!"

He glanced round and saw Poole, a wizened, dark-haired individual with recessive eyes, blush and hug his bag tighter. All the best in his life was crammed into that bag, out of sight, so that he might earn a position as a mediocre preventer of the young.

"Swotting away, I see," said Stott to him.

"I haven't even read yesterday's lectures yet," said Poole, turning away and heading upstairs, his eyes screwed up behind his glasses in a girn of concentration.

The bell tolled. The quad filled with monastic and nun-like shapes fading again into the concrete. Rollo appeared mysteriously still at his side. He liked Rollo. Though he was unaccountably brilliant, when the occasion arose, he was also aware of the uncomfortable panorama beyond. It was a pity his awareness had no issue except in calculations regarding engines, pistons and table-rapping. When he spoke, his voice was a monotone metallic as a low-pitched bell.

"We had a nice time last night," he said. "Quite spooky. The table answered three times. You ought to try it."

He spoke without moving his lips, looking straight ahead. His eyes were of evanescent blue. He was strangely attractive. He was Banquo.

"Coming up to class?"

Class today was the weekly rambling lecture on Gothic architecture by Professor Gow, delivered in German and illustrated with lantern-slides. As it droned on, and the Roman arch was succeeded by the Norman arch and the final crown of the Gothic arch, David had plenty of time to think. He was tired of being dogged by the Goths. To the Professor every close in Glasgow had a Gothic arch, or should have. There must be some mistake.

He thought of the problem of value. It was the first attempt David had ever heard at a rationale of things. Value, of course, was purely economic . No attempt was made to link it up with value in any other sense. That would not have been "Pure Economics". It was strange how much vice and abuse and debased living was connived at by "Pure" Science and "Pure" Economics. They dealt with the skeleton in the cupboard — Economic Man. Yet, one would think, there was a Political *Philosophy* or there was not. It seemed no, there was not. Philosophy, too, was studied separately, as "Pure" Philosophy, under many guises, the latest of which was the "greatest good of the greatest number", while the world outside was falling completely apart. Nevertheless it must all have been relevant *once*, say during the bourgeois revolution in Scotland, when Watt harnessed steam, and the necks of millions of his fellow countrymen, born and unborn. It all meant nothing whatsoever to Rollo, who could, however, regurgitate it with a quiet efficiency. Lecture-room or barrack-room? David was not quite sure which. What a pity there was no Department of

Social Psychiatry to give the old place a good spring-clean! Already he could see large spider-webs forming on the ceiling and on the stairs; large wrinkles growing on the forehead of the professor, and on his breast great silver fish, that might be the Legion of Honour.

Once or twice he had indeed caught a glimpse of vanished splendours, even in German. During the capping ceremony in the Great Hall, for example, the whole audience of students and visitors had stood and sung 'Gaudeamus Igitur' and other student songs. They sang with such fervour, he felt he was unknowingly attending a mysterious initiation, like those of which his father had told him in the Masons. ʾThese graduates in robe and gown acquired significance as part of a freemasonry hitherto unsuspected. For a moment they gathered the force of Druids. What could it mean but a survival of belief in the only community worth having — the community of the intellect? What had he lost in Whitehall but that same sense of community? Surely that was why he had listened to the waterfall behind the stairs, trying to remember and recapture that comradeship?

In the evenings, in the German Club, they sang old drinking songs and ballads of the 'Wandervogel' deriving from the days when travel for a student or apprentice was a convention having the weight of compulsion. Then there was all the vast community of European Humanism to be explored, with its craftsmen and students. Now there were few craftsmen. Their tradition was being ground underfoot by capitalist society. A gulf divided the "intellectuals" and the "workers", as if students and apprentices had not belonged together from time immemorial in the only association ever known, the association of creation, and the only Republic worth having the Republic of Work and Thought!

The Sorbonne, with its various colleges of the nations, lived on in the Nations of the University of Glasgow, though no one dared remind the Scots student of their ancient ties with Paris, and the "Auld Alliance" was become part of the same drunken impotent sentiment attendant on "Burns' Nicht".

In those days, he felt, life was accepted as picaresque. Goethe wrote his *Wilhelm Meister* but the *Sorrows of Werther* no longer convulsed a generation that had buried natural feeling with the impact of Freud. The world was imagined to be crumbling because perruques and back-scratchers were no longer *à la mode*.

He, too, would have his 'wanderjahre', in which he broke with everything and everyone, and sought his own era among the friends of Ronsard.

"After all," he said to Roilo, "the English universities destroyed Humanism. They moulded education around the growth of an Empire, and reduced the Universal to the Imperial. They and they alone are responsible for the mortal wounds inflicted on the modern world in the name of Physical Science and Imperial Government."

"My foot," said Rollo.

"What is the aim of education?" he asked. "I say to produce free men and women, responsible for their actions and decisions, and of independent spirit and judgment. Instead, what do we find? A host of echoes of the imperial spirit. A set of clerks in the Imperial Civil Service. Education by the die-stamp."

"Balls," said Rollo. "Balls."

"All right, Milton, Newton, Smith, Shelley, Mill were all civil servants manqués. Scotland never had a court. There was no Fergusson, Burns, Dunbar or Henryson. English art and letters since 1800 have shown unparalleled development.

"What are you talking about?"

"A nation of clerks," he said. "And a nation of office-boys to the North."

"Remember," he went on to Rollo outside, "the Renaissance was no divine accident. It was not discovered like America, by any Columbus of a monk. It was the expression of the rise to power of the bourgeoisie of Genoa and Venice and the Hanseatic towns."

"The monks preserved the manuscripts," said Rollo, "in their cells, all through the Dark Ages."

"In their body-cells?" slavered Stott.

"Yes," said David. "Yours are adapted for a different purpose."

"What's that?"

"To serve as hogsheads for bearing whisky down to posterity."

"Hurrah! Here's to the good old whisky, it makes ye feel so frisky!"

"In what did the Dark Ages consist?" asked David. "In the fall of chivalry, or, shall we say, the decay of feudalism. It was the period

135

when power was becoming centralised into the hands of princes who beat their rivals down. There is nothing sacrosanct about tradition and family or the age of murder. Absolute kingship, divine right, was the first blow at feudalism, not the invention of gunpowder, because it was the first blow at chivalry. It was the first manifestation of the future struggle for naked power, and the birth of power-politics."

"Sure," nodded Stott. "What the hell did Edward want up here? The Hammer of the Scots? Well, he got a hammering all right! "See approach proud Edward's power, chains and slaverie!'."

"The bourgeoisie did not rise to power till after 1789," said Rollo.

"They rose to world power then," said David, "but they had lost their *raison d'être*. The Renaissance was finished. Why, do you think, was there no renaissance as we know it in Russia? There were Chronicles there, as old, if not older, than those of Froissart, those of Nestor and Avviakhim. Why?"

"The Russians were out of touch with Europe," said Rollo.

"I'm out of touch with this," said Stott, "bugger this for an argy-bargy!"

"What Europe? Venice and Genoa. There was no bourgeoisie in Russia. None ever grew there. Theirs is the Twentieth Century Renaissance, the Era of the Common Man."

"Bullocks," said Rollo.

"If you say so, perhaps," said David, "but I think not."

"Why doesn't Gow say all that?"

"You *are* a bastard, Davy," said Stott. "You'll get no marks for that high-flown tosh in June. You're nothing but a sucking bolshie."

"Your mother must have been frightened by the Bogey-Man on the stairs," said David. "Besides being useful for holding up a hat and filling a fortuitous space between the ears, that portion of bone directly above your nose can be used for visualising sights and sounds and links unapparent to the naked eye. Did you know that?"

"You bleedin' pig!"

"Stick to the prescribed books," said Rollo.

"No, they present the Renaissance as a sudden and unaccountable treasure-hunt. A vast Hunt the Slipper, an archaeological expedition into the deserts of history, and by God they *are* deserts!"

"Nothing of the kind."

"It was less a time-discovery than a passing of the arts of culture into new and eager hands."

"Ooh, I'm a fairy," shouted Stott, gadding about and throwing his books in the air.

"I don't agree," Lew said, coming up. "The paintings, the writings were already there. All that was lacking was the will to explore them by those who had the power to sway men's destiny. Why should they? They had all they wanted. Their interest was in ignorance and superstition. That is what is meant by reaction."

"What do you mean, all they wanted?"

"The power of initiation and decision. The bourgeoisie raised these to new heights, with the force of revolution. You will never have your National Scotland," he said to Rollo, "as long as the bourgeoisie retain the power of initiation and decision. Growth of empires was incidental. Power had already passed to the middle classes. They created the civilisation of the Adriatic in the Middle Ages. They failed to create any in Sheffield or Pittsburg. There was more raw material there for manipulation."

"Bullocks," said Rollo again.

"I suppose you think this bloody place is civilised because you can have a cup of coffee in the Union for 2d," said David.

"You old Gow," hissed Stott. "I've a good mind to drop you one."

He and Currie were invariably together. They hunted in pairs, Stott and Currie, the one with the long jaw of the kangaroo and the same height and slouch, looking for something to put in his pouch; the other the bright weasel, teaching his grandmother to suck eggs.

"What does your mother vote, Wullie?" asked Stott in a sing-song whine and whistle.

"Tory," said Currie. "She doesny know what she's daein', but I'm going down to the Corporation today to see Bailie Giemuckle. There's a teachin' job goin', and tae hang wi' bein' put on a waitin' list!" he chuckled, slightly slavering.

It was cowardice that inspired his ambition. To Stott, on the other hand, the Varsity was a free bank where the blank cheque of a degree might be cashed, which by some incomprehensible miracle was at once exclusive and universal.

"Have you been to the Adviser on Careers yet?" he asked.

137

"I'm going now," said David.

"For Pete's sake don't say you want to be a teacher!" gittered Currie.

"Why, is the profession overcrowded?"

"Overcrowded? It's worse than puttin' your name doon for a hoose, intit Harold?"

"Aye, that's right," said Stott; "honest," and nodded his head in emphasis.

"Whit are ye gonny be anyway?"

"I think I'll try to find out what being a man is like for a start," said Rollo.

"Dirty dog. He's a dirty dog, inty Mac?"

"You don't understand."

Hundreds of students thronged the stairs, waiting to see the Adviser on Careers. Every now and then, in the irascible tone of the overworked doctor or psychiatrist, they could hear the scream of the Adviser: "Get to bluidy hell out of here! Next!"

No doubt he was sick of interviewing the prospective leaders of a nation at 2d a time. No doubt he was appalled at these candidates for the world coming up in wide-eyed droves, but, felt David, he might occasionally have remembered that his tragically useless advice had been made compulsory.

He was also the Adviser of Studies, a post he filled equally well.

"What do *you* want?"

"Nothing."

"What are you here for then?"

"On instructions."

"Course?"

"Arts."

"Honours?"

"I hope so."

"What do you mean you hope so?"

"One never knows."

"Subjects?"

"French, German, Economics."

"What are you going in for?"

"The Civil Service, I hope."

138

"You hope a lot, don't you? Come back next year."

It was time he had a drink. They were just open.

"No more today," he shouted through the open door.

Stott and Currie were waiting in the quadrangle.

"You ought to take philosophy," Stott said.

"The history of philosophy," said Rollo. "There's no philosophy in this place except the philosophy of bowdlerism."

"I'll buy it," said Stott.

"Hee-hee-hee," Currie tittered.

"It is a racket," David said. "Rollo's right. It's not a question of believing in something or investigating something up here, but of being able to read the minds of lecturers and examiners and serve up in a palatable way what is wanted upstairs. With the proper kitchen-maid mentality there is no telling how far you will go."

"Is that whit ye do in Economics?" lisped Currie.

"I believe in limiting population, but not by discouraging marriage," Rollo answered.

"Surely ye know that marriage is only a fertility rite?" said Currie in surprise, laughing and baring his teeth like a horse.

"I can see you limiting population, you ram, you," Stott said, jaw more pelican than ever. "You would press on the means of subsistence all right you would."

"We all press on the means of subsistence," said David; "that's what we're here for."

"You don't quite get me, does he, Wullie?"

"I hope no'!" sneered Currie, convulsed.

"Malthus gives a static picture of a dynamic society," said David. "What is needed is a sociology of change."

"Whee-whee, Stott, look," said Currie, "ain't she a nice bit?"

"She's certainly a hot momma," Stott said. "I wis an accident. Were you, Mac?"

"Do you use contraceptives, Mac?"

"You know, these airships?"

They gazed at each other and burst into desperate laughter, holding their sides like boxers punched in the stomach. Currie's teeth were clenched and his eyes stood out of the sockets as though he were being throttled.

139

"Jack-of-all-Trades," said Stott.

"Master of One," giggled Currie.

David gazed at them. Their attitudes were frozen compulsion, like the movements of a Javanese dancer.

"You should come into English lit. with us, you really should, Mac," sang Stott.

His lips pursed when he spoke, and his cheeks contracted as if he were sucking something delectable.

"We read the choicer bits of Chaucer and Burns, dain't we, Currie?"

"We sure do," said Currie. "It's all we do."

"You *are* a bastard, Currie; did yer mother no' tell ye?" laughed Stott, shaking his head, so that David could see he suffered from St Vitus dance.

"I suppose you're St Paul?" grinned Currie.

On they raved, in their happy communion of unacted guilt.

"Women to you are unpurged images, are they not?" he said.

"Listen!" squealed Currie. "Who's talking!"

"You don't recognise the voice," said David. "English Lit. and you don't recognise the voice?"

"It's got a cold," said Currie.

"As I said," repeated Stott, "I'm an accident. I used to swim about in a green bottle in a chemist's windy. I came into this world when the rubber tore."

They rolled about the pavement, wrestling and grabbing at each other.

He knew what that meant. All along Buchanan Street where processions of carters in convoy marched proud horses, there were dark and furtive shops disguised as herbalists, and surgical stores, claiming to sell bird-seed and artificial limbs, but dispensing in reality rare books; cigarette-cases, with naked women on the front, containing four sheaths; as well as whirling-sprays, enemas, and other medical items to be sold only under the twin disguises of hypocrisy and pornography.

"Are you taking a degree in French Letters?" sniggered Currie.

A crime was fastened on their hearts like a leech. How did they propose to assuage that crime? By the crime of the usurpation of power. Was there no end to the Hamlet sequence?

"He's the strong silent type," Stott said. "He doesny have tae answer that, do ye, Mac?"

"Hahahaha," Currie staggered as if struck, holding his stomach.

Mary had marked him for life. He could not laugh, remembering the Christmas three years before when she had disappeared along the back in a shimmering white frock, like an apparition. It was then he had thrown an india-rubber into the gas-fire in the room for a bet. Sparking out, it had permanently marked his left hand. The white patch of skin was still there, under the last knuckle, like a weal. At the time he had not realised why he did such a stupid thing. He knew now, watching them caper like monkeys.

The thing seen against all lack of purpose and direction was its soul and inmost spirit. To a novel or a picture the same applied as to the individual life and will.

"Spit it out, Mac! Whit dae ye think?"

"Unless and until we are given full and final freedom we will not accept responsibility. Until State and external authority are dead — together with economic exploitation of one man by another — we shall not act, for we shall be incapable of true action. There will be no action, only reaction; no literature, but only the mouthings of fearful fools; no philosophy and no wisdom, but only the cunning thought that hides knowledge from the majority, to employ as an instrument of oppression. The ultimate power — the sanction of force — must be broken before this book or that book or any book can be given direction or purpose or form, or life itself brought to accept what we are pleased to call responsibility, but which is only awareness of action."

"Hurrah!" shouted Currie.

"Hip-hip-hooray!" screamed Stott, throwing his cap in the air. "Whit a swot, eh Wullie? Where did that come fae, Mac? I know, Stevenson! Or was it Dr Johnson? God forbid it should sound like Johnsonese!"

"I was just practising," said David.

"Well, ye'll get nae marks for that here, willie Wullie?" Stott bawled, and Currie slapped him as they ran off. "The great lexicographer!" they shouted.

He turned and went into French.

It was a currycomb curriculum. The French Professor, precious and precise M. Prince, Chevalier de la Légion, not unfortunately Etrangère, possessed an exquisite accent owing largely to his habit of sucking his beard.

"Balzac est le plus grand romancier!" he said, kissing his hand in the air.

He hissed when he mentioned Flaubert. One did not read Madame Bovary among the prescribed books, but La Légend de St Julien, or was it the tobacco? To him, no Dostoievsky, no Gogol, not even a Zola. Was he, could he be still, a dreyfusard? He conveyed the impression of being a piccolo pétain, with his head so full of flags and trumpets and slightly swashbuckling honneur that he could not hear the sub-machine of his Louis-Ferdinand Céline, in the sewers.

To David, fresh from the Russian class, where at any rate a sense of history was instilled, he represented the punctilious decadence of Tsarism, the satin-bearded, the satyr, exquis.

"Victor Hugo es sans doute le plus grand des poètes francais, " he added.

French poetry stopped at de Musset. There was no Baudelaire, no Rimbaud; Ronsard here like Villon was a medieval aberration.

M. Prince was able seconded by M. Gold, who carried a small Gladstone bag and cultivated a Latin moustache in memory of the Paris buses. Sweeping in on the eddies of his gown, he was greeted with cries of: "Good morning, Dr MacPherson!"

Chief clown in this musical comedy was, however, jovial M. Leblanc, who ought to have been expounding de Maupassant and Paul de Kock instead of seventeenth-century drama. He hoped one day to rise to the position of ringmaster.

If art was a stripping of motives, a search after truth, a process of historical indexing a *prise sur le vif*, the place of these gentry, David felt, was surely the Empire Music Hall, not Gilmorehill.

He was therefore glad when the gong sounded and he could reach the comparative sobriety of the Economics Department, though there, too, nothing was up to date. The very walls exuded weariness in their damp, and the prof. lay across his chair like a tired Roman Emperor in his toga, unable to touch, far less digest, a morsel of the wondrous banquet lying around in profusion; sipping Godwin, putting a fork in J. S. Mill, parodying scripture with a bored gesture, yet the scripture was there.

He dealt with the problem of value at great length, in order to relate it to nothing in particular.

"Wrap up the affairs of State in my fish and chips!" said David to Rollo, but it was no laughing matter.

As the professor rambled on David dreamed an English lesson.

"Let us consider today," the professor said, "the extravaganzas of the word 'shop'. Probably the most important word in English or any other language. 'Nation of shopkeepers,' said Napoleon. Not, you will notice, shopwalkers or shoplifters, though a good case might be made out for the latter, but shopkeepers. 'Keepers of the Privy Shop'. The derivation of shop is not clear. 'I'll shop you,' says the army, which may or may not mean 'I'll treat you as a piece of goods' — an empty threat in any case, for are not soldiers merely the goods sold up the river in the War Shop? Not that the War Shop is a knocking-shop. Heaven forbid. Knock — you may knock — but it shall not be opened unto you, is Holy Writ, or should be writ, but we must not get on to the subject of writs today.

"The shop is one our most cherished institutions. It is mentioned in the Doomsday Book, wherein occurs the entry — Rent of Shoppe — Nil — Desperandum, telling us of the acute economic crisis of the period. One does not even need a shop in order to be able to shut up shop and go home. A shop is literally forced on every infant at its birth — the children's shop. No matter whether it call itself a church, an office, or a gallery of art, a shop by any other name would smell. Psychologically, etymologically, epistemologically, it is still a shop where goods are sold, and here we have the key to the entire symbiosis. The town is a shop. The whole country is a shop, and we had better sell out quick if we wish to make a living.

"Housing shortage? M-yes. But whoever heard of a shop shortage? We talk shop, we walk shop, we tuck shop. Home, Guards, and at 'em! Export or fly! As Chaucer skylarks in the Old Wives' Tale: 'Honey, suet queue, mail ye pence!'."

It might have been said of the Professor that he had spent so much time learning how to think that he never actually thought. He was a sub-division of Hamlet. Moore on Logical Positivism he found so fascinating as a proposition that he sat for hours wrapped in the contemplation of mere ways, incipient channels of thought, angles which, however, never taught him tolerance. Like the spider, looking all ways, he rarely missed the chance of swallowing a passing victim.

"No, no, not fundamental!" he said with a dyspeptic look. "The relation of methodology to metaphysic and to the biology of human conflict is much more cogent than apparently you realise!" Throwing aloft a frown, into the snows of his Tibetan thought, until he could smell the bacon and, in later years, the curtains, burning.

He was an unlaughing dwarf with a brow like a giant John Bull. His temples bulged like the dome of St Paul's, and he knew everything, for he had read all the books that ever gathered around him. He walked, if it is of any consequence, with long flat strides like a determined duck, quite *pregnant* with consequence, eyes huge and revolving, like the butterfly's eyes, imprisoned in a bottle. He rarely smiled. Such is not the habit of those to whom life is earnest, or who have discovered, little by little, that life is real and must be given a purpose, *their* purpose.

When once he did laugh, however, a revolution broke out and rapidly spread to every part of his face. This is not to say it required a revolution to make him laugh, or that laughter inevitably entailed a revolution in his nature. Those with an English love of compromise know how one can laugh without meaning it, so that the personal revolution is not really one, or revolt, laughing, so that the political laughter is real but not a revolution, if you follow. His pupils seemed to pop out of their sockets, and his head jerked forward as though he were being strangled, while his face grew purple. That was the moving into position, the strategy of his laughter. Then he half arose from his seat, propping himself up with stiff arms and a low rumbling came from the direction of his stomach like distant gunfire. By devious routes the rumbling reached the throat. The isosceles triangle of his face collapsed on its apex the chin. The eyes protruded more and more on to the cheeks. The cheek-bones stood out. The man seemed *hungry*! And blood-vessels filled with red made a blotch on the face. It looked like a retching fit, but no, no, no, he hee-hee-hee-heaved and *laughed*, shaking his body and filling with blood that egg of a head — a sack of tilting potato-delight!

"There will be a war. It is absolutely certain," he hissed from between his teeth, eyes poking forward in prophetic trance.

Invariably in his later youth he dealt with "absolutes" and "fundamentals" and other cabers tossed from his gut.

In a way he was a symbol. His books were so many fallen leaves, authors in hibernation. Yesterday a summer-house of culture, a challenging tower of the intellect in the days when each ivory tower shone like a lighthouse, now withered at a breath of war and winter, tumbled into ruins, burned, if necessary, by the new-born pagan suckled in a creed out-worn at the merest hint of a trumpet blow.

He was one of the sects moving in a dream of their own making, a dream not even war or the dissolution of all they held dear could break, the dream that the exclusive ideal, the madness of each would overcome all the others. This was the Imperialism of Thought. Their only belief in democracy was as a vehicle to ensure the supremacy of their particular dream. Would they still cling to a democracy in which their own private dream had been defeated? Pacifism? Personalism? Anarchism? Would they attain that love? The pot and the kettle. The whole political set-up, he felt, as he read Muggs on Political Theory, was an elaborate camouflage for personalities and libidinous leanings. It was a crude struggle for power by men ignorant of conscience, and devoid of reality except the reality of a few small minds asserting their blindness over that of the others.

The one hard fact was a cliché: the means of production were not in the hands of the people. This had been said so often that no one listened any longer, but one day they would have to listen, when internecine conflict would so isolate and destroy the fabric of communal living that there would be nothing left for people to do but direct the machinery of production, much as a passenger on a bus might have to drive it, on finding the driver dead at the wheel.

The gong sounded again.

"Let's get out of here quick," said Rollo.

Every day during break David walked with Lew and Rollo in the grounds of Kelvingrove, his mind caught by the classical lines of a church in Doric style, or the windings of the ardent Kelvin.

"You're so clever," said Rollo to Lew, "you're a chameleon."

"How am I a chameleon?"

"Adaptation to a background of self-colouring is a feature of jungle life," said David.

They walked along towards Keppochhill Road humming the Stein Song.

Keppochhill! — a name full of the sound and fury of the Western Isles, sea and soft rain and landing-stages constantly awash. There were plaids in it, too, and something altogether wild and tameless and immortal. Rollo, he felt, would understand that. Looking up, he remembered as a child going along this street on a tram one Saturday afternoon when the city was gradually growing into a vast revelation. There was a Symphony Concert for Schools in St Andrew's Halls.

The tram was full of boys. As it swayed and rattled, the long pole gave off red and blue sparks. They sang and whistled sitting upstairs in a crow's nest, even passing the loud cemetery with its pearls of lilies and white stones set within rusting red railings of fleur-de-lys that guarded the marshalled dead.

On the other side lay a steep cutting, a viaduct and then a mine. It was absurdly like hell and purgatory. To the boy, the compact ugly images of the town were wedged together so tightly that their associations were difficult to extricate. One had to be an archaeologist to sift their significance. Most people ignored them and sailed about in trams and trains as in a dream not of their own making. They pretended this intensity was not there. They called themselves practical people, surrendering themselves to the blind and ruthless forces that had built up this environment.

Schools for crippled children, iron playgrounds for those not yet crippled, nursing-homes and public-houses, succeeded each other with bewildering swiftness as the blue car sped down its slipway like a yacht. A dizzy coma of whitewash and placards blossomed on a field of hoardings. They read: BEER IS BEST. Twelve hundred and fifty-two shops displayed a myriad of goods in small windows before they reached Charing Cross, and Charing Cross itself was one enormous bay-window of furs, home safes, gigantic castellated wedding-cakes and super undertakings through which these matchless goods might be owned for no less than quite a temporary slavery. No feudal village in the thrall of tyranny, no medieval city in mortal fear of hostile neighbours, nor buried ruins of Colosseum or Carchemish had ever thrown up such a monstrous brood of terrors, such a catalogue of idols of introspection as this modern city of whip and fetish.

The Halls themselves were grim and gray. They were like Barlinnie, or obstacles on a battlefield, imprisoning promise and tokens of thought. Children in a horde stood outside, like beggars, holding warm sixpences. Yet when the music began inside, it set everything dancing, the wires, the seats, flowers, trams, cemeteries and shops, and made the river speak.

On the way back they passed the Kelvin Hall. He remembered that too! All the winter it had been a raging sea of coloured lights and laughter, a vast, impersonal rushing noise, like the wind, filled it like a sail. That was the wind from The Whales.

Every year there were the Whip, the Hammer and the Whales, groaning up and down their green and red and purple turbulent mountains. There was the Hall of Mirrors, where your head was bigger than your body and your stomach bigger than your head and your legs two inches long. That made them all laugh. Different mirrors inside made you different shapes. Even in the same mirror you were a different shape if you walked up close from what you were if you walked away. How could you ever be sure what you were?

His mother was a different shape from his father — but she wasn't really.

They were all comical, spherical gnomes of no meaning but laughter. They were all gaunt, elongated lozenges with no desire but hymns of praise and emptiness. Or else they were bumpy, wart-like freaks, offspring of the illusion of sin. It all depended on the way you looked at folk.

He liked the Fishing Pond. It had real water, not a mirror. You paid 6d for a rod which worked by magnetism, and there were tin fish, of which he caught six. They were more magical than the prize, which was only a small box of chocolates, mostly ginger.

His father preferred the Hammer, where he always rang the bell, or the punchball, which he always nearly burst with a powerful right you could "see leaving the house".

When at last they tired of walking among these vast acres of booths and incalculable enterprise, laden with coloured balloons and pogo-sticks and dolls and wally dugs, they met a smirr of rain outside that melted the lights into liquid roses and crocus.

He loved Glasgow in that dark and mist just before Christmas

147

when all the shops, like Trerons, contained a little Kelvin Hall of jollity and fun, with an office for Santa Claus.

In the tram again he sat back relaxed. It was a blue one, so there was a blue light behind the blue glass knob downstairs. The thing was a blob of swaying clanging light. And, once in the house, he went to bed dreaming of dwarfs and heads balanced on sword-blades on chairs, and of other near-perversions, preferring always the music of the Whales, whose voices were the vast organs of the deep.

"There's Mr Pan," he said, pointing to Stott in the distance, "the boy who laboriously grew himself up by adding to his stature every week until it was taken for granted that his mind was suitable for long trousers."

"Let's avoid him," Rollo said. "We can go into the Mitchell."

His friends were cultured in so far as they had risen above culture. Meeting them, talking to them, were so many parts he did not deliberately act, but was forced to act because of the theatre, the décor in which he found himself, not false, real enough, but not totally he, a scene in which he was being fitted into a jacket too small for him, like Professor Gori in Pirandello's story *Marsina Stretta*, part of a concatenation of circumstance to which he owed no allegiance but the allegiance of affection.

To them, Pirandello was of little interest. They were content with their triple catalogue of books, one for class-reading, one for general reading (the University Library) and one for private reading (the Mitchell).

In actual fact, private reading was both prescribed and proscribed.

"The whole place is for illiterates; no reading but public reading, no thinking but public thinking are encouraged. I can't stick it," said David.

"I'm finished when they give me that degree," said Rollo. "I'll never open another bloody book."

"Lucky you. I want to tear out the Hidden Index. I want to be an 'Unqualified Reader' in some museum."

"You're a fathead. You'll only ruin your eyes."

"The only department worth a damn is the Russian Department."

"How?"

"In Russian literature you find an interest in people of all classes, merging always beautifully with organic feeling for nature and classical language. Read *A Sportsman's Sketches* or *The Death of Ivan Ilyitch* in the original. That interest was the tremendous motive power that shaped the Revolution of 1917, but there is no account of contemporary Russia here."

"They're all Bolshies," Rollo said, "are you?"

"The only vital force in the contemporary world is allowed to rot in a small corner of one quadrangle," he went on, "while vast new departments are built to house the eternal fantastic engineering by means of which Scotsmen try to build bridges to one another."

II

"It gives me great pleasure . . . !"

"Yeah?"

"It gives me great pleasure . . . repeat . . . pleasure . . ."

"Liah!"

"I repeat," said Sir John Suckling, "it gives me the greatest pleasure . . ."

"YEAH?"

"Really!"

He was standing on the platform in the Debating Hall at lunchtime. The place was packed with students in search of a little colic, or bucolic, or alcoholic entertainment from the speakers in favour of the various candidates in the Rectorial Election.

"My purpose in coming here," he said, glancing apprehensively at the gallery, "is to speak . . ."

"Who's stopping you?" squeaked a voice. Two streamers floated gracefully down from the tiers. A long blower almost touched his nose.

"I do not propose to make a set speech and certainly not to outline the policy of H.M. Government. . . ."

"HURRAH! HOORAY! Three cheers for Sucker!"

"But if I can answer any questions, or clarify any issues. . . ."

They stood around watching him, smoking, eating pies, drinking tea, mostly with considerable scepticism. He fingered his tie nervously, Secretary of State for Scotland, not knowing what to expect from these barbarians.

"Does Sir John consider 15 shillings a week sufficient to keep an unemployed man and his family?" shouted an undergraduate, leaping up.

"That raises an interesting question," said Sir John. "The view of the Government is . . ."

"Does *Sir John* consider 15 shillings a week sufficient?"

"You must take into account the price-level and the index figure for the cost of living," shouted Sir John, losing control for a moment.

"ANSWER THE QUESTION! GO ON, ANSWER THE QUESTION!" they cried from all over the room.

"Then there is the point about Purchasing-Power Parity, known as PPP!"

"PPP," they squeaked. "PPP."

It was the chief letter in their vocabulary.

"YES OR NO?" bawled the questioner.

"NO!" screamed an angry Sir John.

"HURRAH!"

G.K.C. was better. He took all the sting out of the attack by demolishing himself.

"I am painfully aware that I am not one of your light Scottish riders," he began; "nevertheless, I think I may say that I attach a great deal of weight to any question. (Laughter.) Whether I am right or wrong, my view is bound to bulk large in any argument. (Renewed laughter.) In fact, I may be said often to dominate the proceedings by the mere preponderance of my presence. . . ." (Applause.)

They liked this cheerful old man and would not permit him to debunk himself. What a pity he was a Distributist. He was the most brilliant of the speakers.

It was all a jape, of course, a "rammy" like Charities Day. Now David remembered how he had envied as a child the gaily dressed students on their Roman carnival. Here he did not care to join in. He could see the junketings were less gay than he had imagined, more reminiscent of the drill and mascara of some weary chorus than of Venetian nights. Instead of masks and palazzi and love under the moon, there were collecting-boxes rattling bones or dice and behind the gaunt Gothic shapes of the hospitals there lay the waxen masks of the dead, to quell his riot. For the others, however, it was still a sheer rammy, a riot of jollity and unlimited licence, although of the meaning of their Saturnalia they had no conception. Only a few sad-faced classicists perhaps, with gold and bronze medals in honour of a defunct empire, stood by and saw, not Donald Stott and Wullie Currie and Lily Weather wearing rumples, but a satyr and a goat and a Maenad, more alive than the gargoyles of George Square.

They walked out of the Union, leaving Stott and Currie, and along the dung and straw-littered cart-track of Eglinton Street, past the Drill Hall of the Rover Scouts where he and his father had once seen the Scots boxers beat the Danes. Carl Hansen was there, the wizard of Rangers.

"The Pope is only infallible when he speaks *ex Cathedra*," said Quinn.

"He's always inaffalible," Rollo said.

"He isn't. That's a Protestant heresy."

"Listen," said Lew.

David looked up at the wires, thinking perhaps a bird was about to sing. Combined, their feet rang on the endless flagstones of nightmare. A city shrouded in a blanket of cobbles wept by his bed in his dreams.

"Listen," said Lew's comforting deep voice, "say the Pope says in private what he said *ex Cathedra?*"

"Ah, but he wouldn't!"

"But just say he did? For argument's sake?"

"Then he wouldn't be infallible in private!"

"That's illogical," Lew said.

"I can't help that!"

Quinn laughed. He was a queer fellow, hungry and desperate-looking. His face was pale, the cheek-bones prominent, and his eyes bulged balefully behind the thick lenses of his glasses. Yet his hair, dried in wisps of innocence, and laughter, were as delicate as his voice. When he spoke, the rising and falling tones were unmistakably Scots, though he was of Irish origin.

"Stuff it," said Rollo. "You're always wrangling about the Pope. Why can't you talk about something decent for a change? I saw Lily today."

"Lily who?"

"Lily who? Lily Weather!"

He thought of the day of the Orange Walk on Balgray Hill, when, all unsuspecting as you were, you would be seized by the shoulder and look up to see an upraised fist and hear the challenge: "A Billy or a Dan?"

It was impossible to guess right. It was Bullies' Day.

"Tell us about her," he said.

"I've asked her out next week."

Rollo was a son of the Manse, proud of his deceased father's library on witchcraft and warlocks.

"Better to marry than to burn, eh?" said Quinn.

Rollo was burning.

"Do you believe in free love?" asked Lew.

"If I can find it," Rollo said, looking straight ahead, carrying his attaché-case like some prim parson.

"Do you?" he asked David.

"I don't know. If free love means a rammy as public policy, no. Most people seem to take it that way. If it means the absence of marriage and the basing of cohabitation on sincerity of feeling, yes, but what does it mean?"

"If your wife wanted a man, could she have him?"

"She probably would. There would be something wrong with the marriage."

"Not necessarily."

"I'd decide that. Not you."

"It's all in Ognyev's *Diary of a Communist Schoolboy*," said David. "In practice it doesn't seem to work."

"You mean people are possessive?"

"Of course they are possessive! How the hell can you possess a woman if you aren't possessive?"

"Possessiveness has nothing to do with it. The trouble is in sticking to principles, revolutionary or otherwise. Love or marriage is a private affair. It must be free. You cannot impose freedom, like the Irish democrat who said 'You are all free to vote as you like and if you don't we'll damned well make you!'" Lew said.

"It's all a question of sex," maintained Rollo. "If the sexual attraction is strong enough. . . ."

152

"French salaciousness," said David.

"It's true," put in Rollo. "Now, take Lily Weather . . ."

"Is she like the weather?"

"I don't know. She agrees with me most of the time. She says it's because she loves me."

"That's bad," Lew said, "bad, bad. If she loved you she'd be the opposite of you. She'd oppose you just for the fun of it even."

"Sex and love," said David, "are like 2 and 4, the one contains the other; but if you go around thinking two *is* four, your measurements will be badly out."

"The Puritan," Lew said. "Listen to the Puritan. Looking for the ideal woman."

The writhing discontent of Glasgow coiled in their bones.

Lew and Rollo were doing well. So were Quinn and Poole. Rollo was outstanding, but careless of success. Lew was steadily brilliant with a tight-lipped brilliance. In the French library, David, however, sat and read the wrong books for hours, Larbaud, Rimbaud, Verlaine, Baudelaire Apollinaire, not the prescribed de Musset and Lamartine, resenting the establishment so soon of alien criteria. In economics, too, Godwin he found more interesting than Mill, and Keynes than Stamp.

"You won't get your degree," Stott said, nodding. He had taken to wearing a cap, what they called in Glasgow "a hooker" or a "skippit bunnet".

"I don't care," David said. "I'm tired of traps and snares. If I could start all over again I'd concentrate on philosophy, though after Wittgenstein it's hard to see what could be done except to create a new organic philosophy. A degree is only the visa on the passport of serfdom."

"Serfs, eh? Did you hear that, Stott?" Currie said. "That's a good one, isn't it, Stott?"

"Are we serfs, Mac?"

"The most backward examples, for you do not yet realise the fact of your serfdom."

"He's a caution," slavered Stott, "in't 'e, Currie?"

He looked at David with menace, shoulders bowed, the long tapir-face drooling.

153

"So we're serfs, eh? We ought to scrag him, Currie. Whit dae ye say?"

"How long do you even devote to Scottish Literature?"

"Four weeks."

"No Chair in a Scottish university. Shame!" he said.

"Listen to the serf," Currie said. "A Chair of Scottish Literature. He wants us to study Rabbie Burns and Harry Lauder."

"Dunbar," David said, "Henryson, the Makars, Fergusson, Hogg, Drummond, Burns, Byron, Stevenson, Hume, Grassic Gibbon, isn't that enough for you to be going on with?"

"There's nae dirty stories in them," Stott said. "We only read dirty stories. That's why we like Chaucer. The Scottish Chaucerians are only derivative, in't they, Currie? They lack Chaucer's genius for the bawdy."

"The body?" howled Currie.

"If that's what you like, why don't you take your degree in pornography?" asked David. "There's a nice list of prescribed books at the Barrows: *Moll Flanders* and *Maria Monk*."

He remembered the purple and crimson covers of books he had seen, like deep-sea fauna. He had come on them one Saturday afternoon, and all the way home, past the rattling trams and red-brick factories, had tried to remember the posture on the cover. It was lurid red and purple, with a girl lying deshabille on the bed, the flesh pale-cream above her stockings, under the title *Damaged Goods*.

Arriving at the house, he found no one in, and stood looking at a puddle stretched halfway across the road. It was a soft yellow round the edges. Children with sailing boats of paper and matches for masts were kneeling by the side of it, pretending it was a pond. Standing there, he felt the liquidity and liability of everything — the sky brightening up after a shower of rain, like a tear-stained face; the chalked sandstone walls of the houses glistening like the hide of a beast, and the sliding ooze and worms lured up through the spongy ground by the sound of rain, coiling pale in the soiled water.

Even his memory of the picture faded fast. He could not hold it. The woman became floating and shadowy, but the conception of the picture remained. Did people think like that about women? Were women really like that?

His aunt came along the street with his mother and they went into the house together.

"I suppose I'll be seeing you here with your girl soon," lisped his aunt, with her red smile.

"No, you won't," said David, angry and embarrassed, thinking of the one he liked and feared in case she should become one of those living mummies.

For a moment he saw the picture again clearly, and then his aunt's voice re-echoed in his ear, ancient in its "harpy" wisdom: "Oh, yes you will. Boys are all the same."

She made him prefer the picture to reality, the lurid to her, while children sat before the puddle pretending it was a pond although there was only the puddle. They had no pond of clear water.

"We don't know anything about Maria Monk, do we, Currie?" he heard Stott say.

"Na, tell us about it, Mac."

"Yes, come on, tell us. What's she like?"

"She's a woman," he said, "not like Lily Weather. She doesn't care about agreeing with you or disagreeing with you, so as to attract you. She has no bait, except her appearance. She's honest."

"Suits us, eh, Stott?" leered Currie.

"Her appearance is everything desirable. She has full breasts, well-rounded hips, just the right curves, and a lovely face, and she is content to be herself because she feels how real she is."

"Where does she live, Mac?"

"She lives on the covers of a book on a barrow in Renfield Street," he said, "where you put her."

III

"And how are you getting on with your lessons?" asked his uncle.

"I don't have lessons any longer. I have lectures."

"Well, lectures then," laughed his uncle, waving his hand as he sat himself on the window-bottom to watch the trams at the foot of the hill.

"I'm still learning."

"What are you going to do?" asked his aunt, peering at him as though frightened or puzzled, wrapping her fur coat more tightly around her.

"I don't know."

They were waiting for his father to finish tea.

"How's business, Johnnie?" asked his uncle in quite a different tone, partly worried, partly patronising.

"OK, Norman; a bit slack."

"Aye, it is that," his uncle said, paring his nails with his fingers.

"What do you think of things?" he went on, turning to David, as if he had just remembered. "You're studying economics aren't you?"

"Yes."

"He's a Socialist," his father said as if secretly glad, though he himself was a true blue.

"What? No' a spouter?"

"There *is* an unemployment problem," said David coldly.

"Socialism won't cure it," his uncle said. "You can't change human nature."

"The gap in your argument is a chasm," David said. "You imply unemployment is in the nature of things; also that it is necessary to 'change' human nature to cure it. Ergo, you can't change human nature. A large statement, coming from one who is said to believe in Christianity, and also a tragic one."

He was quite white.

"Christianity is different."

"What do you think your Christ would do," said David, "if He came into Glasgow now? Join the Kirk? Read *The Citizen*? The Scots have lost historical vision. They seem to have lost a sense of the eternal as well. A greater pack of money-grubbers and robbers would be hard to find. They are probably the one nation to *sell* their country, and later to hush up the deal and boast of it."

"What do you mean?"

"Read Burns on the Union:

   'We're bought and sold for English gold
   By a parcel of rogues in a nation'."

"That was a long time ago," laughed his uncle.

"It's now a national custom. It would not be so obnoxious if it weren't wrapped in so much religion. Glasgow, according to an English parson in tonight's paper, is a city of top-hats and churches. He thinks he is praising it! The Stock Exchange has taken over the Kirk!"

His uncle laughed uneasily. His aunt paled and bit her lip.

"It's right enough, Norman," his father said. "Religion and this money business don't mix. Not that I'm much of a one for religion."

"God and Mammon," said his mother.

"I'm neutral," David said. "You're the Christian. Or should it be Pauline? Christ, you know, did not want to be worshipped, but emulated."

His uncle rose in a fury.

"Ye can't change human nature," he shouted.

"Do you imagine that your career in usury has the remotest connection with Christianity? You are elevating your own faults into universal ones, like the capitalist everywhere. You may be right, but if you are, let's have no more platitudes about education and democracy."

"My oh," said his mother, "these boys are on the wall again. I'll soon put a stop to that."

She, too, was white with anger.

"I'll burn the balls that come over, I will."

"They're *devils*," she said.

"They're not," said David. "They're boys."

"I was ten times worse than they are, Teenie," said his father with a gust of sanity.

"They're your Socialist friends," sneered his uncle. "What's yours is mine and what's mine is ma ain! Eh?"

"If your creed is different," said David, "what are you belly-aching about?"

There was a sudden silence.

"It's sixes and saxes," said his mother surprisingly.

"Norman," said his aunt. "We'd better go."

Her face was drawn.

"Eunice will be waiting."

"Aye, O weel, goodbye Teenie."

"By heavens," said his father, "you certainly shut him up."

"He's my brother," said his mother, weeping.

"He asked me what I thought," David said. "I told him. You had a father as well who lived in this same house and had the very same trouble with your brother. He stood for something else than narrow-minded greed."

"He widnae come and see us at a'," his father said, "if it wasna to collect the drawings every week for his bank."

"How dare you!" his mother said. "He comes to see me!"

"All right, all right, have it yer ain wey!"

"Oh dear, oh dear," his mother whimpered, "what I've tae stand! Some day I'll just run away, I know I will, some day!"

Her mouth began to work spasmodically, up and down, and no words came. She was drifting into a state approaching hysteria, in what he thought a subtle assertion of her own will. He saw his father pale and grow alarmed. Going up, he tapped his mother smartly on either cheek.

"Stop it," he said. "Don't frighten Dad like that."

He had done it more for her than for him, but that was the way to say it.

"David," she said, sobering at once, "how dare you! I can look after myself, thank you. You are exceeding your competence."

Afterwards his father thanked him.

"Ye're no' very fair to your uncle," he said. "He offered to put you through your studies if anything happened to me."

"It was a nice thing to offer," said David, "but what makes him so sure I'd accept?"

"You shouldna say these things. You only hurt your mother."

"I'm sorry, Dad."

"I'd rather have seen you a boxer," he said, "or a mechanic, but I see you can do other things. Good luck to you, my lad. Don't be a wild man though."

"I'm not as wild as I sound sometimes," he said.

"And don't, ever, hurt your mother."

"I'll try not to," he said, "but I think I know her sometimes as you don't."

"Don't be too sure," his father said, smiling. "Now I want you to pay attention to this bit of lamb I bought today. It'll melt in your mouth."

He held out his palm. On it lay a choice piece of meat, like a large red jewel.

"Ye'll no' find the spit o' that on a king's table," he said.

Wrapping it up as if it were a gold nugget, and putting it away: "Come awa' into the room," he said, "and we'll hae a crack."

"How do ye like living in High Cartcraigs?"

"It's wonderful," he said.

"Norman didn't want it, so I bought it. This is where your mother's family really belongs you know. The Laird has a 'Quoich' and a model of Crookston Castle your great-great-grandfather made when he was a prisoner in the Covenanting days."

"Why don't we ask for it?"

"Don't be silly," said his mother. "There's Ian Halley going up to the Life Boys!"

"I said why don't we ask for it?"

"Nancy said a wee loaf would be better to be eaten a day or two old," she said.

"It's ours, isn't it? I suppose he ought not to have been imprisoned in the first place."

"The Finlays first came here to put down the Covenanters. Isn't it funny?" his father said.

"I didn't know that," said David.

"I've a favour to ask ye," his father said. "I want you to come to Fairlie on Sunday. Will you?"

"Yes, of course."

"I'm going out to Sanny's now. Are you coming?"

"I'll get my coat."

He knew what to expect. His father still went to Sanny's Piggery, where he had once garaged his car. Sanny was a boyhood friend of his and they kept up the old association.

"You'll please him a lot if you come. Since you won that scholarship he thinks you're it. He'd like you to give Frank some tuition."

"I'd rather not."

It was more exciting to stand beside a large vat in which pig food was boiling, on a sunny morning, listening to the crack of Sanny and Bob Andrews and his cronies than to go to lectures in the University.

These men meant what they said, most of the time. They lived in a dramatic world equally removed from the dilettante and the bureaucrat.

"So this is him!" Sanny said with a laugh. He was very small. "This is the boy. Ye should be prood o' him."

"I'm still a better man than he is," grinned his father.

"That's what you think, Jock." Sanny gave another giggling laugh. He was wearing old trousers and a belt and clogs. His shirt was open at the neck and collarless. The sleeves were rolled down, and in his mouth, upside down, hung the stump of a discoloured clay pipe. Every now and then he punctuated his remarks with an eloquent spit. His voice was hoarse from much smoking, and husky too with concealed emotion.

"He's a good yin, Jock!"

"He'll have to be a good yin to be as gallus as his faither!"

They all laughed again and David felt embarrassed and miserable because they treated him as if he were somehow different. "Gallus" was his father's word. His father was full of such words. He did not know where they came from, but they sounded good. "Gallus", he supposed, meant "Gallic", "Gaulois", like the garb of Old Gaul for kilt. It might be written "Gallice". It might be a French borrowing. His father would have been astounded to know.

They looked into the huge vat in which the pig food was simmering and bubbling. Sanny stirred it with a long pole. It was overpowering.

"Wad ye like tae see the pigs?" he asked.

They walked round the sties, where old boars and colossal sows wallowed and slept amid glorious filth.

"The dirtier they are, the healthier," Sanny said. "There's a mint o' money in dirt."

He looked like a schoolboy overjoyed at an excuse to become as dirty as possible.

"How did ye make oot last year?" Mr Macrae asked.

"Bad, Jock, bad. The swine fever cleaned me oot," he rasped, spitting quickly and heaving a sigh.

"I'll make a fortune next year though wi' a' they young yins comin' on."

Sanny was always making a fortune. He never did.

They strolled over to the old railway carriage that served as quarters for the men and drank some tea.

"Hoo are ye gettin' on, David?" beamed Sanny.

It was rather a strain till Bob Andrews arrived, with pendent cheeks and a ruddy complexion formed into the jolliest expression imaginable. He was on the dole.

"He's a weel-read fellow," his father said.

Bob was a Socialist.

"Whit dae ye think o' things?" he asked David, directly.

"Rotten," said David. "A pack of criminals in office set themselves up as saints."

"Ha-ha-ha, hear that?" Bob asked Macrae, delighted, as if it were the best joke he had heard in years.

"Oh, he's red-hot," his father said, not at all displeased now it seemed.

"Well, who's no'?" said Bob. "We've had enough o' this for twenty bloody years."

"Ye're no' a Socialist are ye, David?" asked Sanny, paling at the thought of losing his fortune before he actually made it.

"He's a bit that way, I'm afraid, Sanny," Mr Macrae said.

"Weel, he should ken," said Sanny manfully. "What's gonny happen tae us?"

"More and more crises, and then a war likely."

"Jeez that's a fine way to cheer a man up."

"If you don't alter things yourself," David said, "nobody will do it for you."

Bob nodded cheerfully.

"Ye canna stop it," he said, delighted. "He has haud o' the richt end o' the stick!"

It was distressing that they believed not only in what he had to say but also in the "learning" that was to be acquired at the University. The only learning worth the name was the learning realised in their arms and in their labour, but they persisted in imagining there was another.

"There's only one thing aboot him," Mr Macrae laughed, "he'll no' roll up his sleeves!"

"Ye canny blame him for that," roared Bob. "It hasnae brocht you hellish much!"

F

They screamed with laughter again.

"I work too," David said. "We all work."

All three wore caps. Macrae had a rubber collar and a bow-tie. Bob wore a muffler and lived in a "model". They all remembered more of revolution and oratory and history than he had ever read. They had heard John Maclean and Guy Aldred and Robert Busby, who could sway thousands and might have been Prime Minister in a new revolutionary party but for his sudden, never-explained disappearance. They spoke of men like those as they did of boxing champions who had finally lost their crowns, and now they were listening to him. He felt small and ridiculous. They only listened out of politeness, because his name was Macrae. They had faith in nothing but their own right arm, and perhaps a dim future in which rough justice would be done. Meanwhile it was best to be "gallus", to be cheerful and tough and self-reliant. Awkwardly David felt that he was by no means "gallus" enough in his day and generation.

They had a tremendous respect for what they called scholarship, and yet their sons, the new generation, were betraying them. It was easier to betray them than to fight their errors and prejudice and lack of knowledge, easier to say "yes" and then betray them. They asked for betrayal because they demanded confirming in their prejudices and hates, and thereby connived at the same deadly dangerous social system, and the same stupid errors of acceptance, they wanted to fight. Currie was betraying these men, and he was the most dangerous of traitors since he knew he was betraying. His china-mask of a face — the high cheek-bones and cunning eyes gave him the appearance of a Tibetan priest turned bandit — admitted his guilt and boldly laughed because there was no denunciation. His own father was a worker, but the sole idea of people like Stott and Currie was to rise out of that class and live in a cardboard bungalow full of paper hopes and on some railed-off hill, secure in awareness of a fractional superiority. They were prepared for sacrifice, but it was the sacrifice of others. They were the new generation from which "Scotland" hoped so much, and what they were becoming they did not care. Stott and Currie, identical in bullying egos.

Compared with such masterpieces of synthetic conscience as those "products" of the educational system, David thought Sanny and Bob and his father wonderful people, but it was impossible to make them realise how wonderful they were. They regarded themselves as patient carthorses like the ones in the city, born for toil and sweat and worthy of no more. They talked of "getting out of harness". They were people of humility in that they had no desire for power and dominance. They left that to others, and here perhaps they showed awareness of true power.

"Oh, he's a worker all right," he heard his father say. "He'll read his brain into train-ile some day."

"Hee-hee-hee," laughed Sanny, without taking his clay pipe from his mouth, as if choking. His hands were thrust down into the forepockets of his trousers.

"Ye're an awfu' man Jock."

IV

The people who lived at the top of the hill differed from the people who lived at the foot, along the traffic-lined streets. It was not only that they had a little more money at their disposal daily. The houses at the top were often detached, or "semi-detached", whereas those at the foot were mainly in the form of tenements. Then the walking up and down the hill developed from a simple exercise into a kind of ritual. Unconsciously the hill began to symbolise effort and sacrifice merely by being there. The view from the top was said to "reward" all one's efforts, as if it had not always been there but only appeared, like a magic vision, to those who had worked hard. Yet the sight of the smoking valleys lent a sense of detachment to David apart from any effort, except the effort to get out of the place altogether.

In winter the hill was covered with ice in treacherous webs, over which people gingerly stepped on their way to the chores they called "work", confusing toil with assignation. Sometimes a horse would fall down, and for hours make gallant attempts to rise, thrashing with its hooves on the cobbles and macadam, and striking fire among the sudden sightseers from the roots of flint. On these dark mornings when sparks leapt from the masts of trams, emitting a blue flare, David felt its dim significance and was disturbed at his inability to put the scene into words. Sometimes then in a storm the slates would be ripped from the roofs to sail through the air like magic carpets, whilst the chimney-cans themselves spun merrily like boiling kettles on the hob.

At the very top lived richer folk, doctors and ministers, and Luke Sharp the accountant, whose daughter they said acted "awful well-off" and had a harelip and eyes like two frogs, frozen full of laughter and mockery. Midway lay a row of semi-detached houses, starting with the Hendersons, whose son was apprenticed to a C.A. at half-a-crown a week and wore a bowler hat, and was tall and always clean, past the Pierces, prim, till fat, moustached Mr Pierce cut his throat in a lavatory, and ending with the Simsons, whose walrus father, a locomotive fitter on half-time, had been smashed up on his motor-bike without any compensation. Straggling downhill then to the bottom came a row of little cottages, once whitewashed, now peeled, with small windows and flagstone corridors that made every step a harbinger of doom.

He passed them on his way downhill to meet Maclean. They filled his mind: an absurd, ugly little world of irreconcilables. He was going to a meeting where they would be reconciled. It was upstairs in a tenement. Maclean said it would be good, and at least it was not connected with the luxurious pipe-dreams of the University.

There were two rooms, so small that seven people crowded the house. In the middle of one of them stood a short, plump figure with a coat on. It carried a stick which it kept banging up and down on the floor as it swore. The place was knee-deep in newsprint.

"Well, what do you think of it?" the figure rasped to David. It was obviously a great man.

"There's more intellectual activity here," said David, "than in the University."

"What d'ye expect?" growled the irascible man.

The New Gael. 1d.; The Organ of Scottish Self-Government; Scotland the Milchcow of the Empire (Lord Derby) crashed the headlines on the sleek paper.

"I'm going to build this up till its circulation is in bloody thousands," said the man, and you could almost see the circulation of his blood as he spoke.

"I've been addressing meetings in Edinburgh," he said. "The Fuller Life idea will sweep the country. Of course you are familiar with it?"

"The credit part, yes." he said.

Maclean nudged him. He went on.

"Some people, though, say that there mustn't be enough currency in circulation to buy all the goods in the country, including capital goods, for that would lead to inflation."

"Tripe," said the man, "bloody tripe."

"I make no apology for the economics of scarcity," David said, "but I don't want to be forced to buy a steam-engine. I don't like steam-engines. Yet unless I take part in the process called making a living, and promise to work at making engines and wireless sets and cars and buy, eat and drink and sell engines, wireless sets and cars, I'm called an agitator, not only by the Government, but by everyone, including you and Fuller."

"Bloody tripe," repeated the man, the veins standing out on his forehead.

"Where am I wrong,?" David said, "granted I hate steam-engines?"

"Scotland and Credits go together," the man said, stamping his stick. "You can't have one without the other. You are a clucking anarchist!"

"I am a man who likes to know the name of the street he lives in," David said, "and where he is going. I think James Watt was a bloody anarchist, and a dangerous one. His mental aberrations did in fact change society in the way he wanted it."

"You must have vast credit," the man said, "for everyone."

"Now you blackmail me," David said. "I can only be free, I can only be happy if I buy your bloody steam-engine. Is the country populated with 'teenage morons? What are you trying to do, hypnotise me?"

"Do you agree with the abolition of the price-level?" asked the man fiercely.

"As long as there are prices, how can anything be free?" asked David.

"Look," the man siad, "if you have any difficulties, I wish you would write to me about them."

He had now adopted the superior attitude of the missionary who does not HAVE to save souls for Heaven. His party was one of seven other national parties, though what was national about any of them was difficult to discover, considering that one and all of them had lost, almost irretrievably, every trace of national feeling and consciousness in the frightful greed and disordered chaos of the Industrial Revolution, for which their own ancestors had been at least partly responsible. They lived in the smoking ashes of a country more ruined and plundered than Europe at war. *Glasgow, Lanark, Barrhead, Motherwell,* were as Scottish as *Pittsburgh* or *Magnetogorsk* or *Chung-king.*

"Now what did ye want to go and do that for?" asked Maclean as they went sideways down the narrow whitewashed stair — like those in a lighthouse or a dungeon.

"What Scottish architecture owes to the prison principle is better not investigated," said David.

"He was going to help us!" said Maclean in the gaslit close.

"He calls *me* the anarchist," David said, "while *he* helps *himself*."

"Does that matter?" asked Maclean. "Only Scotland matters."

"Now there's where we differ," said David. "To you Scotland is something tangible, apart from the people. You are like the prophets abroad who oppress the people by talking of the nation, or the warlords in London who even talk of the 'British Nation' — which has as much reality as the American Nation. Did not an eminent English critic recently write that he would not trust the future of English Literature, or even an expression of English Literature, to a Scotsman? Why, then, should a Scotsman be expected to entrust the political destiny of his country to Englishmen?"

"I agree," said Maclean. "That's what I mean."

"Why talk about the 'Nation' anyway? The 'Nation' is a dying faction. You should go on talking of the people. There *is* a Scottish people."

"We must recover a sense of nationhood," said Maclean, "like Ireland."

"I think we must first recover a sense of identity," said David. "Until we know who we are, there's little use in finding out what we are."

"That's too highbrow," smiled Maclean.

Sometimes he looked like Stalin.

It was difficult to reconcile such living movements with the dead and moribund activities going on at Gilmorehill. At least they did not give doctors bodies to dissect which were composed of rotten and putrefying flesh. Nor did they instruct engineers by means of models of Roman and Greek engines. Only in literature and in the philosophies was it necessary to prevent anything remotely touching modern life from being discussed. The Classics, he suspected, were revered for the same reason as Christ or newly deceased poets, that they were dead and their resurrection was not an immediate danger.

He tried to read as instructed, but finding it more and more impossible, looked forward with misgiving to the tutorial examinations.

On examination day, his nerves, uncontrollably on edge when he entered the room, crystallised into strained politeness at the sight of the examiners. He stood, he felt, too stiffly, behind a chair, until the Head motioned all four to be seated.

After an impressive pause, questions burst like bubbles from the pompous historian to be answered in a mechanical falsetto by the girl. It was obvious she had learnt her notes by heart. Her answers, he thought absently, resembled an after-dinner speech in all but the speed with which they were uttered.

Awaiting his turn, he watched the over-fed diplomat across the eminently suitable green baize table, by now as agreeably surprised and now as unpleasantly startled as a diplomat ought. He heard, too, the clock before the bumptious chairman tick with maddening precision. It seemed as divorced from the proceedings as its maddeningly precise owner, who interrupted importantly now and then on catching some familiar name, but more often dozed.

He watched the chairman awake from a daydream to dismiss the girl with one of his outworn platitudes: "You must work steadily."

It was not his turn yet. Playing the same game as the two fat little men, he outdid them in orthodox gravity. They had regulation falsefaces, he an expressionless mask, slightly darkened by the frown that passed over his features.

Catching it by chance, the chairman inwardly approved the results of academic training, while the youth was thinking how damned impertinent were these fatuities to have spent their time conniving at expenditure in blood and lives, while knowing themselves to be incompetent. He resented passionately their dogmatic impudence in teaching and requiring unformed youth to train in their movements and complexes of thought. He was amused at their smugness, sickened at their duplicity and afraid of the mysterious power whose tools they were, a power reducing to impotence by its silent and ubiquitous oppression; the power that lay in the hooves of stampeding herds. Who could restrain or direct this inhumanity? He suppressed an absurd desire to begin by stunning both of them with the clock and started up. It was his turn.

Stumblingly he answered the easy questions put to him. He felt now only contempt for the machinations of Metternich, and though he knew the answers well enough, lacked the desire to express them.

"What happened at the Congress of Troppau?"

He wanted to say: "Austria desired the murder of blasphemous Italians demanding peace and freedom," but instead he stuttered. The corpulent diplomat had a spasm of benevolence.

"The fellow knows, but he cannot express himself!"

The fellow did know. Intrigues by brainless wirepullers treating the earth as their preserve, and eternity as a stopwatch, had cost human puppets their slender lives. Tsars found inspiration for Holy Alliances in unholy mésalliances; honest men sacrificed their country's honour out of patriotism; the vicious circle spun ever quicker and wider.

The fellow could not express himself, other than by action.

He thought of a little yellow nation five thousand miles away which had learned such diplomacy and was blowing to the sky the culture of ages and the wisdom of the world. He wondered how its victim would react, and "express itself"? The chairman awoke.

"Thank you," he said ungraciously. "Come back in a year's time. You will be better able to express yourself then."

Outside, he met Lew and Rollo again.

"Hello," said Rollo, "how did you get on?"

"Horrible. Next year I ought to do better, he says. I doubt if I'll be here next year."

"Why? What are you going to do? You have to justify your existence, you know!"

"For me it is enough I exist. What will you do when you leave?"

"Teach, I think."

"You'll be good."

"I'll teach them the opposite of Rollo's witchcraft in a rational Catholic school," said Quinn with his speared smile.

"I'm going abroad," David said.

Was it running away? From his city? From Mary? From himself? Or to find himself?

"Escapism," said Lew.

"From what to what?" asked David. "Go and paste up a poster if you want your words to stick. There are two ways of looking through every microscope. I'm tired of looking through one end only."

No more sitting in sunlit trams in the mornings, rolling and swaying up to Gilmorehill to stop before the Union. No more gossip before morning lectures.

"I've been writing for GUM," Rollo said, "but their punch-and-pseudo humour does not appeal to my taste."

"Where will you go?" asked Quinn.

"America."

"The new Pilgrim Father."

"I'd only be doing what hundreds have done in the past."

No more Mary Watson, no more evenings at the cinema, no more hope of renewing the friendship. He had a daemon that drove him on, whither he did not know.

Home he went on the rollicking tram to his attic in Cartcraigs, where they now lived, to the silence of the old house and to the tracery of the giant tree, like a woodcut framed in the high-cabined windows, home to the blackbird that sang every morning before his awakening.

How could he explain that he was not going to be a colonist, or an emigrant, or a refugee? Unless indeed he were a permanent refugee from the human filth and ignorance and depression and prejudice and cruelty of cities built by an Industrial Revolution which had made a mockery of man's liberties? How could he explain that he was leaving only as a gesture of war on these and their like? This monstrous perversion of Nature had begun to assume a life of its own — apart from the will of those who struggled in its mire and squalor.

To find a touchstone for the present age they must return not to the Middle Ages, not to the puny French Revolution, nor to any of the metrical measurements of former history, but to Stone Age Man, who by his discovery of fire conquered the animals, only to find them in his brain.

Ever since the Stone Age, man had walked, not upright, as confident scientists had depicted him, in distinction to the ape on all fours, but upon two crutches. One crutch was called Weapon, the other Self-Righteousness. These two were called into being to balance the horrible creature that was first able to stumble about outside its Cave of Terror.

The Atomic Age, or the Age of Space, had knocked away both of these props. The Weapon, just at its most terrifying, was most meaningless, for Self-Righteousness no longer held any justification. Yet was there ever such fear and yammering? Self-Righteousness had never been justified, except as the second crutch. Yet now there was a mass-fear, dark as the Dark Ages.

Man since the Stone Age had sought in the external world for justification of himself. This process he called "rationalism". Now, unleashing even the myriad caverns and corridors of the atom, and still finding no justification of "himself", would he finally see his story as one of growth and maturity? Would he, sooner or later, cry out, throwing away his crutches: "Away with palaces and pomp and courts and finance and authority that bind me like so many threads for Gulliver. I will Live; and for that any 'justification' is both an insult and a mockery!"

Was a new Pre-History about to begin? Were the dinosaurs revived in another form, endowed with power over life and death?

It would be said that the evil was not in the city but in the way the city was run. It would be said that the evil was not the machine but the way the machine was run. In a way it was true. Any improvement in control — especially workers' control — would help to tame the gigantic animal. Only centuries, perhaps, of workers' government could disperse the monstrous creation of unbridled human greed and superstructures on the Ego, into the depths of the countryside where it belonged, so that its political power and perversion would be of no more consequence than slugs on cabbage-leaves. The destruction of this monster was the prime task of all Government. That was the Disarmament of the Mind.

Communists said "the withering away of the State", and were not always too explicit about it. Hobbes called it Leviathan. Fascism was its ally. His mother would have said the "Beast from the Bottomless Pit".

His exile was escapism, for these tentacles were all over the globe. It was an exploration, like the Joycean "silence, exile and cunning", only this time preparatory to attack.

He thought of Mary, the Queen of his Elfland.

Perhaps he was going to find her country.

They were waiting for Mrs Macrae, to drive her down to Fairlie.

"Let me tell you a baur," his father said. "You know Big Jock, eldest o' the faimily, and the most ignorant and unscrupulous as well. The whole distrtict knows him for a crooked fool. Well I went to his faither's funeral yesterday and he was a disgrace.

"He went to lengths in and out o' the business that no' even his brothers would have credited, but the auld man knew it a', Teenie."

"Ach, I've heard a' this before," she said. "I'll away and get dressed."

"During the war every one of his machine-shops was making a fortune, but when one of his assistants tried to buy a place of his own, day ye ken what he did? He did the dirty on him. Although the man was honest and working for him eighteen hours a day, he bribed the factor no' tae let him have it. Twenty years later, he gave that same man a cheap gold watch, 'For 25 Years' Faithful Service'. What a mockery! He wadna take it. I know. How dae I know? I was that man.

"Huh, aye an' afore that even, when he knew his faither was dying and went to see him to thank him, if you please, for leaving him one of his shops, do you ken what the auld man said? 'It's a' richt, Jock,' he said. 'You were stealing it aff me onywey.'

"The dirty swine was pilfering the till and wangling prices for his ain benefit."

"He's no' happy though. That wife o' his is driving him wrang in the mind. The money he made is in her name, and she threatens tae pit him oot unless she has her ain wey. Maybe she's right. He does mess things up, but whit a position for a man to be in! He never gave his son a chance at school, but took him away when he was fourteen for fear he would become what he ca'd a 'wide man'! Now he *is* a 'wide man', dodging work, smoking and drinking, and knowing less about the business even than his faither. He'd have messed up you an' a'. He says to me says he" — his father coughed — "when I telt him aboot ye wanting to go to the University, 'Don't let him, Jock. He'll turn oot a wide man. And then you'll be sorry. It's him that's sorry noo, no' me.

"When you won that bursary, he tried to congratulate me, but I just said: 'Mebbe he's only a wide man, Jock!'."

He shook his head.

"Whit a stumer! Bob Andrews says he saw him one night in Argyle Street at twelve o'clock. The rain was pouring doon, but he didnae seem tae notice it. He was walking along like a man in a nightmare, soaked, and his face drawn like somebody who's seen the horror o' reality. His wife had pit him oot. Of course he goes wi' other weemin, the dirty sod, but she *is* a tartar and the kids spy on him for her. They tell her a' he does, and tell him what to do as weel. Whit a midden! T-t-t! Are ye ready, Teenie?"

"I'm just coming."

"It was her, I bet you a pound to a hayseed, that made him mak' sic a fule o' himsel' the ither day at the funeral, for she'll hardly let him touch a penny, though she has her cars and furcoats and a maid and a' her orders. The auld man was a good yin. When he was seventy he went into a tobacconist's for his usual ounce o' thick black. The counterhand charged him three halfpence too much, and he asked why and said it seemed a bit funny. Then the youngster got cheeky and said something about his ignorance and that it was his age that saved him. 'It's my age that saves you, ye bloody young pup,' said the auld man, 'frae dragging ye ower the coonter and pulling ye ootside in!'."

"He never ca'ed Jock's wife onything else but a bitch."

David sat listening, miserably, wondering how his father would take the idea of his going to America. Would he think he was being a 'wide man' after all?

"Weel, as soon as the auld man deed, the seven brothers made arrangements for the funeral. They were a lovely family really, a' masons — and I wish I saw you a mason — seven is a mystic number in masonry. One o' them's a vet, and one a civil servant. It was one o' the finest initiations ye could see when they were made, seven being the perfect number.

"Teenie!"

"Yes!"

"It's the hauf-oor!"

"I'm coming!"

"Well, six o' them turned up to pay their last respects to their faither, complete wi' top-hats and frock-coats. It was touching to see these six big men thegither, helpless, an' naebody wad hae been mair touched, for a' his hardness, than their faither. But Big Jock was late. The whole company had to stand roon' the open grave, and the gravediggers blowing their hands and the minister looking uncomfortable, as if his collar was too tight. They stood aboot in groups, talking, but you can imagine what the conversation was like in the circumstances. Some o' them took a dauner roon' the cemetery, peeping surreptitiously at their watches, and the minister hid ablow a tree wi' a clump o' whispering weemin. And a' the time the coffin lying itsel' near the grave wi' the win' blowin' the flooers aff it. T-t-t-t.

"Some o' them began to get angry, especially Wallace the vet, and some o' the guests had left the place athegither, when in walks Big Jock puffin' and blowin', his red face like a piece of roasting dough. I can see him yet, snivelling like a dog. Oh he was concerned, for once. He knew he had done something wrong.

"'Gee,' he says, when he came up, looking pathetically at their faces, 'I had to wait hauf an oor. I couldnae get a tram.'

"And he's a man worth thousands, mind ye, maistly left by his faither.

"They looked at each other and then at the coffin. This time the auld man was silent.

"Teenie!" he shouted again.

She appeared at last, buttoning up her coat and peering at him in bewilderment.

173

"That's a marvellous story," said David.

"No' very nice though," Macrae said. "The car's ready for ye, Teenie."

It was a Morris Oxford, 1926. Outside the sun was setting fire to buildings and metal. They had the whole day free, as it was Sunday.

"We'll just take a wee run doon tae Fairlie," he said. "Are ye ready?"

"I'm aye ready," she said, rubbing Meg's face furiously with a wet cloth.

He looked out at the car. It was 14/28 horsepower, and a five-seater tourer. At the back was a luxurious windscreen where his mother and Meg sat peering and wrapped in draughts and blankets. He crouched in front with his father before the aluminium dashboard, remembering the first time they had all ridden together in the car.

"Should we take a run oot tae the Shaws first?" his father had shouted over the windscreen. "We could go through Paisley?"

He coughed and sniffed. It was his habit; catarrh, he said.

"Dad! It's Sunday," his mother said, and that was answer enough. "T-t-t," she went on.

"Whit's that got tae dae wi' it?"

"Faither'll no' like it! Ye ken him yersel'. He's wild if I as much as make dinner on a Sunday."

"He's annoyed if I study on Sundays," said David.

"Whit tripe," his father replied angrily, shaking his head like a terrier. "There's mair real religion in taking a car oot and worshipping nature than in sitting in a stuffy kirk listening tae an auld blether!"

"It needna be a stuffy kirk," his mother replied warmly, "and it needna be an auld blether!"

"Think o' the pleesure we could gi'e him. We could take him a hurl before we gae doon."

"He widnae thank ye for it."

"Weel, damn him then! Are ye coming?"

"I've just this bit dustin' to do."

"Dammit, the car's clean, Teenie," he said.

"All right, all right," she answered, frowning. "I'm shair, it's an awfu' job!"

These remarks were quite untranslatable, being a form of speech peculiar to the person and not to anything else, language or dialect. On the verge of an outburst which invariably threatened to take away any pleasure they had, they started off. Not only were Willie Hughes and all the Hemphills walking admiringly around it, Malcolm slinkingly trying the electric horn, but the Seymours were all staring out of the window, and even Mrs Watson could not withhold a discreet glance. He remembered hoping that Mary saw it too. It was the machine drew their eyes, resplendent in gold and silver, for machines were something of a miracle and there was always a considerable amount of subdued excitement as to whether they would go at all.

After some fluttering with the gears they moved downhill in silent triumph.

"Is it to be the Shaws?" his father shouted back into the wind.

"All right, all right, I'm sure," chorussed his mother, gulping in the wind and biting her lips.

In the Shaws the whole family had come on to the front lawn to see the glittering land-yacht — grandfather, grandmother, and even Mr and Mrs Wood, still smoking her clay pipe.

"Whatsoever next?" chirruped Mr Wood, who was a poet of sorts. "It's a wonderful invention, isn't it, Elizabeth?"

"It is that," she sang, her voice old and reedy, pulling her tweed hat down over her ears.

"Would ye like a wee run roon' aboot?" asked his father. "Just a spin?"

"A spin?" Mr Wood looked startled.

"We'll no' go far, Johnnie," his grandfather said with reluctance, "seeing it's the Sabbath."

He sat in the back with Mr Wood and his grandfather.

"Move up," said Mr Wood crossly, "and let your father in!"

"Oh no," laughed his father. "I have to sit in the front. You see I drive it."

"You do? I thocht it went by itself for a meenit," said Mr Wood.

"Not too fast now," said his grandfather chidingly. "Ten miles an hour will be quite ample, Johnnie!"

They did thirty all the way, and when they came back his grandfather said he thought they had been just a wee bittie slow coming hame.

They always went the same way to Fairlie: out through Paisley, past Coats' Mills, and the Abbey, on to the Waterworks, there to begin the long descent of the Hailey Brae. At the top of the Hailey they halted for ten minutes to cool the engine and admire the view. You could see clearly the Big Cumbrae, the Wee Cumbrae, Arran, and on a clear day, Paddy's Milestone, on one side; and on the other, the Gareloch, the Holy Loch, Loch Long and the Kyles of Bute. Below, as if in an aerial photograph, spread out the lovely crystal reaches of the Clyde.

He could see the red rocks and the rock-pools where he had hunted starfish and jellyfish of all colours, blue and maroon and yellow and brilliant gold, or newts and minute fish. He could see the jetty and the seawall and the scales under the old pier, and the church where they sang in an autumn of amber chrysanthemum 'Crossing the Bar'. Far down, along the shore road, he could see, too, the open bus with the broken springs hirpling into Largs, and Largs itself. There the paddle-steamer lay at anchor, on which his Aunt Nan came sometimes home in summer, though the distance was only two miles, purely for the sake of the sail. And he remembered the tragic run to Greenock by taxi one Sunday morning long ago, when his grandmother had to have radium treatment for her eye; he remembered her pain, and the champagne she had to have when she came home. He remembered most of all the long holidays he had spent in Fairlie, watching the hills of Arran covering themselves with snow, in silence, a bride with her veils, and at night, listening to the sea, as it cast in unceasing motion, its pale white beacons of light, on the shores of Ayrshire, and over all the shores of Scotland.

"We must get on to Nan's today," his mother said. "She'll ha'e tea a' ready."

"It's ma faither I'm worried aboot. I wonder hoo he is the day."

"It's a blessing *she's* awa' onywey," his mother said.

He listened to their appalling comments on life and death as if not his mother were talking but some arch-type of the race. When she huddled up her shoulders and sank her head between them, avoiding other people's eyes, she loosed searching if biting judgments on men and affairs like so many thunderbolts.

His grandmother, he knew, had died of cancer eating its way, like an enormous rat, through the eye into her brain. For two years she had lived on champagne and cocaine, both provided by his father at enormous expense.

The old man had rich white hair and blue eyes. He was always quiet and patient, unlike his wife.

When they arrived at the little gate, faces smarting, Nan rushed downstairs to meet them. She was small and thin, like Lilian Gish in looks, and took short, delicate steps, like a deer. She had not married so far because she had had her parents to look after.

"Teenie!" she said, leaning over the side of the car and kissing her. "Oh my!" She smiled broadly into the air, and as she did so David could see that one of her teeth was silvered over. He liked Aunt Nan because she could always smile.

"Come away up," she said. "Tea's ready."

The little table in her immaculate flat was laden with good things. Through the window at which you sat, you saw a row of pines, the smooth edge of the sea, and then the serrated outline of the snow-capped peaks of Arran. Nan loved Arran and Fairlie so much she seemed to own it all.

"How is he?" his father asked in his direct way.

Nan wept.

"No' sae weel, Jock."

"Life's absurdly short, Nan," said his father in one of his pungent, if rare, pronouncements, and coughed and sniffed. "Too short to mean hellish much."

"That's true, Johnnie," she said, sniffing too.

"Aye," said his mother, looking away as if puzzled, her eyes puckered.

It was their tribute to philosophy.

Whenever his father was touched or moved, he thrust out his lip and his nose wrinkled at the nostrils. David liked that. It was a fierce denial of mere sentiment. Now he stole into the bedroom, looking very fierce indeed, in his stocking-soles.

David was not allowed to go in, "unless he liked". Death was a secret people hugged to their hearts instead of sharing it like the Irish or the Mexicans.

There was utter silence in the next room.

They began to eat — slowly.

At the back of the house — beyond the red wood railway station with its little paraffin lamps, the hills rose in broken, dark-blue bulges, almost sheer, with the fir stampeding across them, or, moving slowly, a clenching rainstorm. Now and then, for a few moments only, a train would stop, hissing a holocaust of steam. The whistle would scream like a shell, and then, gathering speed along the track, the long line of jangling steel and iron would sink into the distance like a stone thrown far out into the sea.

The old man, lying with his back to the window in the silent room, could see none of these things. When he opened his eyes all that confronted him was pale-blue wallpaper, on which flowers in their thousands tumbled out of Greek vases. If he inclined his head a little to the right he could see the wardrobe, tall and dark-brown, like a coffin, and its ornate mirror, gathering ghosts in the darkness.

Carefully he listened as he lay, his white Tam O'Shantered head propped up on the pillow, to the wind, washing round the roof and seeping through the lathes in the attic, through the holes in the putty he had moulded between them. Then, deeper and more steadily, he heard the surf-beat on the shore, a never-ending hush-hush like a pulse, or a heartbeat, or like breath itself. The sound of trees. Branches. These were arms, flowing like pliant and patient strength, and never tiring. The sounds of the house. Springing floorboards, hoarding movement for sudden release, like a human body.

Someone, who, Nan, making tea. A voice. The voice would be Jock's. Trying to comfort Nan, his only daughter. Good Jock. A good son, always. Why comfort? If they only knew how easy life was and how peaceful when one was really adjusted to time and space. Then there was no bitterness. If only he could tell them what had always been his secret, he would be happy.

He had learned it early. When he began to be known as a diver, swimming in the current as silently and cleanly as Nan had entered the room in the semi-darkness there, thinking he didn't see, or was asleep.

One of the best in Scotland he had been. Adjustment to time and space is vital to a high diver. Once he had dived off the Forth Bridge for a wager. Timing was necessary then. His blue eyes, pale as the scallops cast up by the sea, dissolved at the thought into mischief. He seemed to hear his wife's voice saying: "Ye auld deevil!"

Timing was necessary then, but it had been a wonderful sensation, first of all to take the bet and watch the amazement of the chaps in the work. To be drunk with resolution, ready to do anything and confound all who said he couldn't. To sneak away on a Saturday afternoon with a couple of Paisley buddies, saying nothing to the wife, though he knew she would say plenty to him. No' giving a damn.

They had a drink first at Mally's Arms at the top of Parliamentary Road. They paid his fare. Footsteps. Jock coming in. Big feet. He smiled.

It was the first time he had seen Edinburgh, the capital of Scotland. One of the most lasting impressions of beauty he had ever received. A worker in the Cally had little to look at but nuts and bolts starving for grease, pistons thirsting for oil, rails new and rails derelict, engines on a practice-shunt or disembowelling for scrap. He had been a man ministering to machines, and if he wanted to see anything else he must close his eyes, for he could not see through the wall of railway sleepers shaggy as wood-hair and caked with smoke.

If he could hear anything but train-shrieks, whistles, sirens and hoarse orders, he must cottonwool his ears. His ears were full of cottonwool now.

He had looked a long time at the outline of the Castle emerging gray from the morning mist, then light-blue, till finally the rock thrust green and a rich serrated brown, into the clear air. He took a walk down Princes Street then, before he went into a tram and away out of Edinburgh.

He couldn't remember if he had been tipsy. His wife, of course, said that he was a drunken rat and it was a peety he wasna droont to go and do a thing like that. Puir soul. Angry at him loving risk better than her, and loving timing and perfect precision in all things and not just in her.

Then they came to the bridge. And it was off with his things, taking a last look at the worried faces, and stripped, to stand arms outstretched, and the wind blowing through him as if he were a bird, taking flight, and the slow launch into space, with a last, quick kick-off.

Breast against wind to drop like a bullet aimed at the Silver Forth.

The air filled his lungs so swiftly, so cleanly, there was scarcely any breathing at all. Falling thousands of feet through space and time, he was never more uplifted, for his head was lifted back, his shoulders braced back and his arms like wings bent back in passionate surrender and burning quest.

In that first dreadful drop his mind was suddenly shot with memories. His wife leaning forward urging him on, not over the bridge, but from the river, where lay an image of her face. He could not believe it! She who so objected to all his escapades because she thought his first duty was to her, his family, the living, she was urging him faster to come, faster . . . and knowing he was coming, he felt, as the drop seemed to lessen, airily unreal, like a plane landing, meeting in the final moment of love or passionately defying with gravity all levity.

Would he never cease rise-falling? Would the wonderful rush of air never quench his breathing by its very richness? He did not care. Better perhaps if it did, and his questing body, filled with clean pure air, plunge into the restless gray of the Forth, forever to remain there.

"Faither! Faither!" came a scream. Oh horror, Nan! How could she be there! She had nothing to do with his plunge. She could not stop him now he was almost in the water. Terror-stricken, silly girl, would she follow out of fright? She mustn't. It wasn't to be. She wasn't ready. She wasn't born!

His mind reeled as though sick, away from the body, forgot its headlong ecstasy, and throbbed and said strangely:

"Why did you do it Nan? Why did you do it? You've made it harder."

"I couldn't bear to see you, faither, like my mither, dying," she sobbed, head bowed.

He leaned back weakly on the pillows. The air was suffocating. If only they knew the delights of timing and how important it was — if only they knew!

"He's no' long for this world noo, Nan. Ye must be prepared for that," his father said.

Afterwards, when they were driving home in the car, came the moment David was secretly dreading.

"Well," he said, "you are twenty-one now. There's £100 in your name in the bank on your coming of age. What are you going to do with it?"

"Go to America," he said.

"America?"

Macrae turned and stared at his son, taking his eyes completely off the road. The car swung wildly, along the walls overgrown with shaggy red moss on the shore road.

"Why? Whit is there there for you?"

"I don't know. I want to find out. I may stay and I may not. You say the money is mine. If it is, I go to America. If it isn't, I stay here and don't touch it."

"Oh, it's yours right enough. Only don't do anything hasty. There's George Aitchison went to America, and as soon as he landed he saw a hold-up. He caught the next boat back."

"I won't do that," David said. "I'll stay a year at least."

"You could go to an English university, Oxford, say. I'd help."

"I don't want to go to Oxford. I want to get out of the country."

"For good?"

"For a bit anyway."

"What will you do over there? Aitchison was going to make golf balls. He was good at that. What can *you* do?"

"The first people who went to America did not know what they were going to do."

"No."

"The main thing is to see this island from a distance first."

"As you say, but I'd rather you didn't go."

"I have to go. There's nothing for me here. It seems if you are not prepared to connive at the destruction of Scotland, there's no room in it."

"Now you're talking tripe."

"All right. Only I'm not the first to leave Scotland and those who left were by no means the worst."

"If you want to go I can't stop you; but think it over, David, and think of your mother. She would like to see you settled down. I had such plans for you. You were going to join the Masons."

"The Masons have always interested me. What are they all about."

181

"I can't tell you 'what they're all about', but I can tell you a few things. I wish you'd join. It would be a great help to you when you were abroad."

"I don't want any help. How did it all start?"

"You're one of the 'Illuminati'," said his father. "You've taken the oath."

"What oath?"

"In the name of the crucified Son,

"Swear to break the fleshly bonds which still bind you to father, mother, brothers, sisters, husbands, wives, relations, friends, sweethearts, kings, superiors, well-doers, or anyone to whom you owe loyalty, obedience, gratitude, or service. Know God, Who saw you born, to live in another sphere, which you will reach when you have left this pestilential earth, the cast-out of Heaven. From this moment on you are freed of any oaths to your country or its laws. Swear to inform your new superior of all that you have done, taken, seen, heard or read, experienced or divined, and to seek and discover that which your eyes do not see.

"Live in the Name of the Father, and of the Son and of the Holy Ghost."

"It sounds rather wonderful," he said. "Where did you learn that?"

"I know a thing or two," his father said. "Remember when we used to go to see Henry Baynton in 'Hamlet'? I wish you could have seen 'Oedipus Rex'. We could have done a lot together."

"I think we could. We still might, one day. Who were these 'Illuminati'?"

"An eighteenth-century sect, springing from the Templars. There were then the Freemasons, the Manicheans and the Templars. The original Masonic ceremony is said to have been that of Hiram Abi the Architect."

"The three sects originated among the builders of Egypt, who later went to Greece. They had a holy order, and regarded themselves as having a holy mission. In Greece, of course, the Egyptian names changed to Greek: Osiris became Bacchus, Isis became Ceres. They built theatres and played in dramas, after Thespis, the creator of the art of tragedy, had seen one of the builders holding a dialogue on a table at a Bacchic feast. They acquired the sole right of building temples, theatres and public buildings.

"Then three hundred years before Christ the King of Pergamo gave them Theos as a spot to live on, and there they organised groups, societies, colleges, synods or lodges."

"I wouldn't mind being a theatrical mason. How did masonry start?"

"There are many stories. It seemed the Jews, too, practised this type of building, and were associated with the Phoenicians in the building of the Temple of Salomonis, under Hiram. The builders could not all speak the same language, some being Jews, some Egyptian, some Phoenician, so they had to recognise each other by means of signs and secret words. Hiram Abi divided them into three, craftsmen, apprentices and masters. Apprentices were paid at Column B, craftsmen at F, and masters in the middle room. No one was paid until he proved his rank. Three of the craftsmen, afraid that the temple would be finished before they reached the grade of Master, decided to wrest the secret from Hiram by force, so as to pass as masters in other countries. They were Jubelas, Jubelos and Jubelum, and they killed Hiram Abi by the East door, burying him on a mountain with an acacia on top.

"Before his death, however, Hiram had sent for the Cedars of Lebanon to use in building the temple at Jerusalem. No one knew what to do with these. The King despatched search parties to find the body, and told them to note the gesture they made when they did find it and the words they said among themselves, as these would have to replace the lost secret. They put on their leather aprons and their white gloves and when they found him, buried the master in Lebanon. They still try to find that word and sign."

"It doesn't sound quite like my job," he said.

"You don't know your job yet, do you?"

"No."

"However, there is another story. Manes, founder of the Manicheans, was born in Persia about 220 years before Christ. At seventeen he was bought by a rich widow in the town of Ctesiphon, who brought him up and gave him his freedom, making him her heir. He began to teach the creed of Soytienus, according to which there are two principles of creation, the good, spirit, light is God, and the bad, matter and darkness is the Devil. He was influenced by Zoroaster. He called himself an apostle and wrote an evangel dealing with the transmigration of souls, forbidding the killing of animals and the eating of meat. He attained fame under Harmuz I of Persia and called himself Paracletus. Harmuz died, and the new King commanded Paracletus to perform a miracle. He did not. He was stripped, skinned and stuffed with straw.

"His followers then started a ceremony like that for Hiram Abi, and the higher ranks of freemasonry. They all stood round a coffin, the same number of steps down as the freemasons, but the figure was not that of Hiram whose secret they sought, but that of Manes, whose death they were to avenge. This was duplicated in another sect organised in honour of the death of Jacob von Molay. The only people on whom they could avenge themselves for the deaths of Manes and Jacob von Molay, the one executed at the end of the third century BC and the other at the end of the fourteenth century, were — the Kings. So Continental freemasonry became very political, unlike ours."

"You haven't told me very much really, have you?"

"I can't. I've told you, you're one of the 'Illuminati'. That is why you are going away. Would you like to join before you go? There was another death. The death of Christ! On whom do we avenge ourselves for that?"

"I don't know," he said. "I can't join anything. Where is my blue shirt, mother? — at the laundry?"

His mother wept. His father put a brave face on it, trusting he said in his son's judgment.

"Ach, a cunny min', David," his mother said with an expression of distaste.

"You're a helluva man, aren't ye?" his father said as they arrived home.

"I got a tin of beans from Miss Sveso, wait till ye see the size o't. I says to her I says says I, 'Miss Sveso?' Where are you going, David? This is a fine tapsalteerie!"

"Up to the attic."

It was the only place where he could study, where he had once read

Nansen. He could see right up Pollokshaws Road from there, and watch the green and red cars come lurching and swaying down from Dumbreck, Bishopbriggs and Bellshill. As he moved through the house he loved, he felt he was moving in several dimensions at once. There was the bedroom as it had been in the time of his grandfather, with a small fire in the grate, littered with Victorian knick-knacks. He remembered being taken upstairs to say goodbye to his grandfather, who was lying in bed. The old man was gentle, yet gruff. His beard prickled David's face. Afterwards it seemed that he had been dying, for he did not come downstairs anymore. In the same room his Aunt Mary died. It was all brown then, as if the sun were concentrated inside the room and you could touch it. The coffin was brown too. Near it lay his aunt under veins of blue marble. It was all unreal, one of those conjuring tricks in which someone lies down in a box and then disappears because the hand is swifter than the eye. All the time you knew they had gone behind the scenes and it was only a trick, so you concentrated on the mystery of it, and pretended to be puzzled and even frightened at the mysterious power which had accomplished it all. Only, now he wanted to talk to his grandfather, he could not.

There was the library where he had worked for so long; the attics where he had read *Tom Finch's Monkey*, crawling up the steep stairs to a breakneck height. How different the house had looked with the various generations living in it! In his grandfather's time it had been severe, uncomfortable and very dusty, steeped in prayer and sanctity from which the only refuge was the attic.

When later his cousins had lived there it was a merry bedlam of shouting children, much as in the time of the original school. Aunt Bessie spent all her time making wonderful dessert-puddings. And through it all blazed the enormous fire on the hearth, that never seemed to go out, with the bells for the servants, smuggled away in cobwebs in the high corner.

They were all there still for him.

Why did they not claim the "Quoich"? Why did his mother not listen when people spoke to her? He read the chapter in Hume Brown called 'The Scottish Wars of Independence' and went downstairs again. He had not read it since he was twelve, and even in school it had not been considered very important really. What was important?

"To play the game," his father said.

"To live the Christian life," his mother said. "Oh yes, David."

Surely what was important was to know what was going on in the world? No one ever mentioned that. The schools taught the past. To them the present was a controversial issue and the future a probable sin.

Entering the kitchen, he remembered his grandfather playing on the violin 'Rantin' Rovin' Robin', and through the window saw again the dusty, hallowed hollytree wrapped in spiders' webs, and the prickly old bushes that were part of an older Scotland than he could grasp.

"If I can leave my son better off than I was, and he does the same, and that goes on for each generation," his father was saying, "'to me that is progress. . . .'"

"You should at least have finished your degree," his father said to him as he went in.

"Not if I'm one of the 'Illuminati'!" he answered. "When I went to see the Adviser of Studies I found there was no serious advice to be had. The University was a factory for teachers and scientists, not a place for learning, which is essentially disinterested. I might have taken a degree in Philosophy, or even in Economic Science but there are no opportunities for research there, as there are in Physical Science, and armaments and the weapons of power. Disinterested thought is not encouraged. I don't belong there."

"Go to London," his father said.

"That is no better," he said. "Scotland was the first nation in Europe to declare itself a nation. It gave the idea of nationhood to the world, but now it seems as if it will be the first nation to die. That does not mean that, like so many of my countrymen, I intend to become a form of Englishman."

"It's beyond me," his father said. "I don't want you to be anything but what you are, but how will America help that?"

"All vision is a help," said David. "Neither nationalism nor religion nor any affiliation so far means anything to me because they are not wide enough. Only the world is wide enough."

Everything was the same, yet not the same. The gray ruined walls and the dripping evergreen and the feathers of frost on ferns and rocks were the same, but leaving everything was different. He thought of the fall of lawns at Gilmorehill away into Kelvingrove Park, and of the strike of the wind in the small cloisters, and the beauty of the scene clung to him like a dream. The train moved on with increasing speed towards Greenock, but it was moving along the path through the rhododendrons behind Cartcraigs and it was whistling through afternoons among the ossified and undone history in the Art Galleries. As it screamed and hissed in anger, a woman opposite rose and put her head out of the window.

He was leaving Scotland, and not only Scotland but all of his previous life, perhaps for always. At the Tail o' the Bank stood a large ship, all ready to sail, her bunkers gritted with coal, her furnaces red with clinkers. Round her rose the mountains, rolling backward in motionless waves from Arran to Ben Lomond and Loch Long, the "Loch of the Ships". They were The Guardians.

Living, he thought, was always a stage cleared for action. He remembered the old man in the hardware shop, old Sneddon, selling the odds and ends of an existence he could no longer order or control, limping against fate.

"How are you, well?" an old dame simpered.

"Well, but poor," tittered old Sneddon nervously, an eternal image.

Had he seen there a spirit, isolated against that background? What remained when he had nothing to cling to at all? Was that his soul, that bald radiance?

The decks were cleared for action. There was no other action than this final one in which he moved and had his being. There never was. Now he knew. The greatest things were space and the emptiness of space called time. The "Ding an Sich", this was it, the thing seen against all lack of purpose and direction, was only to be loved, as a child is loved.

The whole world was a great empty stage on which the antagonist sought to create a final lack of purpose and direction so that creatures might be loved; a great empty stage on which no one had ever acted because no one had ever appreciated the stage, the audience, the act, the scene, the décor — or the nature of the play.

He saw a young Black Watch officer holding high his head, not knowing why, wearing his kilt like a bustle, quite divorced from war and the terrible knowledge of war.

He saw people in a passing train, girls looking out of a window, men smoking or reading, penned in space and time, again in isolation that would be theirs always. To interfere, to help, was dangerous presumption. Their lives, their souls, were theirs. The responsibility was theirs. He had his own life and his own responsibility.

Living was a game of chess, or a vast design, a piece of music, a pattern of achievement. A sister was a sister and not a sister. She played her part and was a sister, having elected out of space to do so. "Be sister to my tragedy." There was in sisterhood a relationship like a geometrical design. So there was for a sweetheart who was and was not, in eternity.

"One of the 'Illuminati'," his father said. "From this moment on you are free from any oaths to your country or its laws. . . . Swear to break the fleshly bonds that bind you still to father, mother, brothers, sisters, husbands, wives, relations, friends, sweetheart." Sweethearts — he remembered Mary — bless you, Mary — and to seek and discover what your eyes do not see. . . ."

He stepped down into the Pilot's cutter. His childhood was left standing on the pier, pulling chocolate out of slot-machines, hammering out the name TARANTULA for his yacht, waiting for the *Davaar* to come in from Campbeltown, standing by his father and mother. The cutter smelt of fish. That was Fairlie and the herring-boxes stacked for transport to London and Glasgow. Sidings of silvered scales like slippery sixpences. His aunt passing in the gray, old open-air bus. Goldfinches, mavies, gannets and heron like metal on the beach, in splendid chorus and incomparable ballet, dancing beyond the windows. The dot on the horizon was the *Queen Mary* coming up. It grew larger. Noon stood still. The sun swelled like a seed. You could see the silent bows of the ship, swollen now, cleaving the water without a sound. It was very mysterious and beautiful to be waiting for the *Queen Mary* that morning, arriving after the *Davaar*, and *The Marchioness of Breadalbane* to sail to Macrihanish Bay. How lovely the names were! The *Queen Mary* was faster than *The Viper* although *The Viper* was fastest in Ireland.

The slowest was *Eagle III*, but she was old.

Every widening ripple was a year. This ship was still larger, a floating generation. He strained his eyes through the light morning mist. There was no one to see him off except the hills and the river of his childhood. That was the best way to go. Now the liner was near; he could see a great hole in her side let down like a bunker for passengers to enter.

In he walked, and through a narrow corridor carpeted with silence, like a hospital, so ill for a moment he felt. On the deck the ship's band began to play 'In My Solitude' and the ship seemed an empty shell.

Only the gulls fluttered over the rain-swept decks.

A spotlight of sun touched the Cumbrae and it shone like amber.

The temples of the engines seemed to throb with music. The hills began their slow and solemn march past. He felt very moved. Now, for one wild moment, he would have liked to dash ashore with the pilot, and sit at the window in Gourock with Miss Gray, or in Helensburgh with the Friels, or in Fairlie with Nan, watching the waves, when a liner passed, coming in like cream-cruds. His country suddenly became very small and very beautiful, like a precious stone with a bloody history, lying in the outstretched palm of a dealer and a charlatan.

Fairlie and Millport and Dunoon, and Innellan and Rothesay and Kilbreggan and Arran, and Brodick and Lamlash, Lochranza and Lochgilphead stood up and bade him goodbye.

On the quays behind, a few stacks and chimneys still stood up like old women in gray shawls waving white handkerchiefs of smoke against a mournful background. He thought of his mother in the Shaws waving at the London train as his grandfather had waved from the old doorway. He thought again of Cartcraigs.

For him the family belonged to that house, and could not leave it altogether. It was not just a house, it was an experience, an assembly-point, a memory they all shared, uniting them no matter where. This was the meaning of "living". No wonder the Scots were called "fey". He would not have been surprised in the least to have seen his grandmother emerge from the cupboard below the stairs leading to the attic, holding in her hands a pair of ancient ladies' boots.

"Awa' wi' ye," she would say, waving the boots at him. "You an' yer fancies!"

That was because she did not want him to know too much, and because she was a very brave old lady.

A cold wind blew up in his face flakes of salt, cold as the water pouncing and worrying the rocks ashore.

Then the vast hand of the sea reached up and wiped away the inarticulate map of the fighting city, and, walking to the bows, he stood in the inscrutable future.